PORTAGE
To The
INTERIOR

A Russian-Alaskan Life

BY THAD KEENER

ISBN: 979-8-9908020-0-1
Any references to historical events, real people, or real places are used fictitiously. Names, characters, and places are products of the author's imagination.

Book design by Gisela Swift
Artistic story maps by Vojin Kremic

Front cover map - PiADyshev, V. P., Faleleef, C. & Russia. General Staff. Military Topographical Depot, A. N. (1826) General'naia Karta Chukotskoĭ Zemli, Aleutskikh "ostrovov" i sievero-zapadnago berega Ameriki. [Saint Petersburg, Russia: Military Topographical Depot] [Map] Retrieved from the Library of Congress, https://www.loc.gov/item/2018688693/.

Back cover map - Lewis, J. F. (1862) Map of Russian America or Alaska Territory. [S.l] [Map] Retrieved from the Library of Congress, https://www.loc.gov/item/99446183/.

First printing edition 2024.
Keenaway, LLC

PO Box 83757
Fairbanks, AK 99708
thadkeener.org

Gratitude.

Like a salve upon a burn, like a cool breeze when stuck in a hot room, like a day of rain after weeks of drought, gratitude soothes the human spirit.

Table of Contents

Introduction 1

Maps 5
    Russia
    Russia-America

Part One 11
    Beginnings
        Pride - April, 1829
        Fear - May, 1829
        Humility - May, 1829
        Faith - June, 1829
        Elsewhere in the World
        Trust - October, 1829
        Awareness - January 1830

Part Two 87
        Courage - February, 1830
        Strength - July, 1830
        Anger - Fall of 1830
        Modesty - Winter of 1830-1831
        The Ever Changing World
        Gratitude - 1831-1833
        Wisdom - 1833-1836
        Family - 1836-1867

Part Three 181
        Lieutenant Allen - 1885
        Years Roll By
        June 15, 2023

Closing Notes 205

Introduction

Alaska, the Northwest chunk of the Americas. It is more than a location, a land filled with riches. It is an internal place that humans hold and nurture and, having achieved it, few let go.

The natural resources of Alaska are immense: gold, timber, salmon, and petroleum that fuels the economy. The location, two miles from Asia, offers unparalleled strategic advantages, and our Arctic positioning to Europe is just being explored.

But it is the internal personal resource gained in Alaska that provides a drive and wisdom few places can replicate. The summer heat of a desert, the social connections of city life, or the vast horizons of the oceans have forever provided humans with rich insights. The old sea mariner holds a vision through the hurricane that few understand. He earned it and is not fool enough to let it go. The savannah rancher sees all and is comfortable standing naked before the storm. He brings this with him to town, to the cities, and enriches his life with this strength. A desert man comes close to an Alaskan. The raw brutality of the heat, the death it brings, and the knowledge of how one survives molds a human. Such characteristics advance the person wherever they may roam.

Being an Alaskan is a spectrum, a wisdom that only you know. The person gains life advantage through trials in Alaska. It is a wisdom that one learns from moving through an experience. Why does Alaska provide a richer internal experience than others? You'll know when you know. When you live the vastness, remoteness, wilderness that is unparalleled on our planet. You see things differently when the scope of its northern winds are confronted.

People quest for these experiences throughout the planet: the incessant city lawyer, the striving Hollywood actor, the southern football player. It is well recognized that these experiences create a richness that few let go, and so it is with Alaska. The rancher in northern Montana only needs to drive north to understand the differences between the two states. The Montana experience has a richness, but it does not have an Alaskan richness. That is fine.

To understand Alaskans is to understand this definitive internal experience and internal wisdom bestowed upon these people living in the far northwest corner of our continent.

Lest we forget our brothers across the sea, our Siberian neighbors. Colder and claiming an incomparable history, our neighbors offer a mirror to our boreal lives. Do they not take outside winter baths while at public schools? Do they not have freezing winters and forest fire summers that make ours look tame? Is not their gulag history one of humanity's most brutal chapters? We could easily lose our wealth if we fail to recognize human patterning.

An Alaskan is not an arrogant, egotistical person. They recognize their safety and success relies on the other. A dominating Alaskan has not found themselves in genuine need. A show-off cannot build community which keeps them sane in a land of eternal darkness. Around an Alaskan you will experience patience, despite the dangerous moment, that creates success.

Scanning each moment, an Alaskan can appear to others a bit preoccupied. On the frontier rarely is there not an issue to be monitored. Many issues just need watching and the patience of a skilled person to tend them. The Alaskan becomes a contemplative person through the rigors and demands of the environment. Internal monitoring becomes as important as watching the snows, moose, mosquitoes and so on.

The Alcan drive to Alaska will bring this out in a person. Easily routed from your hometown, today's digital programs give you not only the driving miles but the time it will take down to the minutes. Reasonable and doable are common replies, but most drivers know to take a moment to learn the stories and read the online reviews that save one a lot of time and energy.

Miles from nowhere, in a growing Canadian Rocky Mountain snowstorm, I passed a slow-moving, Texas plated, SUV driven by a young woman. She had come far, had a long way to go, and now the remoteness loomed large. Whether her knowledge of her vehicle or sheer personal drive to push the car forward had dropped, her driving style looked floundering. At the Muncho Lake gas station I waited while the snow swirled and was able to get confirmation she understood the dilemma. Twenty inches later, wind-driven snows hardened into drifts, the remoteness, the lack of cell coverage for miles, made the freezing rains of Sand Point, Idaho look like a walk in the park. We were 750 miles from the mountains of Alaska, plenty of time to really get to know yourself.

Not that we should seek such adventures to develop our characters, Alaska reminds us excuses don't count. Slow down, check-in with yourself, and make sure you're going the right way.

…

Aaron Katz is our story's protagonist, and he's a Russian Jew. He probably wouldn't like being called Russian, but in time, he would understand. Russia was a monstrous contiguous nation in the 1820s. Stretching from Europe to just north of San Francisco and back to Asia. The cultures within this empire were vast. The character of the nation is difficult to describe without including this diversity. Additionally, Russians had occupied France after the Napoleonic Wars. There, soldiers absorbed much of the philosophy they had fought against, Liberty.

Like many today, half of Aaron's Alaskan adventure is getting there. His Judaism is illuminated, as are Russian Orthodoxy and Indigenous ways. All have a developed approach to the sacred which is unfolded in the story. All use the art of storytelling, which reminds us of both the uniqueness of an individual and the transitory nature of life.

Mussar is the daily journaling Aaron does throughout his life. He strives to understand. If he is to wander the desert, he will use the time to study.

Here are a few translations that will help. Most are Yiddish, the language spoken by millions of Eastern European Jews.

Adank - Thank you
Bema - Lectern in a synagogue
Bris - Jewish male circumcision on eighth day
Bruder - Yiddish for brother
Bubbee - Yiddish for grandmother
Chai - Tea
Chyaa tsal - Athabascan boy
Czar - Ruler of the Russian Empire

3

Dachas - Russian country homes

Decembrists - Russian revolutionaries exiled to Siberia

Eenaa'e - Athabascan mother

Foter - Yiddish for father

Goyim - People who are not Jewish

Gut Margn - Good morning

Haver - Jewish study partner

Katorga - Russian forced-work prison

K Chertu - Russian for 'to the devil'

Kippah - Jewish head covering

Mezuzah - Jewish prayer on doorpost

Moter -Yiddish for mother

Muselmann - Yiddish for Muslim

Mussar - Jewish moral daily practice from Lithuanian

New Archangel - Russian-American headquarters, today Sitka

Oh Kvell - Prideful exclamation

Pale Settlement - Border where Russian Jews were exiled

Qahal - Jewish town leadership

Rabbi - Jewish teacher and service leader

Russian Orthodox - Christian Religion of Russian Empire

Saba - Hebrew for grandfather

Shmegegge - hot-air, petty person

Shvester - Yiddish for sister

Synagogue - Jewish house of worship

Tato - Ukrainian for father

Tzava'ot - Final letter from dying Jew

Vozok - Russian for an enclosed winter carriage

Yeshiva - Jewish religious school

Zei Gezunt - To your health

Zin - Yiddish for sons

Maps

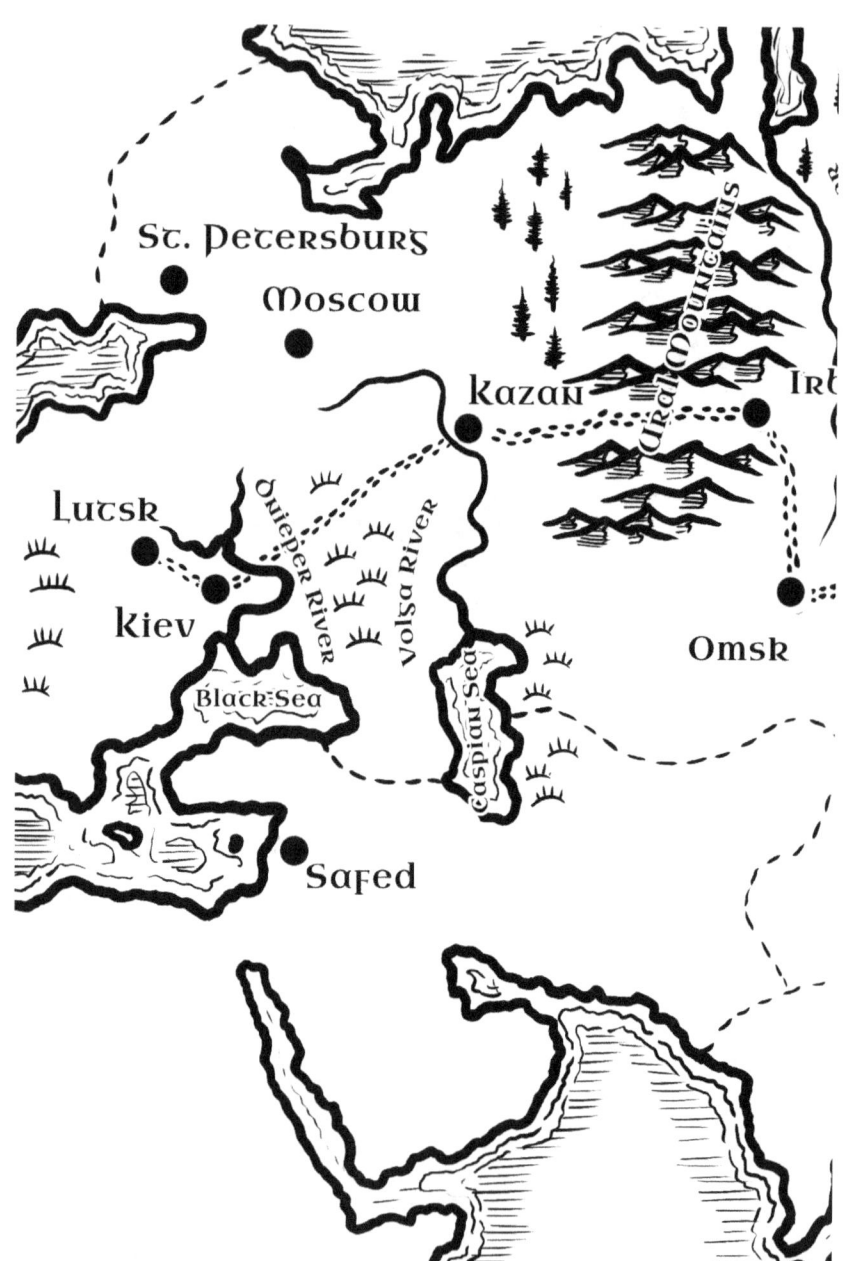

St. Petersburg

Moscow

Kazan

Ural Mountains

Irk

Lutsk

Dnieper River

Volga River

Kiev

Black Sea

Caspian Sea

Omsk

Safed

Russia

Aaron's Travels 1829-1830

Ob River

Lena River

Tomsk

Lake Baikal

Verkhne-Udinsk

Amur River

Irkutsk

Nerchinsk

Kyakhta

China

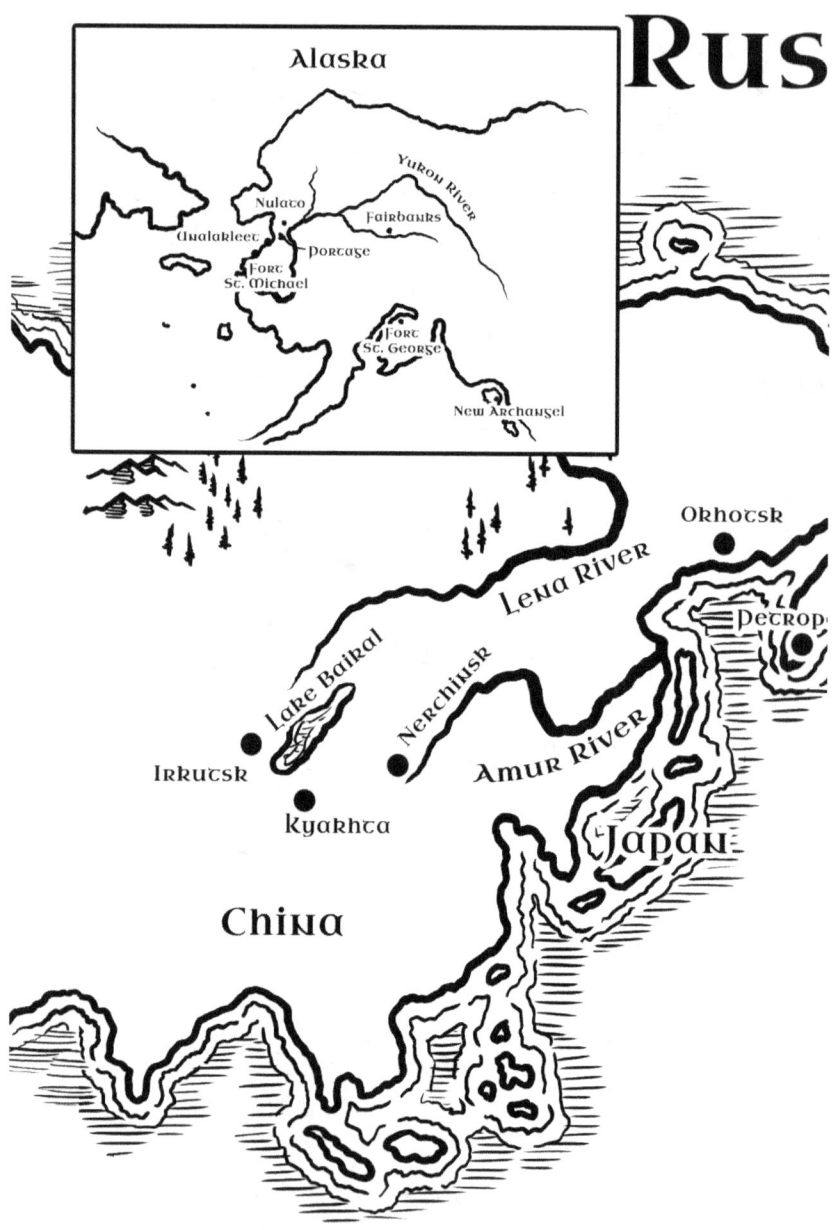

Rus

Alaska

Yukon River

Nulato

Fairbanks

Unalakleet

Portage

Fort
St. Michael

Fort
St. George

New Archangel

Okhotsk

Lena River

Petrop

Lake Baikal

Nerchiusk

Amur River

Irkutsk

Japan

Kyakhta

China

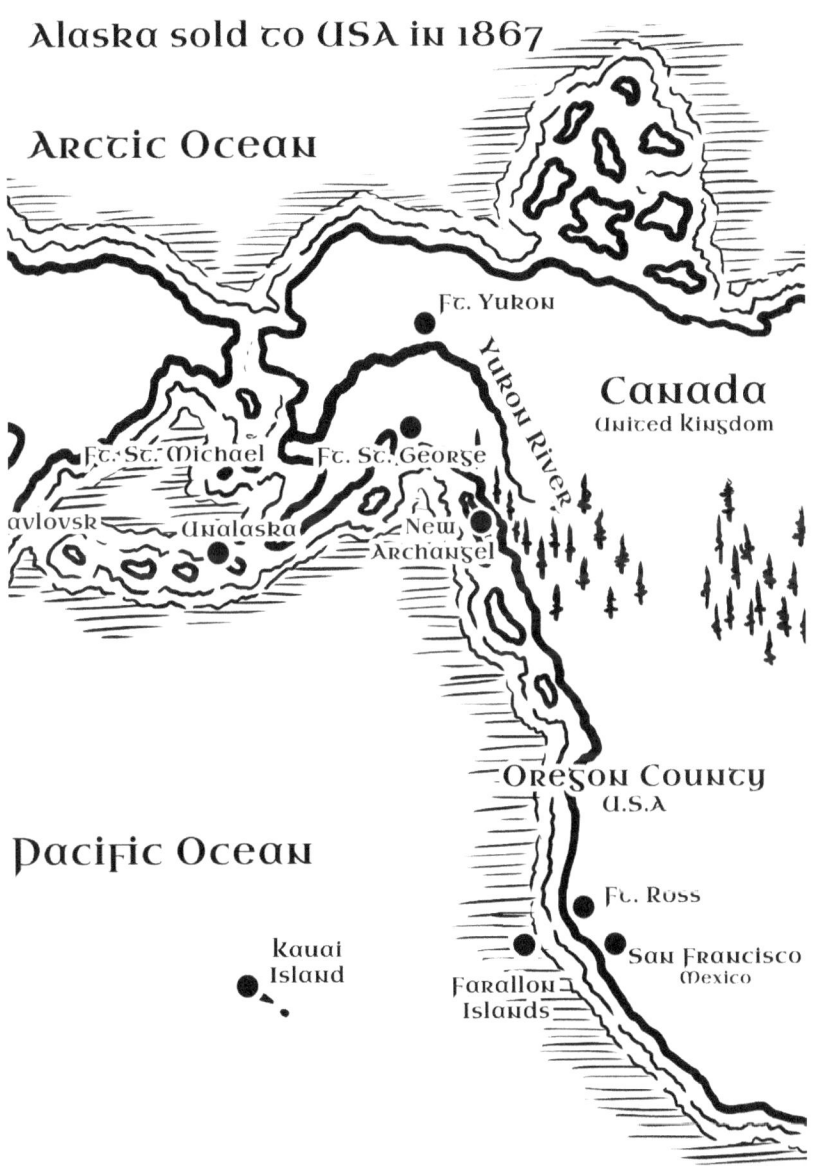

sia - America

Alaska sold to USA in 1867

Arctic Ocean

Ft. Yukon

Canada
United Kingdom

Ft. St. Michael   Ft. St. George
avlovsk   Unalaska   New
Archangel

Yukon River

Oregon County
U.S.A

Pacific Ocean

Ft. Russ

Kauai
Island

San Francisco
Mexico

Farallon
Islands

Part One

Beginnings

Our story begins in a small thatch-roofed house on the edge of Lutsk. In the spring of 1829, it was Russian, though newly acquired Russian land since the division of Poland. Lutsk straddles the Styr River, which flows to the Dnieper and then the Black Sea. Like many rivers in this part of the world, it watered rich farmlands with few barriers on the endless Eurasian steppe.

Chelm Street was a street behind the main road leading north to Mylushi, which followed the bends of the Styr. Along the Mylushi Road, in this part of Lutsk, one could find stone or brick homes. The few citizens who had money wanted others to know. Being set back, Chelm Street did not have such citizens as many were not citizens.

Lutsk was within 'The Pale of Settlement.' When Russia annexed the land, the people were a mixed bunch, but mostly not followers of Russian Orthodoxy, not citizens. Partially as a buffer, partially to assimilate, Jews were forcibly moved to the Pale. With hardly any economic prospects, life in the Pale was a struggle. The waves of poor Jewish exiles from the Russian Empire created much talk in the markets, synagogues, and homes.

Our thatch-roofed house had constant visitors. During the summers, the moter (Zelde) would sit with her friends out back under the summer kitchen awning. A well nearby was shared by her two neighbors, her milking cow, and her son (Aaron). On this north side of the house, you would hear talk. "I heard the Zemnovs are moving. This town is losing some of its best people. What are we to do?" Zelde would spend as much time as she could with her friends as her life was busy being the only parent at home.

Her husband, Joseph, had been gone for over two years. Her eldest, Joshua, had left not long after her husband, following him east. *"East! G.. forbid!"* Joseph followed Lord Muravyov, a Decembrist, who was lucky to be alive. Their years fighting Napoleon and occupying France had forged a lifelong bond. Lord Muravyov, who knew a thousand soldiers, picked Joseph to be by his side. It was because of Joseph's people skills, his ability to smash through obstacles, to find solutions in the middle of disasters. More importantly, it was his ability to speak so many of the needed languages: Ukrainian, Polish, Russian, Yiddish, Lithuanian, German, and most importantly for Lord Muravyov: French.

One cannot talk about Decembrists without understanding the impact of the French, their ideals, and the years Russians, like Lord Muravyov and Joseph, spent occupying France where they were steeped in these new ideas of 'Liberty.' When Lord Muravyov and Joseph returned to Lutsk, they joined the new 'Union of Salvation.' Together, they worked their connections, spreading the ideas of 'Constitutional Monarchy' and the 'End of Serfdom.' Within time, their ideas did spread but landed them in one of Earth's most foreboding pits of despair: Siberia.

For Zelde he was gone, her eldest was gone. They were not going to bring home a chicken for Shabbat dinner. They were not going to bring home a new coat or boots for Aaron. They were not going to help the countless Jews who filled the streets and slept under her backyard kitchen awning. But they did pay for Aaron to attend yeshiva. Like Joseph and their eldest, Joshua, Aaron attended the Lutsk yeshiva. A fair distance across town, Aaron had been a regular at the school for nearly ten years. Zelde was soothed by this when she listened to Margo talk on and on about her boy, who worked for the best carpenter in town. "I know Margo, you've got the best son a moter could ever want." "Of course I do. We work hard for what we have, unlike so many of these new people. Worthless!"

During these cool spring days, it was the sunny front porch that housed these talks. Nina, her neighbor, spent more time with her than her children, who constantly looked for food. The southern view of Lutsk, the expanse of endless farmland, the countless souls struggling for a living, the sunrise and sunset could all be seen from her porch.

Pride - Spring, 1829

Are we not quickly pulled by the sweetness of pride?
Worse than jealousy as the energy we receive intoxicates.
Most hide in the warmth or boast at the power.
But when our conscious mind wakes, we know the
dangerous dance has begun.

Fool is the one who maintains confidence in the
face of misunderstanding.

Yet, lack of pride produces unneeded hurdles with others.
Like the spinning circle of Yin and Yang, you need to keep
moving to stay balanced between light and dark.

"Aaron, go to the market. I don't want to ask you again."

"But moter, I'll be late for school. I'm never late. Rabbi Hulstein will be shocked!"

"Rabbi Hulstein, Oy! Today, you are taking these buttons and pins to your shvester in the market. This is not an option. Now go!"

If he moved quickly, as he knew he could, Aaron would be to the yeshiva with time to spare. He checked his coat pocket to confirm the small hard roll for lunch. He looked down at his coat hem, tattered, like the rim of his hat. Further down, his boots were fraying patches upon blown patches. None of this mattered, for underneath he had the best socks a man could desire. *'Socks can make or break a man!' Adank, moter.*

"Zei Gezunt," Aaron spoke as he kissed the front-door mezuzah and walked out onto Chelm Street. He was seventeen going on twenty-seven and felt larger. The bag of buttons and pins swung from his hand and he ran a bit on the dusty road as the sun peeked over another thatched roof. The streets were buzzing with waking Jews new to Lutsk.

"Gut Margn," Aaron blurted more than enough as he moved to the center of Lutsk. The market was where everyone went, and Aaron rarely missed an opportunity. A woman walked by with a chicken under her arm and he stopped. 'Such a fine chicken!' His large overcoat was wide open and furled like a cape unless held. It was going to be a sunny-cool spring day.

"Ah, my favorite shmegegge!" cried Estle from her table. Aaron twisted his nose and dropped the bag on her table.

"Moter said you need to bring her a big fat chicken tonight."

"Tonight? Why tonight? Oy. I have an idiot for a bruder." Estle's hair was covered, her shawl was the newest piece of clothing between both families, and her smile could melt the cold north winds. "I'll stop by tonight. No chicken!"

"Zei Gezunt shvester." Aaron knew Nathan was a good match for his sister. He was sad the young man lacked anything to talk about besides Israel.

Booths, tables, people, Goyim (more than he knew), dogs, cats, even a goat roamed today's market. Lining tables were last year's apples, beets, carrots, and turnips, bolts of cloth, sheet metal tableware (everyone wanted sheet metal tableware), rakes, used coats, boots, and best of all custard pies like the ones his moter would make. No time for idleness, Aaron was building his kingdom, onward.

Aaron was taller than most his age. At seventeen, he knew he was changing by the way people looked at him. Friends of his moter would say he was 60% his foter, but 100% Zelde. This confused him and he more than once thought about this math as he walked to and from the yeshiva. *That makes me 40% foter and 60% from my moter. Right?'* His sister said, "You are 100% moter. You're becoming more like foter, look how tall you are. But you, you're cute. Foter is a man."

Foter is a man, of course! He is a rabbi, a soldier, a veteran of the Napoleonic Wars, and had spent a year in Paris reminding the French who had lost the war. More importantly, he spent a year soaking up their fervor for 'Liberty!' Foter would go on and on about the way things should be, when moter was not around.

Foter would sit on the porch, talking with his friends, and Aaron would listen through the thin wall of their thatch-roofed house. Stories about voting reminded Aaron of the Lutsk Qahal. Other stories highlighted the grandeur of France because they believed all should have such grandeur. When he said all, he meant all and talked about the end of the Pale, the end of Serfdom.

Some nights, men from the Lutsk Qahal would sit and shake their heads, claiming, "Joseph, you will bring trouble upon you and your family. Look at our lives! As bad as this is: the hunger, the lack of work; things can get worse. Why poke a bear!" Foter would smile and stick out his bearded jaw, giving few the courage to say more. "We get what we ask for. I ask for more!"

When the men of the Qahal would leave, the others would come closer, including those from the shadows. Recent immigrants, who had not two sticks to rub together, sat for hours getting to know their new neighbors and the wild stories of freedom, voting, and Liberty.

On other nights, Rabbi Mechlenburg would sit with foter and discuss mussar, their moral daily practice. Rabbi Mechlenberg was a Lithuanian forcibly moved to Lutsk and in time became the head rabbi of their beloved synagogue. In Vilna, he had studied mussar, the Jewish daily practice. Foter had heard and yearned to learn more. One night it would be about courage, another evening about strength. The night they talked about anger foter talked so quietly Aaron could not hear. Rabbi Mechlenberg was older and gave Joseph much of his patience. Moter always warmly greeted Rabbi Mechlenberg and shooed the others away with spit and then some.

These were long-ago evenings. Those memories, however sad they made Aaron feel, made his hour walk fly by. Indeed, he was early, with time to spare.

The one-story, tile-roofed yeshiva had several windows along the southern wall. To the east, one had a bucolic view, not so looking west to the many storehouses. A courtyard and large sycamore were out back, students would congregate there during breaks. In the small front yard, Aaron greeted boys and men as they came to study. Men in their long coats would brush the dust off their boots and pants before entering. Several had the beginnings, if not developed stages of hunger. All removed their hats, exposed their kippahs, and kissed the mezuzah upon entering. Aaron continued to greet and wait.

Mikhail arrived a bit late. He was a year older, but shorter than Aaron. Mikhail was Aaron's havruta partner for the past four years. An earlier study partner, Noam, G.. *rest his soul,* had died crossing the Styr when it was not completely frozen. Besides his moter, Mikhail was the closest person in his life. But like certain family members, Aaron never felt that he knew Mikhail, though Mikhail knew him better than his moter. Together, they had discussed hundreds of Talmudic topics, revealing and challenging each other's beliefs. Mikhail was a thinker, one who watched, analyzed, and rarely answered Rabbi Hulstein's questions unless called upon. Mikhail's family came from a big city in Russia where they had worked in the government. His foter 'carried an air' when he walked the dusty streets of Lutsk. They had purchased a stone home, destroyed in a fire, and were rebuilding.

"Gut Margn," Aaron expressed more with his smile and hug than his words. Mikhail clasped him back and looked deeply into his eyes. Mikhail's curly hair flopped out of his hat, his kippah was lost within. In his hand, he carried a bag with his lunch and a bit extra. Mikhail entered the yeshiva without saying a word.

The little study tables filled the large room. Chairs, stools, and long benches along the walls were all claimed, most for years. The older students, men in their mid-twenties, manipulated younger students' behavior to be the recipients of their chairs when they graduated. Aaron sat on his stool across from Mikhail, their coats and hats on pegs by the door. No fire today.

Rabbi Hulstein entered from the backroom, his office and yeshiva library. His presence turned heads, his focus on his steps, then eyes on his students caused silence.

"Shalom." He placed a large, leather-bound book on the bema. "What have you used that was not yours?" He paused and scanned the room again.

"Where's Feivel?" No one answered.

"What have you broken that is not yours? What did you do?" The thinking from the older students was palpable. Mikhail blinked a long blink.

"Does your worker replace your broken rake? Do you buy a new one with your own money for him to use tomorrow? Should you expect your neighbor to replace your rake he borrowed and broke?"

Aaron thought about Nina's children, who came over every night. They not only took things, they broke more cups and plates than he cared to count. There was no way Nina would replace those items.

"You are obligated to know these answers. He who wanders the desert should not waste his time. Study." Rabbi Hulstein spoke his words like threads connected to a rich past. It was common for students to record his lectures.

"Consider the four guardians of objects: the unpaid, the paid, the renter, and the borrower. Use what you know to build the best questions for what you don't know, yet." A command Aaron had heard a hundred times.

"Well my haver, what say you?" Aaron leaned on the little table, Mikhail sat straight on his stool, eyes almost at a squint. He was more distant today than most. Aaron waited and felt the heaviness of Mikhail's mood. "Tell me my haver, what sits on your shoulders?"

Mikhail turned his gaze on Aaron and gave him a bit of a smile while his eyes retreated further. "Rabbi Hulstein knows much. He can tell us more. Feivel won't be the only one." Cryptic words for Mikhail, but not an answer.

"You have broken my mood, my haver. As a borrower you will not be expected to replace, but I do wish you would." Aaron gave a chuckle, which was not answered. He turned away to gain a moment. He saw older students deep in their questions, younger students playfully engaged. Rabbi Hulstein stood at the bema watching his students. Uncharacteristically, Aaron approached him.

"Shalom Rabbi Hulstein." Aaron's pause was not acknowledged. "Is all well today in Lutsk, Rabbi Hulstein?" The uncommon question roused the rabbi from his thoughts. His eyes met Aaron's, who saw an old man wrestling with powerful thoughts. "Ah, my young man. I have seen much in my life." The rabbi turned for the door and Aaron followed. The sun was warm but the spring air was cool. Outside, he looked up and down the street. He did not find what he wanted.

"How old are you, Aaron?"

"I turned seventeen this January."

"And your foter and bruder, have you heard from them?" Never had Rabbi Hulstein asked about his foter or bruder, though he had known both.

"We received a letter from Joshua when he arrived in Nerchinsk." It had taken six months for the letter to arrive.

"Your foter always believed in a better life. Lord Muravyov knew this power and wasted it in the wind. Both would break in two with this world they left behind." A harsh claim knowing where they were broke most upon hearing its name. "Has your moter spoken to you about the army?" He paused, looking deep into Aaron.

Aaron did not know how to answer. Of course, he knew about his foter's time with Lord Muravyov, the wars, the talks, the death of the Czar, and their failed revolution for all. Foter had followed Lord Muravyov to Siberia, bless all there, and Joshua had joined the army to be posted with Lord Muravyov and foter. The strings that pulled these actions were the same that paid for Aaron to be here today at the yeshiva. What was Rabbi Hulstein asking?

"I am seventeen years old. I will study under your guidance for many more years, until I am a rabbi like my foter and bruder." His words fell flat before Rabbi Hulstein, who turned down the street.

He knew Aaron was not his foter, nor his bruder. His spirit had floated under his moter's guidance, as any moter under her condition would have wanted. Somehow free from the pain of his life, Aaron must be blessed, and he was. The Muravyov family had taken care of his schooling, giving a small fortune to Rabbi Hulstein. Few could pay his fee, any fee, but few could not work during the day and study. Why should such a calamity fall upon such a blessed young man? He walked further.

Lunch was not much different from the morning's limited talks. Aaron nibbled his roll according to its hardness. He appreciated half of Mikhail's apple while they sat next to the sycamore. Later, he noticed too many gaunt faces as he walked home, sunken eyes. Several bodies were lying against buildings, an uncommon behavior for anyone in Lutsk.

…

Aaron and his moter attended the synagogue meeting. She did not explain and Aaron grew unsure if not a bit concerned as they sat waiting. Members of the Lutsk Qahal rarely came to their synagogue made of plaster, not brick. They sat looking at the Jews as if they themselves were different.

Rabbi Mechlenberg called out for quiet. "I asked the Qahal to speak tonight. Please listen. We have much to discuss."

A man wearing a fine jacket with silk trim spoke, "Thank you, Rabbi Mechlenberg. We will share the proclamation and then let you discuss. We have but three weeks before we need names."

Another finely dressed man stood. "Our numbers have grown. The officials claim we have over 8,000 Jews living in Lutsk, an outlandish count." Here his face grew indignant while the faces of parents grew tight. "The Czar expects twelve more this year than last." And the congregants erupted.

"Crazy! Not possible! No way!" Calls from congregants grew louder. "You took my Isaac last year. Are you now wanting my Zavi? You'll get my fist!" The Lutsk Qahal took the storm as a wolf watched a deer, looking for weakness.

Rabbi Mechlenberg spoke, "People. People listen. There will be thirty-two men from Lutsk. I have been told to only give fourteen names."

"Only! Kill me now!" cried an old man.

The congregants cried out, hugged each other in anguish, and looked across the room for other young men to send into the army besides their own. These were the Jews who had time to come to an evening meeting. Hundreds of other moters and foters roamed the town trying to feed their families. These families were ripe for the picking and drew the anger of congregants.

"Take them from the streets! You could catch ten in a minute with one loaf of bread!"

Rabbi Mechlenberg stood, "Enough! You are both correct and … this is not who you are. I know you, David, you speak to protect your Ari. We will be thoughtful. We will protect those needing protection. But first, we will challenge this number!" The congregation cheered at the last proclamation.

The Lutsk Qahal was affronted. "Don't test. You are lucky it is not twenty. Rabbi Anshel's synagogue will name ten but would gladly give you half. Your neighborhood has Jews living in the streets. Shameful! Don't test our patience. You have three weeks to send us names." With that, the finely dressed men stood to the astonishment of the congregation. The Lutsk Qahal had spoken and walked in file from the synagogue.

...

Together, Zelde and her son of seventeen years sat by a fire under their summer awning. Clouds hid the moon and stars. The cow and chickens watched their caregivers in the flickering firelight, unsure about their actions.

Two years ago, Zelde had sat there with Joshua. She couldn't believe it was happening again. Back then, Joshua had a plan. In fact, the plan had been hatched before Joseph left. Ahead of his exile, Lord Muravyov paid Joshua's army commission. This was unheard of, but then with great wealth came great powers, even for the convicted. What officer would want a Siberia commission?

As Zelde shared and explained these details, ones Aaron had known but not understood, his lofty spirit collapsed. Deeper than he realized, an inner pride for his life, a love, a passion, and a true honor for his people crumbled.

In the twisted firelight escaping from an old summer oven, a grieving moter mistook her son's silence for strength. She poured forth her misery, her struggle to live in Lutsk, and her despair since her husband had left. The tired moter gave details to her son-in-law's dream of Israel and how it would come true for her. Her son Aaron would take the message to his foter, as no letter could explain such a story. Thus, it was to be.

The fireside image of a man was not silent from strength, but from the vivid death images he held about Jews in the Russian army. It would be freezing to death at one's post over another beating in the barracks. It would be pieces of his body strewn across a battlefield. Cannon fodder was a Jew's quickest exit, for Russians didn't want their sons blown to pieces. His mind was not listening to his moter's details or her pain or what now must happen. All he heard were the cries of his friends mixed with his own on wasted Russian lands.

That night he began his mussar work. His foter had given him twelve small cards with the attributes he should follow. Each day, he switched the card in his pocket. Today's had been Pride. In his journal, Aaron wrote his first entry.

April 7th, 1829

Pride -

- *Pride in my family's porch and my foter's belief in a better world*
- *Pride in my studies*
- *Pride in my moter's custards*
- *Pride in my fast walk*
- *Pride in my socks*
- *I would give all my pride to finish my studies with Rabbi Hulstein*
- *What use is pride if you are ignorant of the laws and ways for a good life?*

Fear - May 1st, 1829

Far more for the unknown than for what stands before us, humans are a fearful bunch.

The rustle in the darkness is rarely understood as the scurrying mice.

The slight from a friend is misunderstood as anger instead of the bad day she is having.

We let fear run our lives and our anxious reactions control those around us including the ones that love us.

A hovering mother does much because of her fear instead of love.

The aggressive father yells because of his dreaded repeated failures instead of accepting.

When the object of our fear is revealed, acceptance as well as progress follow like rains on dry lands.

Czar Nicholas was called 'Haman the Second' by many Jews because of his aggressive restrictive laws. To many, he killed his brother, Czar Alexander, and for soldiers like Joseph, this was too much. The Decembrists had brought French ideals home, but Russia was no France. Their weak attempt to overthrow Czar Nicholas was easily crushed. The high social status of so many traitors confused the Czar and more than enough were given exile as an option to their swinging from a rope. Lord Muravyov convinced Joseph to join him on what seemed like another adventure. The Siberian exiles would change the country, change the Taiga, the Boreal Forest, the mines, the frozen land, the brutal expanse. Their educated minds and passions would thrive and expand in the harsh, cold environment. They would either thrive or die. By the thousands, before even reaching Siberia, and by the tens of thousands exiles would die once there.

The 'Exile in Siberia' trail was also the 'Chai Route' to St. Petersburg. The samavors of Russia brewed the Chinese tea that traveled back from Siberia on what they called the 'Chai Route'. One could be the greatest merchant in Russia or one of its greatest criminals; it all depended on which way you walked.

Zelde had talked at length with Samuel when he delivered Joshua's letter two years earlier. Samuel was one of those rare Jews who could travel. His trade should have made him richer than Solomon, but the authorities gave him his passage so they could steal his profits. Traveling the Chai Route was not a walk in the park, and when Zelde saw him again, he had aged ten years.

Samuel looked at Zelde, "You're going to Safed, Israel. Where did you get such an idea?" He stroked his beard and leaned forward. He wanted to know.

"Our rabbi knows another Lithuanian rabbi who has contact with Jews in Safed. They've been there twenty years. It is not easy, but it is not Russia. Nathan knows more, including the best routes through Russia and the lands of the Ottomans. I have thought about this enough to make my head boil. I will go with Estle and Nathan. She will one day be with child and will need her moter. They have saved, I have saved and can make some selling of my life here in Lutsk." She emphasized her words, so Samuel knew her intent. Emphasis or not, Samuel knew such a journey was dangerous. Leaving Russia would need official signatures.

"Nathan, I've never heard of him. If he is so powerful, I would know."

"You are a Russian. Nathan's family is from Vilna. You both are new to Lutsk compared to my family. We helped your moter and foter when they were sent here. They didn't have more than a sack of sheet metal the day they arrived. Samuel, I remember the day of your bris. You have grown into an important man. Listen to your Zelde. I am going to Safed because I want more for my grandchildren than this prison."

Samuel had little to contest. "Nathan has papers from this rabbi in Safed?" What other way could a Jew leave?

"He has, and he has signatures from above."

"You mean Muravyov. Don't think they won't know. You take risks upon risks." Zelde looked Samuel in the eye with a fire he knew wouldn't be quelched. "Honestly, Zelde, things are only getting worse. In Kiev, they talk about a Polish revolt. G.. forbid! I know too much not to expect this land to be burned and flat within five years." Samuel shook his head. He was beholden to Lutsk as the Zamov family controlled his life. He returned to report to Zamov, but his travels provided multiple homes throughout the vastness of Russia. Samuel had reconnected with family friends in Kazan, who still worked the sheet metal business.

"Tell me more about Aaron." Samuel knew few Jews questioned as much as he. If there was going to be a successful future, he needed to know the smallest of issues.

Their plan was both simple and too simple. Zelde knew her husband's, bless those in Siberia, ability to speak many languages had been his ticket out of Lutsk. She knew the same would be for Aaron and had taught him all she knew. Besides Ukrainian, Lithuanian, Russian, Yiddish, and Hebrew, Zelde had others teach him French, German, Polish, and a bit of Turkish. This pleased Samuel. He needed merchants who could trade with anyone. More importantly, he needed ones that were smart. Samuel knew about Aaron's years in the Lutsk yeshiva, a rare education. So Aaron would be his assistant. Also, another mouth to feed.

There would be no pay for Aaron. He would need to do as he was told and take risks few grown men would want to engage. The road was long to Kiev. To think Kazan was far was a joke. Kazan was to the moon and back and not even halfway. Cold in Lutsk was a summer day where they were headed. Aaron could easily die on this journey. What would Zelde think of Samuel then?

The two discussed and questioned and argued for hours out back under the summer kitchen awning. Zelde was trying to grasp a big idea few understood, other than Samuel. In turn, he was trying not to further frighten a moter who was abandoning her son. Samuel had been brought up with at least some manners.

Yet, was this the right line of action for such a young man? Looking more like a wilted flower from his unbearable life, Aaron could hardly rouse himself to listen through the thin walls of his thatch-roofed house. His mind was deep into stories boys had told him about cantonist schools, where they sent Jewish boys to become Russian Orthodox. He was twisted by the twenty-five-year army enlistment from which no one ever returned.

...

"You will go with Samuel and do as you are told." What more does her boy need to understand, thought Zelde. He was escaping the Pale before the Army grabbed him.

Aaron looked at Samuel, then at his moter. "I am to tell foter you have moved to Safed?"

Had his brains fallen out of his head? Zelde raised up on her toes, grasped her arms around Aaron's neck, and pulled him close. "Have you not been listening?" Zelde stared into his weak eyes. "Aaron." This was not her son, her happy, few cares in the world walk in any weather child. Zelde softened for a brief moment. "Oy!" and it was gone. Her hard life had drained her. This was the best for all. Did he think he could hide in the yeshiva forever?

The family was moving, splitting, changing, but it had already done so years earlier. They were correcting the physical, which had not kept pace. Zelde believed in Nathan. Her strong-willed daughter would not have been with anyone else. Zelde was right to do so and would one day hold her grandson in Safed. Aaron was a healthy, growing, educated yet naïve young man getting ready to see the breadth of Russia. He was also a Jew. Russia did not love her Jews.

"Aaron. You will be shaved and clothed. Go to Gabriel and go to Zalman. You need your scalp showing and your feet and back covered in good leather and cloth. They will understand."

Aaron looked at Samuel, who threw his chin towards the door to get him moving. Was this kid going to survive?

"Zelde. Where we are going, the sun can rise and set without it rising here in Lutsk. Your son will see wonders few can imagine. He will get to see the heart of Mother Russia." Samuel wanted Zelde to trust all would be well.

"Good." Zelde was done. "We are all going to see wonders. Great.

You sleep here tonight and tomorrow you go. Take Aaron. I have much to do and need him on his way." The well of emotional love was beyond dry. Samuel at twenty-six, traveler of all Russia, never having attended yeshiva, was going to be a foter figure.

Recorded in his journal, under the mussar title of fear, Aaron wrote:

- *A spring lamb is hung by its hind feet, so fear does not taint its meat*
- *My meat is so ... tainted*
- *My stomach hates itself*
- *I will never see Rabbi Hulsten again*

... and his pencil stopped writing when he realized all would be lost.

Humility - May 1829

*The head is bowed, one steps back before one approaches
and the person of your endeavor relaxes despite the
experience of being attacked.*

Why create more trouble for oneself?

Do we not remember humans are a fearful bunch?

*Like balancing the energies of pride, humility
too can cause imbalance.*

The weak dragon upon piles of gold will be killed.

A boastful enemy will be silenced when captured.

*Awareness of one's behavior is a prerequisite
to being an adult.*

Aaron showed Samuel his bag. A minute later, it was half the size. What surprised Samuel made him turn to Zelde. "Does a moter have one more pair of these fine socks?" Samuel's smile was as wide as his arms. Zelde threw him a pair.

Aaron's new long coat, boots, and haircut made Samuel twist his nose. Zelde pulled Samuel aside. "You will have to go. Go quickly. I cannot survive watching you drive away." Of course.

Aaron was wearing his new purchases, the old hat covered his bare scalp. Zelde wrapped her arms around him like the moter who brought him into this world and cared for him these past seventeen years. "Make me proud, Aaron. One day, when this Czar leaves this world, I will see you, your brother, and foter in Safed. *Bless them. Bless you. Go with G..'s love and peace.*" Zelde looked into her son's eyes. They showed a new understanding. Good enough. With that, she turned and went into her thatch-roofed house.

Aaron stood looking at the door, the thin plaster wall, the porch, the thatch roof. Samuel turned Aaron's shoulder and pushed him forward and up into the cart.

They were nearing the southern bridge across the Styr when Samuel shook Aaron from his face-in-his-hands cry. Aaron looked down to see a blurred Mikhail standing beside the road, as if he had been waiting. Aaron wiped his face and wiped it again as Samuel stopped the cart.

"Aaron." Mikhail held an envelope out to him. His tone was both upbeat and caring, not a normal Mikhail. "Are you leaving?" The obvious answer need not be spoken. "I have done the same myself, Novgorod. I've written you a letter and another for friends in Novgorod. If you pass through, you visit them." He said this more to Samuel, as if it were a command. Aaron took the envelope while still seated. Then he rose and hopped down to embrace his friend, his haver. Mikhail cared for him. Aaron was not alone. He would not forget his yeshiva study partner, never.

Down the road, Aaron began to open Mikhail's envelope. "Ahh…no!" Samuel looked at him with stern eyes, then softened. "You keep that envelope until the day you need it. There will be more than enough of those." Aaron tried to muster a reply. He simply put the envelope deep in his bag.

The cool May air had warmed into a fine morning. Beyond the town, light green fields of wheat stretched for miles. Samuel held the reins as if he were part of the cart, part of the team of horses. They moved at a real clip, not your plod-on-the-farm walk. Aaron noticed the quality of the cart, a large waxed tarp over their supplies, the newly oiled leather tack, and muscles under a sheen on the horses. These were not the farm animals and wagon Aaron was used to seeing.

"What a gut margn," exclaimed Aaron.

Samuel felt the young man's shift. 'Ugh' as he remembered the up and down emotions of youth. "Tis fine. This road is better."

The horses were moving at a fine trot. Aaron looked at the freshly graded gravel, not his Chelm Street dirt.

"We make good time on these roads. Who wouldn't?" Samuel gave

Aaron the reins and instantly the horses knew. "Ayap! Go on!" he yelled and the black horse on the left turned his ears forward and renewed his pace. Aaron held a rein in each hand as he had been taught to do, loose but not so loose they didn't know he was there.

Samuel reached behind, moved the waxed tarp, and pulled forth a small bag and canteen. He stretched his feet out on the footboard. He smiled.

"There is mud," Samuel shared, "so thick it can swallow an ox. You move fast when you can and walk when you can't. This is easy. No load, no product. Bless us… no bugs!" And Samuel gave an emotional, "Whoop!"

Poplar, birch, oak, maple, pine, and spruce filled the woodlots, and sprouts of wheat filled the fields. As they drew closer to a town, dairy cows, steers, ewes, and lambs grazed the spring grass.

"Do you have any idea how far the Mines of Nerchinsk are from here?" Samuel saw the complete absence of understanding in the boy. *'Not now Samuel,'* he reminded himself.

"When I was about your age, I was doing my second trip to the lands beyond Lake Baikal. The Chai Route keeps Russia moving. Without our work, without our suffering, the fine people of St. Petersburg would have only hot water in the samovars. Don't forget this as you suffer each step of the way. It'll make you feel better." He ended this with a sardonic smile, something Aaron missed. *'May this road be not so long,'* thought Samuel.

"You can have your choice tonight, cart or beneath. I don't care. It's your night to choose." Samuel felt magnanimous offering the choice to Aaron. The quiet seventeen-year-old looked straight ahead, held the reins a bit too loose. Samuel took them back.

"Do you care?" asked Samuel.

"What?" Aaron had not understood. He slept regularly on the floor in the corner of their thatch-roofed house. He had expected they would reach a similar thatch-roofed home tonight.

"You can have the cart. I'll set you up tonight. Tomorrow you can have the dirt." Samuel ended this as if the ground was worse than the cart when both had their pluses and minuses.

"Did you study with Rabbi Hulstein?" Aaron asked, as if he wanted to discuss.

Samuel would end this now, half a day into their journey. "Listen! I'm not going to put up with your 'holier than thou,' I attended yeshiva. My moter pushed me out at thirteen after years of working me like a slave with every neighboring farmer. Too many mouths to feed. The lessons I learned came hard." *G.. bless.* He had told himself to hold his arrogant tongue.

"Ok," Aaron said with resolve, something which surprised Samuel.

The men were working through their hierarchies: fiscal and physical, intellectual and emotional, you name it. A fast-moving cart in the vastness of the Russian Steppe was in reality a small room with colorful landscape paintings and windows which never closed. The older one knew the dangers of expecting too much. Did he not remember the time his crew left him and his wares by the side of the road? Was his arrogant tongue not to blame? The younger one sat a bit taller, if not with a smile.

Later, "What brings your smile?"

"Rabbi Hulstein would probably tell you the story of Eliezer." At this Samuel, against his will, hmphed. "Eliezer was a proud farmer who never learned to read...."

"Oh, I know how to read." Samuel nearly lost it, then clamped down. "I can read several languages, including a bit of Chinese."

"Good. I hope to learn a bit too." Aaron said this with a straight face, with almost no acknowledgment of Samuel's anger.

"Eliezer was not the man you are. He read the land, the animals, the seasons. He knew when to plow, when to plant, when to harvest, when to cut the saplings, when the lambs were to be born, when to store extra water. He knew the land like others knew the Torah. A rabbi came to his farm late one winter evening asking for shelter and food. Eliezer sat with the learned man as they ate mutton soup. 'Rabbi, what should a man like me do to become a good Jew like you?' Eliezer asked in the hopes his hospitality would gain him a small leg up in this world. 'What?' replied the rabbi. 'You ask me? It is I who knocked on your door late at night, a foreigner in a foreign land. I should ask the same of you!'"

"I know how to read the land and animals. Heck, I can read people." Samuel wanted Aaron to agree.

"That was a good story." Samuel continued. "I'm supposed to say Eliezer was smarter than he realized."

"Sure. Rabbi Hulstein shares the story to remind us we are all wrestling with what it means to be a good Jew. Even Moses failed to make the Promised Land."

Samuel was stunned. *'Ok, What! Moses didn't make it to the Promised Land? But he was the greatest Jew ever. He gave us the Torah. He never made the Promised Land?'* Samuel's thoughts swirled. He looked at Aaron, who continued to stare ahead as if in another world.

"Is your moter going to Israel because God gave the land to the Jews?"

"She goes because Estle goes, who in turn is following her husband, Nathan. Nathan goes because he will die in Russia having no skills. That's what Rabbi Hulstein says. He also says my mom wrestles with night angels like every other Jew. She wrestles the best way she knows how. But don't wrestle so you go lame like Jacob. Rabbi Hulstein says everything in moderation except my moter's custard." Aaron laughed. Samuel looked ahead, like he was in another world.

With a bit of dramatic flare, Aaron pulled forth a full pan of custard hidden in his bag. Samuel pulled the cart off the road.

While traveling, Aaron knew he could not do his prayers like normal. Throughout the spring, partially for fun and because he had been told to by Rabbi Mechlenberg, he had practiced his daily prayers (waking, washing, eating) while doing normal activities and then he would stop and properly do the prayers. His fast attempt conflicted him as they ate custard in the shade of an poplar grove.

"I keep my money in my boot. Don't let me lose my boots." Samuel's laughter brought a smirk from Aaron. "Seriously, you need to be safe. I keep coins in my pocket but my money, I keep under the boot liner, in a hole I carved out of the heel. You need to think about what you should do." Aaron said nothing.

"You have money. Yes?" Aaron continued to say nothing while he looked at the ground.

"You don't have any money! Oy! You have more than a year's journey and you don't have two kopeks. What was I thinking! You lived in squalor. Your roof was going to fall in, another reason your moter was moving. Look at you! You look like you live on two slices of bread a day."

35

Aaron turned and smiled at Samuel. He spooned another scoop of custard into his grinning mouth. Through the thick custard, "I don't have any money. What I had I gave to my moter." Aaron continued his smile, bringing laughter to the pair.

As dusk deepened, they found a small clearing behind brush growing along the road. They were miles from the last village. The summer light would last while they cooked. Samuel figured they had traveled close to 50 miles, a distance nearly unheard of. If they had roads and weather like this, they would be in Nerchinsk before winter.

Travelers passed. Each time, Samuel would face the sound of the moving wagon. "You'll learn, my little twig. The first lesson in being a safe traveler is not being surprised." He banked stones around the fire and tried to shield the top. He went on a bit more than normal with the fire, trying to impress upon the young man the need for attentive behaviors.

Samuel had removed the waxed tarp to reveal travel supplies Aaron had not considered. Shovels, axes, poles, rope, blankets, boxes of food, four bags of horse feed, jugs of water, what looked like animal skins, more boxes of things, and sheet metal pans wrapped in fabric.

Samuel looked at the sky. A few stars were popping out after a perfect spring day. He grabbed a blanket and threw it under the cart. He pushed wagon supplies to one side and laid another blanket out for Aaron. "You can pull the tarp over yourself if the weather changes." He was done and walked off into the woods.

The horses were hobbled and grazing on the spring grass. They had quickly gone through their rations of grain. A stream behind the poplars had filled their bellies. Aaron smelled the air, listened to the insects and bird calls. Overhead, stars were trying to fill the sky. The handful of clouds parted, letting a waxing moon illuminate their edges. Treetops moved in a gentle breeze. Aaron had not spent many nights out of Lutsk, none in fact.

"Ye. Rabbi Hulstein taught us many things." Now, Samuel was ready for a story, a rare treat on the road.

"A rabbi and several merchants, with their merchandise, were sailing the Black Sea. Bandits chased them down and boarded their boat. They took everything of value (personal coins, the merchants' goods) and left.

At port, the rabbi, lacking any coins, went to the yeshiva and found work within the day. Later that week, he was called to City Hall to vouch for the destitute merchants in need of charity."

Aaron paused and breathed in the moonlight that slanted through the poplars. He listened to the leaves rustle in a light-warm breeze.

"'Why do you not ask for support?' asked one merchant. The rabbi answered with a story. 'A prosperous merchant had a wife known for her generous spirit. Eventually, he fell on hard times and died with enormous debts. His wife and children pleaded with authorities for defense from the creditors. All the while, she continued to pray at her husband's grave and for those who had no one to recite the Kaddish. When the day came that all of her household belongings were forcibly removed, a disheveled man asked what he was witnessing. The workers said she had debts that must be paid, at which the vagabond pulled forth a wad of bills and asked how much. To this day, she continues to pray for her husband and for those who have no one to pray." Aaron paused and then continued.

"Years later, the rabbi's son had grown into a fine young man in need of a profession. Who do you think he ran into?"

Aaron waited. Samuel shifted his blanket. "You mean the rabbi from the boat?"

"Ye. The rabbi who told the merchants the story."

"Well, was his son not a rabbi?"

"He was studying to be one," Aaron replied.

"The young man ran into a rabbi with no skills except the ability to tell dreadful stories."

"I hear you." Aaron gave a chuckle. "My answer was he ran into an army officer and that was the end of him. Rabbi Hulstein had no answer. He said your answer reflects your character." Samuel kicked the bottom of the cart.

"Dream better stories."

…

The next day was better as they had an early start. Samuel was boasting about nearly 75 miles in one day, and the horses could have done more. He was giddy as he made camp.

"Gather some wood for the fire. Get those large rocks over there." Samuel was in a good mood.

The commands roused Aaron from his bliss. It had been nearly two days of nothing but sitting in a cart. There was his occasional story, but nothing to do was unheard of in Aaron's life. Gathering the wood and those rocks were his first chores and woke him from his holiday. Was this the merchant's life? Samuel kept talking like Siberia was beyond the moon. Were they not going to be there in record time, especially with these horses? Besides his bottom, ugh, this was his best two days ever!

The rains started before sunrise. The little trench he had dug did nothing. Soon, Aaron was sitting on his haunches beneath the cart. The large tarp draped over the edges and water poured down the sides. The rain fell harder and Samuel groaned from underneath the tarp. "Get up here. We can wait this out."

Hours later, the hard rains had shifted to a constant downpour with wind. Samuel had been out to check on the horses who had hobbled over into the trees. "There is no point to this. Let's go."

One wheel would drop into the mudhole, twisting the cart over to one side. Then up and out and down went the back wheel. The horses were not in the mood. Samuel was not in the mood. Both he and Aaron were being dumped on and then there was the mud. Their hope lay in a kind farmer and his barn, which was just ahead. Samuel had been saying such for an hour.

A long stretch of standing water lay in front of them. "Go on. Get out there and find out how deep." Samuel watched the young man splash into the water, pass the horses with muddied underbellies, and nearly disappear mid-way through the water.

"I think this is a creek," called Aaron as he struggled back up its hidden bank.

"I thought as much," replied Samuel.

Aaron had not oiled his new leather boots. He knew when they dried, they would be three sizes smaller. He needed to keep them on, but he was as wet as a drowned rat. Samuel's gear was repelling the water, and he had a large-brimmed hat under which he could hide.

"What do we do?" Aaron added a bit of misery to his words. He sat next to Samuel as the rain came down in sheets.

"We have to go back." Aaron moaned. Samuel worked the horses backward to a spot where he turned them around. It would be at least an hour before they spied any barn.

That evening they listened to the rain run off the old lean-to's roof. In several spots, water found its way through, but the ground inside stayed dry. The horses were dried, combed, fed, and left munching at the back of the lean-to. The farmer hesitated more because he didn't want to come out into such a storm. Samuel was thankful he knew Polish and had coins handy. The damp cool air was taking its toll, but fires were not allowed in the lean-to. Samuel obtained two large hot turnips from the farmer for their dinner. They went back for tea and the farmer gave Aaron two more large turnips to stuff into his boots when he would take them off. "You look like you've never been out of your mother's house." Aaron thanked him and drank all his tea.

Which kept him awake late into the night. Rain and wind continued to splash against the lean-to. When the storm noise lessened, scurrying creatures were heard going here and there. Eventually, the critters found him and the supplies in the cart. Aaron flung the tarp in their direction. He was not getting to sleep anytime soon.

His thoughts did eventually drift away from the storm, the splashes, the scratching, the gnawing. He recalled nights in his thatch-roofed house when storms sent streams of rainwater into pans laid around the floor. His shvester would let their moter lay in bed and by candlelight protected their belongings. After one heavy downpour, during which Aaron had stayed under his blanket, Estle poured an entire pot of water on him. His shvester and moter laughed. He could do nothing but join.

The next day, under a heavy fog, the road was a disaster. The farmer calculated the route to the nearest bridge would add a good day, if not some of the next, but the creek would not go down for three. Aaron swayed so much riding the damaged road he got blisters from holding his seat.

After a week, they were a little more than halfway to Kiev. Samuel was glum.

"This story has been told several ways, but let us call it Asher's story." Despite the depressed atmosphere, Aaron had energy for a story.

"Years ago, Asher, a young man, had a dream. He woke and drew a design for weaving without human hands. This was an early mill, though no one had a clue. He worked every free moment on his invention. The exactness of his invention needed metalwork, which cost money. He had none. At the advice of his rabbi, he went to a rich elder and explained his need. When pressed for details, Asher withheld. So, he promised to pay double the loan amount if he failed to make payments, an extreme rate for anyone. Walking home with his large pile of coins, a highwayman found Asher. The thief pushed his dagger at Asher's heart until a small hole appeared in his coat and Asher relented. Asher lost more than his large bag of coins. Back in his village, he told the authorities his story, which they thought was outlandish. The next day, police caught the highwayman robbing another. They did not find Asher's coins. The thief adamantly disagreed with Asher's story. In the end, the highwayman's crimes got him years in jail where he died. Upon further suspicion, examination, and investigation, the authorities convicted Asher of financial fraud and sent him to prison. There he languished, losing all hope. Eventually, the elder from whom he borrowed demanded Asher work off his loan. Out of jail, Asher did every bidding imagined by the elder. For years, the hours moved slowly. A decade later, the elder called the double loan complete and asked if the now trained Asher wanted to continue in his work. His new position provided good pay, and he once again dreamt of completing his invention. As life has a way of balancing out, a group of women collecting mushrooms came across a hideout in the woods. Inside, buried under a pile of debris, the women found a leather bag filled with coins and the receipt for Asher's loan. Of course, the women had heard about Asher's prior conviction and all set off for his home. When Asher realized he now was a wealthy man, having both saved and been blessed with his money returned, he knew his dream would come true. When the weaving mill started making profits, Asher set half aside so he could fund other people's dreams. He lived a long time with great awe for life."

After a pause with no comments, "It's you, Samuel. One day you'll awake to a fortune staring you in the face. You need to wait a bit longer."

"Me." Samuel's voice was gruff. Then he smiled and giggled a bit. "I do like dreaming of wealth, but I'm not sure what I'd do besides ride behind two fine horses such as these." Aaron agreed.

…

Three and a half weeks after leaving Lutsk, they reached Kiev. Samuel had drifted into his hard travel mode. He expected this. He knew how to travel like this. Samuel did this for his living. Travel had worn Aaron like his new boots, sporting scrapes and cuts and grains of sand embedded deep in the leather.

Three weeks had been an eternity. Aaron and Samuel had stopped telling stories, had nearly stopped talking. He did his chores. He hung on for dear life. Aaron nursed his hands in private and looked dumbfounded upon the sheer power of the horses, who snorted with excitement as they entered the city. All Aaron could think about was a hot bath, a luxury his empty pockets could never afford.

From the edge of Kiev, Aaron recorded in his journal.

Humility-
- *I can't make it. I'm not made for this work. I don't have the strength*
- *Humility sneaks up on you like a specter. It can envelop you like darkness*
- *I pray I make my moter proud*

Faith - June, 1829

Like any skill, if it is not used and used properly it won't work when it is needed.

For some, faith is the strength not to engage another's viewpoint, their personal way and words are true.

Consider a simpler version: faith is the belief that everything will be for the best, you are supported, you are loved.

Faith that you are loved and all will be well is a superpower.

During the summer of 1829, Kiev was still transforming from a Polish to a Russian city. In the 40 years since the Polish partition, Kiev had seen a gradual increase in Russian elites replacing their Polish counterparts. In the long process, there was a local increase in 'Little Russian' or Ukrainian being spoken, a sign of their rising aspirations. Add the forced movement of Russian Jews to the Pale, Cossacks from the Ottoman Wars, as well as a few traders from just about everywhere. One could feel the city's vibrant community.

What Aaron saw made his head hang lower. He understood much of what was being said, but his lack of energy and the people's 'cityfied' engagement humbled his approach. Samuel had left the cart and horses at a livery, telling Aaron to enjoy the free day. He would be back before sunset, tossing Aaron fifty kopeks after they had eaten a full breakfast.

This part of the city was several blocks from the Dnieper; they were still on the Right Bank. Aaron walked out of the little breakfast room to a bustling street. Aaron was used to lots of people. He wasn't used to these.

The young man had enough connections in Lutsk that his open engagement was nearly always met by friendly faces. Not so in this city. He quickly learned not to laugh or smile or greet people with warm welcomes.

Aaron stood at a corner and watched the movement of people, carts, wagons, wares, and even stray dogs. He stood, slumped shoulders draped by his worn, new coat waxed to repel the rain, oiled boots not looking new. He gazed blankly at the city life.

"Gezunt." She said as she placed a ten-kopek coin in his hand. The woman was dressed in fine clothes and held her head with an air of independence.

"Adank," Aaron said automatically before he understood what was happening. He looked at her face, familiar.

"Where are you from, my young man?"

Aaron slowly began to comprehend. He had done this himself countless times in Lutsk and handed the coin back to the finely dressed woman. "I, I am from Lutsk." The woman's arms folded, not accepting the coin. "I am not an immigrant. My family has lived in Lutsk for generations." His confidence rose, and he tried again to hand it back. He smiled as he stood taller.

"What are you doing here? No one likes loiters, young men standing outside of shops."

"I am traveling to Siberia." His phrase fell flat and brought a shock to the woman. "My father is there," Aaron added, trying to smooth over the faux pas. "I am a trader." Maybe that would help.

The woman looked him over, took back the coin, and walked away.

Slumped shoulders and his blank stare returned. He shuffled through the dirt and grime of the streets with no goal in mind.

The young man was stuck in his head. Partially sent there to escape the pain of his body, but it was not all physical. Homesickness was gnawing away, leaving little room for the wonders surrounding him.

Aaron's shuffling brought him closer to the Dnieper and closer to other Jews walking the streets. Dazed, confused, these people were hungry and lacked shelter. Then doorposts sprouted mezuzahs, and for a moment he saw an older rabbi surrounded by students walking with purpose. Aaron sat on the banks of the Dnieper.

'What is wrong with me?' The sight of engaged students had nearly brought him to tears. He missed his Lutsk yeshiva, he missed his haver, Mikhail, he missed his thatch-roofed house, he missed his moter. But the young man didn't understand this and sat in his befuddlement, his misery.

Boats were moving to and fro on the river. Upriver, he could see the stone bridge crossing from shore to a little island and then shore. On the island, he could see kids playing and women gathering green shoots growing near the water's edge. They wore such brightly colored clothes. Aaron could see the glint of jewelry on bare arms and necks. He looked away, glanced at his dirty pants, boots, and coat. He pulled his journal from his black coat. Aaron did not own any jewelry.

Aaron looked up his mussar entries for modesty: *learning to transform anger for self and others.* 'What?' *Not downplaying oneself, but not flashy as to be seen.* Aaron wasn't sure he had written these. Then again, the past three weeks were such a blur. Was he angry? Was he being seen?

In truth, Aaron didn't understand how to take care of himself, especially while on the road. He didn't understand the toll from travel and, importantly, travel that exposed him to the elements. Maturity takes time.

Aaron wrote in his journal, *'Modesty: the king wears street clothes to learn what the people think of him. He wears his robes to tell them what to think.'*

Back at the livery, Aaron brushed the horses, including below their knees, still caked with mud. He went back to the small room for a bite and asked the woman if he could get a bath with his few kopeks. Thirty minutes later, he was soaking in sheer bliss.

Samuel secured them a room for the night with a fellow trader. Aaron found his corner, fell asleep in less than a minute, and woke more refreshed than he could remember.

"I thought we would trade horses here?" Aaron stated as if he knew something about trading horses.

"Hmph. Why would I want to trade these fine beasts? They have a lot more pull than anything you'll find here." Samuel paused. "The road is long. For now, these two are perfect. There will be a day, hopefully not too soon, when we will need to find fresh ponies." Nearly two days in the livery had revived the spirited animals.

Aaron marveled at the stone bridge. He saw the children and women again on the island. A colorful bunch with a colorful covered wagon pulled across the shallow waters to the island as if they were on holiday. 'Holiday.' Aaron had warm feelings for that which he did not understand.

Traveling west across the bridge were large groups of immigrants. Aaron had seen hundreds in Lutsk, but here were hundreds trying to cross one bridge. A detachment of soldiers guarded the bridge entrance. They were harassing the elders who were haggling about payments. They spoke to the soldiers and turned to their families, speaking both Yiddish and Polish. One spoke in Lithuanian, words Aaron rarely heard besides coming from Nathan and Rabbi Mechlenburg.

"Did we pay to cross this bridge?"

Samuel looked down and replied, "Did you not see the badges on the front harnesses?" Aaron had not. "The soldiers know we are conducting official Zamov business. It is both my ticket to ride and my leash. Like I am your leash. Yes?" Samuel was hoping for some understanding.

Aaron had stopped listening to Samuel's Yiddish and was listening to a woman scream such foul Polish he blushed. Her husband bent his head further while her young child wailed louder.

"Do you understand Aaron? We are all tethered." Samuel looked at Aaron, who had turned to watch the screaming. "If she doesn't stop, the soldiers will make her stop. We all can only put up with so much." Samuel gave his, "Ayap!" and the horses picked up their pace.

Later, "Kiev, is as far as your mother and sister have to ride. They can float all the way to Israel from here." Aaron didn't understand and Samuel knew, then and there, that he understood much more than Aaron about geography.

"What is the capital of Russia?" Samuel asked in a gamey tone.

"St. Petersburg. Right?"

"What is the capital of France?"

"Paris."

"Good. Now, what is the capital of the Ottomans?" Samuel asked with a smirk. "Your mother and sister are going there."

"What..?" Aaron was confused. He knew of muselmann from Rabbi

46

Hulstein. Weren't Ottomans and muselmann the same? Why were his mother and sisters going there?

"Constantinople." Samuel let it sit with the young man. "What about the Persians?"

"I don't know. Why are they going to the capital of muselmanns?" Aaron asked in bewilderment.

"Capital of the Ottomans. The Persians are muselmanns too, but they are at war with the Ottomans. Tehran is their capital. Your mother and sister will live within the Ottoman lands. Safed is located there. Did Rabbi Hulstein not teach this?" Samuel had heard about Jews pushing untruths about who owned Jerusalem.

"The Turks? Rabbi Hulstein and Rabbi Mechlenberg said Jews were given space to be in Safed. Are they the Ottomans?"

Samuel was going to have fun working this edge with Aaron.

He needed topics to fill their time. Samuel didn't have the nerve to tell Aaron that Kazan was a thousand miles away, four-times what they had just completed. The roads could get progressively worse. They wouldn't get there until after the High Holy Days. Something he knew would hit Aaron hard. Moreover, Kazan was not halfway to Nerchinsk.

During their second week from Kiev, Aaron saw the remains of what humans could do. Carts and crates were still smoldering, birds were pecking at horse carcasses, and shallow graves, some dug at by stray dogs, dotted a far corner of the clearing. Colorfully painted planks reminded Aaron of the children and women by the Dnieper in Kiev.

"Gypsies. Don't worry when you don't know what happened," Samuel commanded.

Debris along this road was becoming more common. Sometimes the furniture was still intact, like a chair waiting to be put back in place. Most of the time, debris and human waste made traveling here far more noxious.

Soldiers were more present and always had the right of way. Samuel would pull over until they had passed. They were nearing the border of the Pale of Settlement. Mother Russia was ahead with its heart for them to explore. Or so Aaron would playfully think.

One day across the boundary, they came across a road crew having chai. A road crew, the road was being graded! On the back of a small wagon, a large samovar was serving endless chai. Russian men chatted away in the shade on this late June day. Large mules were being watered out of their harnesses. The grader was a wizard's contraption with metal teeth.

"Viktor! You'll never finish!" cried Samuel as he hopped down from the cart.

"Is that you Samuel?" The two bear-hugged and kissed each other's cheeks.

"You're such a glutton for punishment. You're off for Siberia. Again!" Viktor laughed at Samuel.

"And you, you never find the warm office. Amazing you don't get lost out here." On and on, the two jabbed at the other.

Twenty minutes later, after exchanges of chai for tins, the road forward was noticeably smoother.

"I met Viktor one winter outside of Irbit. He was plowing towards the market. I stayed behind him as the snows were deep. I even helped him a bit when he needed it. At the market, and what a market Irbit is, only in the winter, we enjoyed spending the long nights sharing stories. You know he's been to Okhotsk. I heard a rumor that your brother went there." Samuel was excited. He was remembering other years like they were long ago.

"We'll get a sleigh when these roads ice over. You'll learn to pray for iced roads." Samuel looked at an astonished Aaron. "Don't worry. You know those skins in the cart, don't touch them. When the temperatures drop, we'll start using them. There is nothing like a reindeer hide when you're outdoors in the cold." Samuel gave his habitual smirk, not expecting anything from Aaron.

"I'm ready now." Aaron had a point, but Samuel wasn't going to agree. Not yet.

Aaron learned to predict the days and at night, took better care of himself. Occasionally, he was making the morning fire before Samuel. The horses drew Aaron, and he tended to them more for his needs than theirs. Aaron had not spent much time around horses since his foter had left. He and his moter did not have the money. They seemed to understand Aaron's need to connect.

Late one morning, two old women, with sacks on their backs, were walking the other way. Samuel stopped and called out, "Bubbee, where is your horse?"

Aaron noticed the old women weren't like other women in the area. Their clothing was similar, but the patterns were unique. As were the ways they tied their leggings and used animal skin foot coverings, something Aaron had never seen. Kerchiefs covered their heads and colorful shawls draped across their shoulders. "Karelians," Samuel said in a soft voice. The old women kept their pace.

"When you see a Nenet or Buryat, you know we're getting there. I imagine these women were sent to the Pale. They don't need to be asked twice. They get the job done."

Banter between travelers appeared to be the rule. It was not uncommon for Samuel to spend 10 minutes yacking with another. While they were sharing much about the roads ahead, they were also socializing, which was sorely missed on the road.

Passing another going your way turned out to be another story. If the driver was in a mood, he would speed up enough to make passing his team dangerous. Stuck behind the slow and mindless traveler, Samuel would yell and scream all kinds of words at the driver. The horses would shake their heads and stomp at the slow pace. Threats would ensue and once Samuel jumped off his cart and ran up and onto the other wagon. Aaron rescued the reins, though the horses had already stopped. They had never seen this before. How the men didn't come to blows is a credit to the commerce code.

Crime on Russian roads ended brutally thirty years earlier. It had not been uncommon for bandits to control vast swaths. The decree to rid Russia of bandits included no quarter. Bandit corpses were nailed, hung, displayed where they fell. Impeding commerce was a capital crime. Thus, Samuel cursed the slow pokes and they, in turn, cursed him, nothing more.

June turned into July and then August. The biggest difference was the bugs. There weren't any. When they had started, swarms of mosquitoes would keep them up at night. Both the horses and humans wanted to keep moving, to stay away from not only the bites but the buzz, which could drive one mad. The constant moving had helped. They had made good time.

Hints of yellow appeared on the birch leaves. A flock of small birds lifted from the road. A dampness enveloped their mornings if not days. Summer heat had played its last hand. The cool mornings were a reminder winter ruled these lands.

Samuel had purchased a good chunk of beef. At night, the two would roast chunks on long sticks. The grease would drip and flame in the fire. Fewer and fewer travelers passed as they rode further east.

"I'm going to teach you some sheet metal work in Kazan. You need to have a real skill. What we make we can sell in Irbit at the fair." Samuel looked at Aaron for a thank you, but was ready for anything.

"Is Kazan where your parents used to live before they were sent to Lutsk?" Aaron did this kind of speaking into the air as if not speaking to anyone. "I am coming to believe they may have been in the sheet metal business." Samuel was stunned the young man had uncovered so much from so little.

"Good, little twig. Kazan was our family home. My grandfather hauled the first sheet metal roller east of Moscow. My foter grew up in the business and had to sell the shop when forced to the Pale. Yegorov has made a fortune with the rollers. I trade for him and give him good prices and he has taught me the trade. With the right tools, I can now make money." Samuel pointed with his chin to pans wrapped in cloth.

"We'll give Yegorov our time and then he'll let us use his shop. I've heard some plates and pans are now painted with thick shiny paint, hard. If we can figure this out, we too can make a fortune." Samuel knew a lot about what people wanted. He knew becoming rich was a delicate dance between men like the Zamovs and Yegorovs.

"How much 'time' are you talking about?" Aaron had turned and looked at Samuel. "Why would we take time from traveling?" Aaron's tone rubbed Samuel wrong. He held his first words.

"We will take a break in Kazan. These horses will bring us more in Kazan than further east." Samuel slowed down. "We may get four horses and a sleigh for this set-up." Samuel had taught Aaron his 'I've had enough,' look and shared such now. Aaron wasn't listening.

"Why would we waste weeks in Kazan? It could be months before the roads are iced enough for a sleigh." Aaron's emotions were flailing his arms, then his hands held his head.

"One doesn't cross the Urals in late autumn or early winter." Samuel was keeping his cool. "One waits for good iced roads or waits till summer. Otherwise, such a fool would be lost." He was still calm and felt his words were being heard. He was pleased with himself.

"You've known this all along. So why did we leave Lutsk when we did? We could have stayed months longer. Was this your ploy all along, to get me to work in some sheet metal shop in Kazan?" Aaron's emotional arms had come back.

Samuel kept quiet. He hung on to his calm despite an internal wave of anger. The young man knew nothing. Did he not remember what his moter was trying to do?

"You'll get out of Kazan what you put in. If you work hard, and I know you can, you will fill your pockets at the Irbit Fair." Keep it positive, keep it positive, Samuel said to himself. "Irbit is the biggest fair you'll ever see. Metal pans, pails, and plates sell like sweet treats. If we can paint them, we'll be the hottest booth there." Samuel smiled his big smile. Aaron groaned his big groan. Samuel had kept his cool.

Leaves swirled, fell in yellow streams of birch and red streams of maple. September had brought frosty mornings, cold rainy days. Samuel shared a wool-knitted sweater and Aaron tried to hide inside his long coat, mile after mile. Sunny afternoons were like finding a warm tavern. The horses would step a little more lively on such days.

The forests had grown. No longer were the woodlots for dachas. These were primal forests not completely axed. Far from any river to transport, these woods held a magic difficult for Samuel to ignore. Aaron knew stories like Hansel and Gretel. It was from woods such as these that the witches made their brooms and flew at night.

"Are you the wandering Jew?" Aaron had a way of being both funny and offensive. Did he know what he was asking? Samuel didn't show any response. He could feel Aaron getting worked up.

"I hear stories, even Rabbi Hulstein, I know, I know. Rabbi Hulstein would bring it up. What I don't understand is how Russians, educated

Russians, can believe such a story. The answer is directly in front of them. The Wandering Jew is forever wandering because his home has been stolen, once again!" Samuel didn't know the young man had such thoughts in him.

"How can these people preach love and then steal in one breath?" Aaron was on a roll.

"Never say that again. Not around me." Samuel's tone was clear. "The Wandering Jew is practically part of their religion. I've heard this Jew was at their god's death. When Russians believe such a story, it is going to be hard to change." Aaron didn't want to listen, he wanted to complain. Then he looked around and took a breath.

"Goblins lived in the Lutsk yeshiva and hid things from Rabbi Hulstein."

"I've met plenty of trolls. And all of them speak Russian!" Samuel had plenty to share but didn't want to scare Aaron. Well, not too much.

"I was making a trip by myself, never do such if you can help it. There was only one bridge and these big Cossack trolls wouldn't take my payment. Then things got worse." Samuel could see Aaron filling in the blanks. "They wanted to join me. Imagine! There are few things worse than having to travel with two big Cossack trolls." Samuel laughed at his story. Aaron didn't get it.

"Rabbi Hulstein says this Jew wanders checking in on all the yeshivas, making sure they are studying. If there is to be a better world, a decent one, we have a lot to learn."

"True, true. One needs a skill if he is to have any future. Why doesn't your rabbi teach you something of value? Something to make a living?"

"What is better than being a rabbi?" Aaron's innocent response shushed Samuel.

At night, now that it was colder, Samuel used the tarp as a tent. While Aaron made the fire, he connected metal poles into ones long enough so when underneath the tarp, Aaron could sit comfortably. The reindeer hides were heavenly. Aaron had never felt comfort like this and slept deeply.

The land was changing, a flat expanse replaced the rolling hills. "We are getting close to 'Mother Volga'," Samuel said thoughtfully. "Yo-oh heave ho. Hmph. Yo-oh heave ho. Hmph," and Samuel laughed at himself. He was never interested in being a river trader, though Zamov had asked many times.

Three days later, they were waiting on the bank, looking across the mighty Volga. On the far shore, Kazan's Kremlin (fort) was an impressive sight. Aaron had forgotten what stone buildings did for one's spirit. The permanence of such could be felt at this distance.

The ferry contained sloshing horse-dung water. Waves crested over the upriver gunwale, causing the animals to stir if not buck in fright. With his blowing white beard, the ferryman gave not a care, despite calls from finely dressed men. At a small island, the passengers transferred to another, more stable ferry and then the shore.

Aaron's mussar journal now had pages and pages of his reflections. He read his entries for Faith:

- *Faith is Trust*
  - *- Trust - I am a good person*
  - *- Trust - I will be cared for*
- *Faith in others is as adventurous as faith in self*
- *Have faith in a higher goal*

He leafed through pages of his thoughts. This reminded him of his havrusa work and Mikhail. Was his journal now his haver? Would he ever have another study partner?

Aaron realized much of what he read was childish, silly thinking. Is this what Mikhail listened to? Had he been this juvenile at the yeshiva? Ugh. Would he ever become wise? Embarrassed, but distracted, Aaron wrote a note about seeing a young woman with pink leggings in Kazan.

Pink!

Elsewhere in the World

Second mate Katz, Aaron's brother, watched the sunrise over the coastal mountains. A light breeze joined the moment. The Ches'ma rose and dipped with the waves. Four bells rang. Captain Petrov would be in his cabin for the rest of the watch.

Joshua stood tall, calmly assessing the moment.

The sailors knew he was getting promoted and agreed amongst themselves. He was fair, consistent, and a quick learner. His people skills were blunt but appreciated, as when Kerchov was arrested. They knew, he knew, they were enjoying the sunrise, but he was not ordering them to move along. New Archangel would be sighted in the next couple of days. This had been another successful trip.

The quick Alaskan fortunes had long since faded. Gone were the days of endless sea otter pelts filling ship holds and making men ravenous for more. These days the sea was silent. The people were silent, if not rebellious to the evil inflicted upon them. Seal furs might become a similar fortune. Salt would make a run for it. Trade and its needed infrastructure were slowly taking form throughout the eastern reaches of the Empire.

"Will you join us again, Golubev?"

"Aye, sir. I have little luck on land. I like to think I could make a go of it, making barrels or such down south, but I'm not much good." Golubev was worn for twenty-three, a broken hand had never healed.

"You know your way around this ship better than most." Joshua continued to look ahead and to the sunrise. It was a fine moment. "One winter we'll stay on Kauai. I hear Captain Petrov mumble more than usual about these cold winds."

"Fine by me, sir. One gets used to sleeping outside and never getting cold." Golubev nodded. "Ayup." He moved along the gunwale checking the ropes.

This was Joshua's third voyage south. He had struggled crossing from Okhotsk, skipping the Aleutian Islands. Everyone had struggled. Three sailors had died of illness, a terrifying experience as the ship had only so many places to hide. Joshua had prayed and given thanks for his position of rank. His second mate bunk gave him space from the sick men. Now he was closing in on New Archangel. The ship holds were filled with salt, seal furs, and food supplies for the coming winter.

He would spend the winter in the hillfort at New Archangel. Maybe he would join another ship for Fort St. George, or maybe he would get lucky and go back to Fort Ross. The farms around Fort Ross calmed his soul. He felt the memories of his home and the vast fields of wheat. In truth, he would enjoy being somewhere else besides New Archangel for the winter. The gray days, the damp-cold winds, the endless rain. He was not one to drink, as the others spent much of their winter days. He was not one to do much but check in with the sailors, his captain, and help around the fort as needed. What was the last book he had read?

This was his new life. Soon he would be thirty, older than most second mates. It was such a novel concept, being an officer in the Russian Navy. He had always considered the military, even feared being drafted towards the end. He had commissioned as a naval officer before he had ever seen saltwater. Had he not joined his foter, he would never have considered this life. But Siberia was brutal, beyond brutal.

"The English are being downright aggressive. If things don't calm down, we may have a fight." Captain Petrov was not as tall as Joshua, prone to sleep late from drink. This was early for him.

The Ches'ma had three small-bore guns on the bow. Besides them and the six rifles locked in the captain's cabin, the ship was relatively weak compared to most navy ships. Joshua had a hard time imagining engaging in a battle at sea. What was there to imagine? Everyone dies.

"Yes, sir." The second mate stood taller. He knew how to take orders. He had trained his whole life. Captain Petrov liked this about him.

"We'll have to catch up this winter. I know you have a story or two I haven't yet heard." The captain smiled. He enjoyed his winters, one long social drinking engagement.

Something was building, Joshua knew not what. If he were to be promoted, what would change? He was not becoming rich as a navy officer. Life at sea was tolerable, but it was also incredibly boring.

Further south was what he wanted. Fort Ross was where he wanted to be stationed, but rumor was the English would soon end it. As Joshua looked at dead ends, he felt a rising tide would one day move his world.

What Joshua rarely thought about was his years at the Lutsk yeshivah, nearly twenty years of study. The countless hours could be summed up by his ability to humanely follow orders. Captain Petrov saw this, so did the sailors. He competently conducted his business but added a flavor of humaneness in a world of routine brutality. In truth, Joshua was far more sensitive than others knew.

The man who saw the brutality of the world and actively engaged it was Joseph, Joshua and Aaron's father. His years with Rabbi Hulstein had taught him to do one thing, argue. Lord Muravyov learned this early and allowed Joseph to fight most of his battles. If not fight them, he had Joseph at least run interference, so he didn't waste time on trivial issues. Joseph could see this, but he didn't have the power to stop it. Nor the desire to, as he enjoyed the contests as well as the victories.

In Nerchinsk, Joseph had stumbled more than he let on. There was no angle to position his arguments. There was not enough of anything to argue over. No one had what they needed. Arguments were not happening as orders were stated only once. And besides, he was always tired, if not always sick. Joseph had never felt the same since they arrived in Nerchinsk. Siberia had kicked him hard, and he had not risen up.

Daily the toil of labor, of inadequate tools, shelter, clothing, food took its toll. Joseph believed in his elevated position through Lord Muravyov, but that only went so far. His head was still shaved, infections still oozed, and his status was rarely recognized. It was not he who was the convict.

"Joseph, do not forget we are to build a better world here and then expand to all of Russia." Lord Muravyov stood outside his short-walled hut, a guard nearby. He held his gaze over the valley, his hands behind his back. Though he did not labor all day mining silver, he still felt aches and pains.

Joseph breathed in and held his torment. He tried not to cough. The vision of a better world had slipped from his grasp weeks ago. He was trying, with all his might, to stay alive. Never one to get sick, his usual rough character had reflected his body's ability to rumble with the best. Had he not traveled the world, seen countless deaths, and survived? Intuitively he had known what to eat, when to drink, where to stand, and thus he had not one scratch from his countless engagements. Was it not his fierce character that had scared all the others away!

"This evil ..." Joseph paused. "This Czar will not be long ..." He stood taller. "His wickedness is ... easily seen. Others will stand ... correct the wrongs." Joseph was exhausted.

"True, true. We will wait and gather strength." Lord Muravyov smiled as he looked upon the men below. A deep cold was descending, one more common to his January. He would spend another winter at the mine. His fellow conspirators encouraged him to come to town, but he would have to leave Joseph, who was not allowed. They taunted him with food reports. It was not easy being an exile.

The Nerchinsk hills were not the mountains of New Archangel. These hills were weathered, icy winds rolled over them, slowing not the least. Winter was descending like a curtain drop, the next act would have to wait till it rose again in spring. For all the fires smelting silver ores, Nerchinsk was an extremely cold place.

Nearly six-thousand miles away snow fell in Safed. Zelde, Aaron's moter, looked outside. No one. The snows were untouched. Their room was warm enough, there were sounds of life. Why would she or others want to get wet and cold?

Hilde was visiting. She lived two blocks over. They met at the market when each overheard the other's accent. Both of them were from along the Dnieper.

Estle, Aaron's sister, was sitting, and Hilde was beside Zelde, looking out the one window. Chai was steeping. They would soon have a light meal.

"Why would anyone like winter?" Zelde had always hated the winter months. The dreariness, the darkness, the suffering all pointed to death. Noam's death, Aaron's study partner, had nearly given her a heart attack. It had been Aaron, as the one first reported to have fallen through the ice. When he was found safe with Rabbi Hulstein, she cried for her loss that she knew one day would be real. Life was much suffering: 'Prepare yourself!'

"My foter took grain to Moscow when the snows came. He said it was much easier. I never understood." Hilde enjoyed her memories. "He was a big man and used the lord's big horses. The wheat sacks were stacked as high as a hill. Ours were but a few, but what a difference those made. We lived like lords compared to the youth today." Hilde smiled, remembering remnants of old Poland before all was consumed by Russia.

"I bet your synagogue was made of brick." Zelde's words were her attempt to support Hilde, who had lost everything. Several years ago, her husband and son had been arrested for tax evasion, a complete farce. The family had nothing and thus had no means to extract the men who died in chains.

"It was. Cherkasy had everything we ever wanted except defense from the Cossacks. Every time we were on the wrong side of the river. We rebuilt many times until we learned to move downtown. Our synagogue looked like every other building. Only the locals knew it as a synagogue." Hilde was nearly seventy years old, she didn't look it.

Zelde looked at her hands. She felt seventy.

"Estle." Zelde hovered over her pregnant daughter. "You need another blanket." And Zelde placed one across her daughter's shoulders.

Estle accepted her mother's care as she knew her good intentions, however frustrating they may be. The escape from Lutsk had at first been a holiday. No one could have predicted the endless bribes needed to move forward. Nathan was smacked around so many times he became unable to engage the highwaymen. Zelde had taken on the family spokesperson role and for this, Estle was most grateful. Her husband was not a fighting man.

Here in Safed, Nathan had blossomed. He was revered as an extension of the esteemed Vilna Gaon. His views were highly respected, and many men came to gain his insights and opinions. Estle knew this and gave him much time and space. She didn't need to say much, as Zelde continually reminded Nathan of his family obligations.

"How is Nathan so respected here, but we must live in such poverty?" Zelde had a tone to her words few wanted to counter.

Hilde sighed. She knew her friend was more on the 'negative' side of life. It was Hilde's hope that her example could guide her friend across. At this moment, she was tired and ready for a bite.

The small charcoal fire had gone out. A coolness was seeping through the room. They sat with their feet tucked in, off the floor. The chai was a welcomed treat, as was the bread. All regretted not having a samovar like they did in Russia.

"Your Nathan is all the talk. I heard he may be hired to argue before the magistrate in Acre. You are blessed."

Estle gave a warm smile.

Zelde sipped and slipped into a memory. Each sip reminded her of her front porch in Lutsk. On the porch bench, she had watched life rise and fall. There, a warm cup would energize her. This cup brought forth Joseph's face. He was leaning forward, speaking much with his hands and his beard stuck out like a weapon. His thick hair was his robust character. It was a painful memory. She remembered this was a life of suffering and she stiffened herself.

In fact, at that moment, all the Katz family stiffened, and held an alertness. Zelde felt a twinge, which was quickly banished. Joshua, who may have started this alert moment, continued such during his watch on the Ches'ma. Joseph did his best to stand next to Lord Muravyov, but succumbed to the bench outside the hut. It was Aaron who truly felt the power of the family moment. A wave of warm air, probably from one of the numerous furnaces in Kazan, lifted Aaron to memories of when they all sat together in their synagogue, the whole Katz family. Aaron knew his family was blessed, that he was blessed, and the struggles he experienced would pass if he could find his way forward to his father in Siberia.

Trust - October, 1829

Faith and Trust, they live on the same street.

Trust in people, trust in things, trust in judgment, and the philosophy one is walking.

Trust means nothing if it is not successful more than half of the time.

Trust until - keeps one from wasting energy and time worrying.

Gaining another's trust can have more to do with the other person's issues.

Usually, it is best to call the spade a spade.

Trust is positive energy.

What Aaron could not put to words was his growing trust in himself. He had learned the routines of the road. He had battled through storms and lack of water, angry people, and boredom. His skills had brought him through and his positivity had helped when a sickness made him question everything. While he saw the fruits of his work, he was too close to gain perspective and thus trust.

Samuel saw it. Long ago, he started believing in Aaron and his ability to get the work done. Furthermore, Samuel started believing in how he engaged Aaron. In a flash of maturity, Samuel realized he was seeing himself grow.

Kazan was a frontier city. Each time Samuel visited, he saw and felt the changes: the new people, the new ways of doing things. Waves of change flowed through the city like the mighty Volga. Its location made Kazan both a producer for and a storehouse from the frontier. Upriver, one could connect to Moscow and St. Petersburg. Downriver were trails to the Don and Black Sea or floating on the Volga to the Caspian Sea. East were the Urals, Siberia, and the flow of goods from China. Produce it here for the frontier or store what came from the east for the big Russian cities.

Ironworks had come to these crossroads almost sixty years ago. Samuel's grandfather immigrated from Germany with other iron tradesmen. They introduced 'puddling' to the production of iron, creating a higher quality material. Samuel's grandfather took steel bars and rolled them into sheets. The frontier people and beyond clamored for his product. The real money came from working the sheets into useful everyday items like plates, pans, bowls, pails, and cups. Rust was the big drawback and plagued the mass production of these items.

Two blocks from the iron smelters and north of Kazan along the Volga, Yegorov's shops were gray, wooden, and one of the few with metal roofs. Belching black smoke filled the streets. Wagons pulled by tired mules and oxen filled the muddy roads. Working men were everywhere, creating an industrious atmosphere. People were making things. They were making money.

Yegorov did not frown, but he did not smile when he saw Samuel. He was standing outside of his large shop talking with men while looking at pieces of steel piled in a wagon. "Samuel," Yegorov announced, as if it marked a shift in time.

"You are so happy to see me, Yegorov." Samuel kept his gaze on the man as he concluded his business.

"Samuel, I am behind on everything and the people around me are idiots. These men are trying to sell me old scraps, which are scraps because they break like cake. No good. Why would I want to buy?" Yegorov looked at the men pulling their heavy wagon down the muddy street. "I have buyers for all I can produce." He paused and looked again at Samuel with a smile. "You have caught me frowning atop my pile of gold." He spread his arms and tossed Samuel back and forth in a bear hug.

"Yegorov, today may be your lucky day!" Samuel smiled his big trader smile and unpacked his scheme to the budding industrialist. They walked up the street and turned back, heads lowered, both calculating numbers Aaron could hear. Impressed, Yegorov turned to Aaron and welcomed the 'little twig', shaking his hand up and down. Together they walked into the sheet metal shop, hot air hitting Aaron like a house-sized oven. "You'll get used to it. We stoke the fires first thing and try to roll by noon. We're getting ready to roll, so I've got to move. Stay and watch, definitely you 'boychik' as I doubt you've seen anything like this."

The factory boss moved quickly to a group of men standing by another doorway. They were shirtless, with long leather aprons and heavy leather gloves. Aaron could see inside from the glow of a full bed of hot coals being blown by huge bellows. Each push of the bellows created a whitening of the light, then orange and red. Yegorov went outside and talked with another in charge of the mules who turned the rollers.

Back inside, Yegorov and the shirtless men pulled a large, glowing bar of steel from the bed of coals. The pulling tongs were long. Aaron could feel the heat at his distance. The men squinted and pulled the red bar onto metal tables. Yegorov gave the bar a whack with his hammer and then a nod to shove it through. The men guided the bar into the spinning rollers, which grabbed and dragged it through. The men dragged the now somewhat flatter bar back around where Yegorov gave it another whack before he sent it through. Two roller trips was the limit before the steel went back to the hot coals. After twenty minutes, the bar had become a sheet thinner than leather, thicker than fabric. The men doused the sheet in a pool of water and stacked it against the wall. On to the next.

"This is a good team," commented Samuel. "Yegorov knows he's lucky. One mistake and someone gets hurt. Never make a mistake when working hot metal." This, Aaron didn't need to be told.

Samuel and Aaron could have the room at the back of the shop. Of course, it needed piles of trash moved out, but the room was free and, of course, warm. The north side of buildings had ice, even a few had remnants of snow. It was October and everyone knew what was coming. An hour after dark, Aaron was lying on his reindeer hide in his corner of the backroom.

His first assigned chore was to stoke the fires on days they were going to roll steel. He had to wake before everyone and light a pile of charcoal.

Lighting the fire was easier with the enormous bellows. Working the bellows was a sweaty and tiring experience, no matter the temperature. Yegorov paid the town night watchman to wake Aaron. Aaron watched coins pass between men, yet had nothing to himself.

Aaron felt being taken advantage of because of his age. Samuel spoke about two months, maybe more, working for Yegorov. This deal made no sense to Aaron. He resented each morning and each additional ask, however nicely made.

Samuel felt like he was giving Aaron a wonderful gift. The young man was learning a trade that could bring him a real living. The best was yet to come. Aaron had not seen Yegorov's craft shop where they made the sheet metal into pans and plates. Some workers created house items like candle holders and lanterns. Others worked on Kazan's industrial needs. The possibilities were endless with this material. On his own, Samuel was snooping around for thick paint to coat and protect the metal from rust.

"Let's move the coal for Yegorov." Samuel was feeling his oats and Aaron was having nothing of it.

"You can move it. I've got the shop to clean and Yegorov wants me to move the steel to the furnace for tomorrow's rolling." Aaron added much attitude to his words.

"You'll miss out on a big surprise 'little twig'." Samuel gave his big smile and received a flat, 'No.'

"What lives on your shoulders?" Samuel looked with as much care as he could muster for this suffering fool.

"I have nothing. I work and work and have nothing while I hear you and Yegorov talk money like it filled a wagon."

"Oy, my little twig. You do have nothing in this world." Samuel made this point to get Aaron's attention. "You want some rubles? You want a piece of the action?" Samuel was hinting hard. Would Aaron bite? Aaron squinted at him sideways. He was tired of all this manipulation. Exasperated, Aaron yelled, "Of course!"

Samuel hoped the craft shop would interest the young man. He didn't expect the boy to take to it like a duck to water. After an afternoon showing him how to crimp and fold the metal edges, how to bend and turn the sheets, Aaron wanted to work all the sheet metal Yegorov would give him. Thus, Aaron learned an important lesson about capital, something he lacked. What he had was a passion for his own coin and a talent for working sheet metal. Both Samuel and Yegorov knew a wise investment when they saw one.

"One-tenth." Yegorov offered Aaron a tenth for when he sold his sheet metal creations. The metal was Yegorov's. All the tools were his capital. When Aaron objected, for that is what he liked to do, Yegorov gave him a twentieth for the first 50 items as a penalty for his impudence. After a frustrating minute, and Yegorov could last all day, Aaron huffed and walked away.

After two hours, Aaron came into the shop with a blackeye.

"I bet I know who gave you that shiner." Yegorov laughed at Aaron. The other men laughed when he told them what Aaron had tried to do. Receiving such treatment, Aaron dropped his head further partially to hide his tears. "What were you thinking? Vasilyev has sold my wares in Kazan for years. He would not put up with some upstart trying to take his living." The men laughed again.

"Then where am I going to sell?" Aaron tried best not to whine.

The men and Yegorov looked a bit baffled. An older man answered, "You're going to the biggest market in the world. Did you forget?" The men were jealous, as only one of them would get to go.

"No!" but Aaron had forgotten. This was not his finest moment.

He turned outside and walked the streets to the river. The November winds blew cold. Rancid coal smoke stung his eyes as the ironworks increased their production during the winter. Shore ice caught floating ice, making a dangerous ice shelf to a small island. *'Why was he so mad?'* He threw what rocks he could pry from the frozen ground. Two broke through the ice while others skidded across, making haunting sounds. His racing mind found something to blame. He latched onto hating being the youngest at the shop. After dinner, Aaron had forgotten how his day had begun.

Yegorov's deal was 10% after he sold 50 at 5%, Aaron would sell a thousand! Importantly, he needed to know what was the best item. After a week of staying low, he went back to Vasilyev's and watched from afar to see what sold. Pans and plates sold well, candlestick holders and candle lanterns sold well too. He needed something different. He watched a dairyman buy a dozen pails for his milk. The dairyman talked at length with Vasilyev. Without hearing him approach, Aaron turned to see Vasilyev standing beside him. "He will buy lids for all his pails, but it doesn't seem right to me." The sheet metal salesman smiled, walked back to his booth, making a fist, chuckling to himself.

Back in Lutsk, Aaron had watched his mom use all kinds of containers for her milk. Most people brought their own bottles. She would pour straight from her pail, through a cloth, and into theirs. His mom needed better pails. Imagine how much milk she would have if she had had two cows.

In the shop Aaron made a lid, then he made a dozen. He knew better than to go directly to the dairyman and had Nikolai take them to Vasilyev. When he returned, Aaron got a nod of approval from Yegorov's shop worker. Nikolai appeared to be Yegorov's man going to the Irbit Market.

The young man from Lutsk could feel the momentum and worked on an extra big pail. The whole point of a milk pail was to fit under a cow, which the extra large one did not. He also needed to correct the large pail's lid, which was difficult to make secure. Personally, he wanted a built-in cup so as not to be slurping milk from a full pail. Aaron then tried a tall standing jug able to hold three pails' worth of milk. Crazy. So he narrowed the mouth and closed it with a long cup. The standing jug weighed nearly a hundred pounds when full. He put handles on his oversized samovar with its funny long neck.

The next morning he went with Nikolai to Vasilyev's. The three went to the dairyman's barns and discussed. Aaron added, "My mom would want one of these. She gave leftover milk to immigrants, which only angered everyone." The men all agreed. "With this, she could keep her extra milk in the cellar."

Aaron continued, "You can sanitize them in a fire, unlike a wooden barrel. Pottery is too heavy for this amount of milk." The men agreed to this, too.

While it was a heavy jug, the cup lid held the milk tight inside. The cup lid was a catchy idea with which the three men took turns pouring themselves a drink.

Soon, Aaron received an order for six. By mid-December, he had made twenty more.

Samuel had been doing his own experimenting with resin coatings. Most coatings on his cups and plates would blacken or crack from fire. Could he get buyers if they couldn't warm their cookware in a fire? The best coatings cooled near the hot coals. He played with this idea to the point of making a box to act like an oven.

In a flurry of a weekend, Samuel painted red all of his and Yegorov's cookware. He liked how the red paint sat thicker on the metal. Combined with the resin and then the baking in his oven, these cups and plates caught everyone's attention. The Irbit trip was setting up to be their best in years.

"There are few stories as good as 'The Three Apples'." Aaron looked for Samuel to agree.

"Ok, I bite. Tell me the story of 'The Three Apples'."

"Oh, no! It's so long and full of suffering. Not today. But it all starts with love. The man is all lovey-dovey with his beautiful wife and does anything for her." Aaron looked at Samuel closer. "Why don't you have a wife?"

"What!" Samuel shook his head. What a kid! There was a long story here too. "I won't do things because she is beautiful. I'll do it because she is my wife."

"Yes. Maybe this is why the story goes so horribly wrong. You know he kills her."

"What kind of story is your rabbi telling you?"

"He doesn't teach us these stories. He tells us to, 'Go and read other people's stories.' There are few stories as good as Shahrazad's. They had to be good." Aaron thought about the Jinns of Arabia. In the north, they probably grew long beards and transformed into bridge trolls.

By late December, the eastward roads had iced over. Snows had fallen for over a month, the mud froze, potholes had filled with ice. When they had arrived in October, Samuel had sold his team and cart. Aaron regretted not saying goodbye to the black horse and let Samuel know. Together, they went to the stockyard.

Samuel purchased four horses and a sleigh, as he had said. On the front harnesses, he hung the Zamov badges. Winter harnesses lacked most metals which burned animals in the frigid temperatures. Aaron brushed the new, shorter, thicker horses. Samuel said they were Nenet horses. Yegorov laughed.

They packed Samuel's sleigh with red tableware. Stuck here and there were Aaron's milk jugs and pails with lids. Nikolai drove Yegorov's set-up, his own sleigh and horses filled with the red tableware. Heavy winter felt tarps replaced the waxed summer ones. In the shop, Samuel built a firebox and stovepipe for warmth in the felt tent. This camp set-up was one in which they could spend some length of time.

The morning they left, Yegorov pulled Aaron aside. "You must stop and visit if you come through again, 'Little Twig'." Aaron blushed with honest appreciation.

...

Seven hundred miles and the Ural mountains separated them from the largest market in the world, well at least one of them. Their four-horse team led the way. When the snows got deep, the two lead horses switched every hour. Nikolai's team appreciated the broken trail on such days.

Nikolai sang to his horses. At the shop, around Kazan, Nikolai never sang. On the open road, he sang for hours, sometimes the same song over and over, to the point of garnering Samuel's ire. Aaron sometimes joined as the songs were simple and the Russian words easily learned. He realized his songs from Lutsk had a rhythm, a complexity unlike most sung by Nikolai. Aaron smiled at his Lutsk memories and sang under his breath.

"The first time I was at Irbit, I nearly died. You must be careful, 'little twig'." Samuel paused for emphasis and gave a snicker. "I was young and naïve. I ran the market like I was at Lutsk and quickly got lost. By nightfall, I had become desperate. I turned down the last row of booths, which led out to winter quarters. I wandered the wagons and felt tents and soon had a group of boys pursuing. When Boris finally found me, I was bruised, bloodied, and without my coat. He beat them, dragged them, and had them locked in the market stocks for all to see."

The younger man from Lutsk didn't know what to say. He couldn't imagine surviving a minute without his coat. "Why did those boys beat you?" What do you say to say such brutality?

"You learned little from your foter," Samuel said this more to himself. "When was the last time you had to fight someone?" Samuel paused, for he wanted an honest answer.

Had he ever fought someone? Aaron didn't know the answer. "I've…" he began, but knew he was going to stretch the truth. When he was younger, his brother would shove him around. On the streets, he had seen many fights and had been hit himself more than he could count. But those were not fights. Rabbi Hulstein had been repeatedly clear about fighting if his own foter had not. "Fighting is for those who haven't studied and learned the right words to say."

"Thank you, Rabbi Hulstein," Samuel added. "You're going to get your face blackened again." He huffed and shook his head. "Keep your fist tight. Let me see your fist."

Aaron made the tightest fist he could and fake punched Samuel, who easily caught it and opened Aaron's fist. "Not bad. Whatever you do, hit straight, hit with your first two knuckles. Otherwise, you'll break your hand." Samuel looked Aaron in the eyes.

Samuel turned and stared forward down the road. Aaron knew Samuel did things like this.

What he didn't know was how Samuel was recalling his foter fighting at Irbit. Boris, what a name, wore his kippah everywhere. While the frontier was more accepting of Jews, and Irbit accepting of all, there were always those who kindled hatred at deep levels. More than once Boris had swung a little cudgel he kept in his coat. His foter was a proud German Jewish tradesman and no backwater Russian was going to tell him what to do. Such thinking always bothered Samuel, though he himself had been known to swing a cudgel or two.

Aaron had filled less than a half of his leather-bound journal. In Kazan, he had gathered extra papers and two new pencils. He drew his milk jugs on these sheets, sketched the shops along the Volga. He tried to map his journey. His drawings were a mess.

Tonight he read through his journal for Trust:

- *Trust all will be good*
- *Trust is found in repeated moments of awareness*
- *Trust when you need something it will appear, though it may come in strange packaging*
- *Trust in Love*

The felt tent was warm. Outside, the short, stocky horses, hobbled, were snorting nearby. Flickering red light came through the cracks in Samuel's little tent stove. Nikolai snored like splintering wood. Aaron trusted tomorrow: *'what he did today he would more than likely do tomorrow'*, and that was good.

Awareness - January, 1830

Countless tasks need attention and we have a tendency to add more.

An accurate list is ridiculous. Most rely on what is most pressing, what we enjoy doing best.

We hear the benefit of being aware, but really?

Do you want to be aware of everything needing your undivided attention?

Your awareness is like a flashlight beam, needed when it is dark.

On the 11th of January, Aaron marked his birthday. He was crossing the Ural mountains in an open sleigh. He was on an adventure to Asia! Irbit held the promise of not only the largest market he would ever see but also the chance to sell his wares and make money. Aaron felt the excitement in his bones.

The young man wrote notes about his adventure on scraps he kept in the back of his mussar journal: descriptions of how he was getting stronger and gaining skills; paragraphs about how traveling with Samuel was a new world apart from his yeshiva studies; entries about his longing for the yeshiva's social atmosphere, the collegiality, and his haver. His beard, what he called his beard, was longer but lacked any fullness like Samuel's or Nikolai's. He was eighteen.

Each evening he waited for three stars to start his new Jewish day, something he had been doing again since they were on the road. During his twilight prayers, he realized it was his birthday. Though he knew his actual

Gregorian birthdate, used in old Poland but not in all of Russia, he followed his Jewish birthdate, the 17th of Tevet. It required a bit of math, calculating his Jewish dates with the Gregorian. It got more complicated when he had to translate to the Russian use of the Julian calendar.

A common question on the road: when would the Irbit Market start? Russian answers with the Julian Calendar dates caused others to pause. While there was a big difference, it became clear most relied on the market opening a moon after the winter solstice. Clear night skies were cold, but helpful especially for dates.

What everyone appreciated was how much easier it was to travel in winter. They filled the sleigh with all their red metal cookware, their supplies, extra sacks of oats for six horses, and their tent charcoal for fires in a land where heat saved your life. The sleigh glided easily, something that never happened in a cart.

Fresh snow provided one of the more playful rides, as long as it was not too deep. The horses pranced higher and Samuel liked to make figure eights when he could get the ponies to comply. Nikolai liked to play as long as they kept pace.

Several enclosed sleighs passed them, moving at nearly a gallop. These vozoks were the preferred way of travel. Some had heat and all enjoyed the glide a sleigh provided. Aaron saw why the Irbit Market only happened in winter.

"Where will we stay at the market?" Aaron was jealous of the enclosed vozoks.

Samuel was aware three bodies changed much. For one, three required more tent space. Then there was the cost for hay, water, and oats for six horses instead of four. The fields for the market booths would fill up quickly. Just as quickly, his supply of charcoal would disappear if he wasn't careful. "If we can't have our tent near our booth, you'll be watching our gear while we sell."

"Oh no, I'll be selling my items like Yegorov said. I plan to make a bundle." Aaron spoke with much enthusiasm.

"You've got a lot to learn about selling. Watch one of us before you try to sell your wares and drive customers away." Samuel both joked and was serious.

"Back in Lutsk, my shvester would sell more than moter's buttons, pins, and custards. She made dresses for rich women. Estle had them pay monthly instead of at once, which allowed her to visit and ask for more work. She said the monthly payments kept her business going. I have seen no one doing this."

Samuel had thought about installment plans but couldn't see how it would work. "Maybe Yegorov could use monthly plans, but he doesn't want to deal with it. He needs the money in hand to keep his steel supply flowing." He was grateful his business didn't have such headaches as Yegorov's.

"If we are at the Irbit Market for more than a week, vendors could use a daily payment plan. They'll be making money each day. I can sell them more when I come around. I bet you hadn't thought of that!" Aaron was proud of his creative business brain.

"You give that a try and let me know how it goes." Samuel was not one to enjoy reminding buyers to cough up money.

After midnight, a powerful winter storm descended on the travelers. By morning, two feet of snow nearly sealed-in the tent. Worse, one horse was lying down, never a good sign. While winter travel was much faster and smoother, care for the horses was doubly difficult. At this part of winter, in these mountains, there was little fodder the men could simply uncover. Water proved to be a constant issue. They had chosen this camping spot for its windbreak, not for its proximity to water.

Eventually, Nikolai killed the horse. Once over the shock of death, Aaron knew 'breaking trail' was the concern. He realized it would probably be one of them. More than likely, himself out in front, trying to stay on the road, trying to stay in front of the horses. He laughed at the thought.

The next day, "We'll stop here." Samuel called it by mid-morning. They had moved, at the most, a mile. Importantly, they were next to a grass-lined river he knew had plenty of water. After an hour of shoveling and chopping ice, their horses had fodder and water to fill their bellies.

Which was a lifesaver because, after the storm, the clear skies let the temperatures drop like a stone. Aaron went out every couple of hours to open the water. The horses were resigned to the cold in a way that allowed them to survive. Aaron brought in more dry branches from the riverside spruce trees.

"It'll be colder than cold tonight." Nikolai chuckled to himself and to Samuel's annoyance.

The little sheet metal stove ate spruce branches like candy.

"We may need to stay here a few days. Until someone breaks trail. There's a crust on the storm snow. It will cut the horses' forelegs. Let someone else do all the work." Samuel almost grunted his words, his resignation to winter.

It took three days.

"Ugh!" was the common, exacerbated call. "What is going on?" Samuel would rant to himself, though he would rarely go outside. Instead, he relied on Aaron's repeated reports.

"First there was darkness." Aaron wanted Samuel to stop being such an unlearned man. "Light and order comes from G.. Storms come from the empty, formless darkness that has always been." Aaron was proud of how the words flowed from his knowing.

"What! So G.. allows these storms though he knows they kill us! Where is our compassionate G.. when we need him?" This kind of ranting was too much for this cramped tent.

"You don't get faith from an easy road." Aaron didn't want to deal with Samuel's anger.

Hours ticked by slowly.

Late one evening, what looked like a herd of vozoks sped through their valley. Nikolai claimed a team of reindeer pulled the front vozok. Samuel felt annoyed by Nikolai. It had been a long three days.

The three went out to inspect the road. It was a pastoral painting: feet of snow lit by a splash of sunset, everything pink and blue. The snow would set up after the deep-cold night. Tomorrow they would make up for lost time.

Getting ready for bed, "Years ago, I fell into overflow. I was two feet off the trail but five feet in water. Colder than this. I stood there in shock as the water penetrated my clothes. My mates pulled me out and rolled me around. Snow sucked up the water like a sponge. Still, I had wet feet and that will kill you. I changed socks, which meant I had to beat my feet back into my freezing boots. Later, I had to beat my boots to get my feet out. I slept with them under my blankets." Aaron stared off into space, giving Samuel the familiar feeling he never listened.

"Point is, fresh snow can hide water. It comes out of the hillsides or from cracks in the river ice. Stay on the trails or be real careful." Samuel knew this young man had never seen overflow.

…

Two weeks later, they were setting up shop at the Irbit Market. Aaron's nose, cheeks, and earlobes had scabs from frostnip. Samuel complained about his hands from holding the reins all day.

Around them swirled a festival of products, an array of people. Gone were the normal dark, dirty colors of the road. Everywhere were brightly colored fabrics, shiny metals, and mirrors for the multitude of torches, lanterns, and lamps lighting the endless market.

Within an hour of arrival, an official approached Samuel. "You've been here before, two rubles. Register here." The tall, heavily clothed man pulled off a furry mitt and handed Samuel a board and paper to register.

"I could have used a pair of mitts like yours," he said with a grunt. He shook his hands to get the blood moving, to get them to complete the registration.

"Four rubles at most booths. If you want a deal, I can set you up. Let me know, three rubles is a good deal. No?" The official handed Sam his mitt. Samuel tried it on. The inner felt lining brought a smile to his face.

"Ugh. Here." Samuel said and handed the man the two ruble fee. "You need to go or I'll spend all the money I don't have." He slapped his back and guided the official away from their booth.

"You'll want this," said the official as he turned and handed him a receipt for his registration and fee. "Someone will be around in another minute asking. So don't lose this." The official looked Samuel in the eye. "Our booth is two rows over. Stop by when you've made some money and I'll get you a pair of these mitts." It was fairly obvious Samuel's hands caused him much pain.

"What did you tell him we were selling?" Nikolai asked.

"I wrote, cookware." Samuel's leather gloves with liners were next to worthless. "I looked through his list and didn't see any other cookware, pottery, anything like us. Things are looking good." Samuel wanted to turn his attitude around.

"Little Twig, you'll want to remember where we are. This place is so big that you can get lost for days. There is so much to see, take it slow. You can rush around and never get to see the good stuff. And don't eat or drink anything until you've watched another. There are plenty of 'bad apples' in a place like this." Nikolai tossed Aaron a ruble. "Yegorov knows you'll do him right. This is kind of a thank you. You understand Little Twig?" Nikolai looked at Aaron. Samuel watched the whole exchange.

"Of course. Thank you Nikolai." Aaron added, "Yegorov." The young man from Lutsk gave a chuckle and put the small fortune deep into his inner coat pocket. He had gained a few kopeks here and there doing extra work, but a whole ruble! He had rarely had so much. If his moter could see him now!

"If you ask too much of a colt, he'll never reach his potential," Samuel commented as Nikolai walked by.

Nikolai turned and with a smile, "You know, this young man speaks nearly eight languages. I hardly know Russian! He is going to come in mighty handy." Nikolai chuckled to himself as he set up camp.

Before they went in for the night, Aaron and Samuel walked the market. It was a cold one, which made each step sound like crunching crisp apples. Ice fog lay here and there, making the torch and lantern light sparkle but weakly. Nonetheless, the market did not disappoint Aaron.

Inside the felt tent, things were a bit more cramped than normal. Nikolai had brought in all kinds of items from his sleigh. "This here is the box, our box. I've got the one key, here, around my neck. We keep all our earnings in here." Nikolai tossed Aaron a leather bag. "Use it during the day. I'll give you some change in the morning. You know how to make change. Yes?"

"I've worked my mom's booth many a time in Lutsk. I'm usually splitting kopeks, not rubles." Aaron imagined piles of rubles in the box by the end of the market. "How much do you think we'll make?"

"There are countless surprises ahead, Little Twig." Nikolai smiled.

"Stop thinking about getting rich. You are the low-man on the pole here. Way above, and I mean way above, is Yegorov. Above him, I will owe a bundle and a half to Zamov." Samuel knew what Aaron was feeling. He remembered. He also remembered the letdown and the long ride home, much less to Nerchinsk.

Aaron muddled to himself in-between his prayers. Whatever Samuel said, he was going to make a bundle.

Samuel lay awake for hours. He played with memories of his foter, Boris, and himself at this market years ago. Where had the years gone? His foter had died too soon. He wanted to know much more. He would never be the man his foter had been, strong like steel-strong, and always ready to engage with anyone. Fearless. He was a Prussian Jew. Why was he, Samuel, afraid of so many things? Was he a Jew from old Poland or Russia? He lay awake and worried the night away.

What he didn't know was how much more his foter had worried the nights away. Before Samuel was born, Boris could complete nothing. He was so afraid of life that he lived at home until he was thirty. He met Greta, his wife, because his parents hired a matchmaker. His dad made him leave the house once he was married. Boris's fear made everything an enemy. He fought his way through life, and a shortened life it was. What Samuel didn't know could fill a book.

Cold.

Despite the reindeer hides and two felt layers, inside the tent all froze. Everything was stiff. Samuel struck a match and saw frost everywhere, including on his little stove.

For weeks they had melted ice and snow in one of their red pails. It barely fit on the little stove, but the snug lid kept the water from spilling. Samuel inspected the paint for damage. He was pleased with his product and would show his buyers how well the paint held up.

The long winter sunrise provided some light for the traders, the snow brightened everything. Tables lined the pathways. Sleighs and tents abutted the tables. Most traders stabled their horses at the livery, probably the most expensive livery Samuel ever used.

To say the people around Aaron were from everywhere was an understatement. In Kiev, there were Poles, Ukrainians, Cossacks, and Russians. Foreign traders mixed in here and there. In Irbit, Aaron was in Asia. Muscovites and Piterechs, people from St. Petersburg, made it known they were the cultured people at Irbit. Mongolians and Indigenous Siberians had the wildest of characters, barking their words. Turks, Chinese, Persians, Arabs; Swedes, Austrians, French, and don't forget the Prussians, they all had their metal trade badges displayed at their booths. Samuel displayed the Zamov badge, or one way or another Zamov would find out.

Booths displayed nearly everything, all shiny and new: metal wares like axes, shovels, picks and farm tools - planters, reapers, forks. Down another row, Aaron found tailors and tanners, jewelers and leatherworkers. The fishmongers sold frozen carp stacked like sticks in a basket. Nikolai had told him to take it slow. But how?

He went back to their booth. Samuel was spinning a large red bowl on his finger while an intent man in a fur hat was inspecting another red bowl.

"You won't find another with such durable paint. Let me show you what a month on the road does to it." After a minute, Samuel emerged with his stovetop pail. While Samuel was away, the man had scratched at the paint with a small knife.

"You can see the color fades a bit, but that is about it. I don't see one chip." Samuel handed over the pail, which still had some water inside. The man looked at the faded bottom. He intently sat the pail down and lifted the lid. 'Snug,' thought both.

Samuel placed the money in the bag hanging from his belt. "You were smart to stay away. Thank you. Men like him get confused by too much talk and will walk." Aaron looked at the sleigh to calculate how many of their items had been sold.

"You sold twenty!" Aaron said animatedly.

"Yes." Samuel was more than pleased. This many at these prices, nearly double with the paint, he could not calculate that high. "Move along Little Twig. Let me do my work. You watch the sleigh and tent. Things are going to get busy." Right he was.

Within two hours, there must have been a hundred buyers. At lunch, Samuel closed the booth so they could count their stock and, more importantly, transfer money to the box. Aaron wondered if the box could hold all the money.

"I'll change the small coins for larger ones. Doing the exchange is always fun. I'll have you and Samuel keep watch." Nikolai enjoyed being

Yegorov's sales agent. He worked at the metal shop for this one trip to the Irbit Market. Why else would anyone work so hard with red-hot metal?

After lunch, Aaron did his share of sales. Their prices were set, the buyers came in waves. It was just work: ask, exchange coins, and provide the item. Over and over. Towards the end of the day, he had men who were looking, not buying. Aaron knew to let them be.

Walking the market, Nikolai ran into his rider. Anton was his traveling companion, his muscle for going back to Kazan. He was a big Russian who carried a long club outside of his coat. On his chest, he wore a Russian medal for bravery, one he had earned against the Cossacks. Aaron knew not to ask.

In general, weapons were forbidden at the market. Anton openly carried his club as he worked security for both the market and for people like Nikolai. Under their coats, nearly everyone carried some form of protection. Samuel had his short club. Nikolai carried a double-edged knife, a dagger under his long coat.

"Anton will watch our wares. Tonight, we are going out!" Nikolai said this with such enthusiasm he was a different man. Samuel gave an energetic, "Hurrah!"

'Unbelievable,' thought Aaron. "What? There are shops here in the markets?" Aaron had seen nothing of the sort.

"Little Twig. There is much you do not know." Nikolai was so joyous Aaron couldn't help but chuckle. He was looking forward to seeing what Nikolai meant.

…

Samuel could hardly keep his eyes off of her. The waitress's repeated glances went along with the festive evening they were having.

"What are we celebrating?" she asked. In person, her beauty was worn.

Puffing up, "We have done well today." Samuel's smile did nothing to hide his interest.

With her hand on her hip, "Well then, congratulations are in order! How can I help?" Her accent reminded Aaron of someone from the west of Lutsk, somewhere further west.

"Your best dinner, bread, and drink. The drink first. Tonight, this young lad will celebrate!" Samuel slapped Aaron's back. "You've done well.

I had no idea those men were speaking French. What are Frenchmen doing here?" Samuel was full of himself. Nikolai struggled to keep up.

By the end of dinner, before the next bottle, the waitress was sitting in Samuel's lap singing songs, ones she didn't truly know. Nikolai and Aaron left. Samuel had made new friends and was nowhere ready to leave.

Nikolai was not pleased. "Samuel knows better than to celebrate this much this early at the market." He spoke in anger and with a bit of jealousy. "He won't be any good tomorrow. His celebration is our extra work. You need to help me remind him when he returns to his senses." The walk home was longer than Aaron remembered. Even with his belly full, he struggled against the brutal cold.

Samuel did not come home. As the market stirred, Nikolai warmed the tent and had ice melting before Aaron woke.

"You know today can be busier. Get ready. I'll open. You can watch our tent and sleigh. We'll switch when the table gets bare."

"Samuel?"

"Not good. He's either frozen in a snowbank or never stopped celebrating. I'm not sure if I care which one." Nikolai was showing his loyalty to Yegorov.

"Shouldn't we go out and look for him?" Aaron hurried with his clothes.

"What? No. Samuel, he knew what he was doing. We've got work to do."

Aaron had seen frozen bodies before, rock hard. Once, he and another helped a man with a frozen arm. He was groaning, but alive, and with an arm of solid ice. *'Ugh.'* Aaron did not feel right.

The morning flew, as did their red cookware. Within the hour, Aaron was helping Nikolai bring out new items, and he took over sales. Nikolai went back and rearranged the cookware and probably stashed his coins.

Aaron moved the material. He wanted to clear the table faster than Nikolai and considered offering deals. The morning events kept him in line and then again, the selling wasn't difficult. Aaron felt the rush of success. His coin bag reminded him how much.

Nikolai closed the booth for lunch. They warmed inside their tent. Aaron hadn't noticed how cold he was until he started to warm-up.

"Give me your coin bag." Nikolai became all business. He dumped the coins on a blanket and counted them, recording the amount in a little book he kept in his coat.

"How much?" Aaron was very interested. He had his own idea and wanted to know if he was close.

"You're a natural." Nikolai, too, was cold and wanted to stay in the tent instead of standing at the booth. He knew better than to answer Aaron.

The long sunset had begun when Samuel returned with the woman under his arm. He was not right. He was happy and all, but not Samuel. Together, they went into the tent. Aaron could hear Nikolai giving him an earful. The woman stepped out and picked up one of the painted plates from Aaron's table.

"How did he do this?" She was the opposite of Samuel, almost serious.

"He worked months on the thick paint. He used red because it was denser than most, because of the iron." Aaron felt her invasive interest.

She smiled. "You've done well. Yes?" Her powerful smile was back.

Aaron looked at her from the corner of his eye. There were real customers. Hadn't she caused enough trouble? "Yes." She watched him a bit longer, then waved goodbye.

…

As their trading ended, Aaron watched Nikolai as he locked up their wares. Their crates in the sleighs now had locks. Maybe they always had. Things were different. Nikolai hid the coin box under blankets in a corner of the tent. Nikolai was excited, worried, and mad at Samuel all at the same time. Samuel was asleep under another pile of blankets. "He won't wake till tomorrow."

Nikolai jiggled his coin bag. "Let's go out ourselves." Aaron didn't miss the disgust Nikolai shot at Samuel as they left.

They went to a different shop and were surprised to see the same waitress. Their arrival witnessed her excitement, something the two men didn't care for. She stayed busily away, which was fine by them.

Aaron had stayed outside the tent to look at the stars when he heard the yelling. At first, he thought it was Nikolai giving Samuel another earful. Then the tent shook and more yelling followed. The scream, a painful scream, moved Aaron towards the tent door. Nikolai fell backwards out of the tent with a man atop.

"Give me that key, old man!" screamed the stranger. He had gained control of Nikolai's dagger and held it poised at his throat. It was Aaron's turn to scream.

He didn't know what he screamed as he rushed the stranger, trying to knock him off of Nikolai. The larger man simply tossed Aaron aside, his eyes focused on Nikolai's neck. "Ay. You annoying old man!"

Nikolai struggled with bloodied hands. He had blood coming from beneath his coat and lacked the strength to fight. Aaron rolled to his feet. He turned to see the dagger go deep into Nikolai's neck. With a twist, the key came off. The man rolled into and then out of the tent with the box now under his arm. His swipe at Aaron was more of a warning. He turned to run.

The immediate whack from Anton's club didn't bounce as much as sink into the man's forehead. He fell like a stone. Anton stood there, a mist formed around him. He gave the man a swift kick. A weak moan escaped the man's lungs. "Croat scum."

Anton went to Nikolai. His blood had seeped into the hardpack and was icing on his coat. His eyes were still and glazing. The cut on his neck was as deep as it was wide, like another mouth. Anton went inside. He called for Aaron.

By the light of a flickering flame, he reviewed the destroyed space. Anton was bending over and it took Aaron a minute to realize it was Samuel. His face had been rearranged, bloodied beyond recognition. Then a gasp emanated from what looked to be his mouth. "What a mess." Anton stood and came back, holding the box. "I'll be back. Do what you can." He left.

With the box under one arm, its key in his pocket, he dragged the body of the robber. At the market office, he dropped the box and picked up jailer keys. He left a trail of blood all the way to the market center and the stocks. As if he were a doll, Anton locked the big man in the stocks and left. By morning the robber was a frozen, slumped form.

Samuel's gasping for air came in waves. Aaron tried to help by wiping away the blood. It looked like the man had used the box to bludgeon Samuel. More than enough. Aaron hoped Samuel hadn't known what was happening.

Anton came back into the tent and dropped Nikolai down next to Samuel. He stood there. "If you'll give me a minute." He looked into Aaron's eyes with a knowledge few men should know. Aaron didn't know what else to do.

When he came back into the tent, silver coins were on both men's eyes. "That should be enough for their burial." Anton had little emotion in his words. "I'll take back to Yegorov what is his. One of these sleighs must be yours. No?" Aaron didn't hear a thing.

Samuel was dead.

Instinctively, Aaron began the Kaddish, the Jewish prayer for the dead.

The next morning, Aaron awoke to Anton moving boxes to Yegorov's sleigh, the sleigh he was taking back to Kazan. He had his horses hitched. Then, Anton was in the tent packing things away, taking them out to his sleigh. A few items he put in Aaron's sleigh.

"Ask for Gregory, he will give a good burial. There are no plots. Everyone lies together, as we should all live." Anton wrapped Nikolai's body in blankets. Once he found Nikolai's coin bag, he looked for Samuel's and was surprised to discover coins in both. "Here." He tossed Aaron twenty-five rubles. "Go somewhere you can make a good life." He looked hard at Aaron.

By the time Aaron emerged from the tent, Anton was gone. Samuel and Nikolai's bodies lay wrapped side-by-side in his sleigh. They would freeze as they lay. Aaron moved an arm, straightened a leg, uncrossed feet.

Aaron stood, looking at Samuel's boot. Stiffness had set in, requiring more effort than he wanted. Thankfully, Samuel had on his moter's thick socks. None of his skin was exposed. The liner came out along with four, twenty-five ruble coins. Instinctively, Aaron dropped them in his coin bag hanging from his belt. Awakened by the clink of coin, he said another Kaddish and went into the tent.

On a blanket, he spread out his coins, a true fortune. He had sold red plates, pans, and milk pails all afternoon without emptying his bag. He separated the coins: 25 ruble, 12 ruble, six, three, and a pile of single rubles along with a mound of kopeks. After counting, he recounted and then counted again. With the kopeks, he made stacks. Three hundred and seventeen rubles, give or take with all those kopeks. Samuel's four coins went into his boot. Another hundred rubles he wrapped and hid in a small pocket in his travel bag. He wrapped a mound of rubles and kopeks in a cloth and set them inside a pail. The other rubles and some larger kopeks he put in the coin bag to hang from his belt. He hurried. Clothes were piled, the little stove was taken apart. Pails and boxes were set near the door.

Mikhail's letter fell out as Aaron was repacking his travel bag. It had been nearly a year. By a candle flame's dancing rays, Aaron read:

To my Haver, my best friend:

You are embarking on a grand adventure. There is no point telling you how wild it can be. Know I didn't travel half of what you will and count myself lucky to have survived. Novgorod is a grand city, one you should convince Samuel to visit. My friends will treat you right, for they know anyone who would be my best friend has the highest of characters.

I have grown so much with you; I don't know what I will do without you. I look around the yeshiva and watch havers fight, stumble, and fail to learn the lessons. Their partners lack smarts, much less any chutzpah. You are the face to my mind. I cannot speak what I think. You did that for me. You are fearless.

One day I will become brave, but it is not today. I shake thinking about the future and hide in my thoughts so no one will know.

Don't stop being brave.

The world is what you make it.

Every day you make it new!

Write to me.

Your haver,
Mikhail

For a quick minute, Aaron envisioned his future. Yegorov would surely give him work, especially after this market. Another option, Aaron could go to Novgorod and stay with Mikhail's friends. A fanciful idea, not one for a Jew. With a surety rare for humans, Aaron decided to continue his journey. He would leave immediately. Yes, before more bothered him like these early buyers calling from the table.

He found Gregory busy at work. On top of his fee, Aaron added another ruble with the intent of doing right by Samuel. Gregory understood.

At the market office, the official expressed his sadness and sympathy. Aaron brought out his pail of cloth-wrapped coins and had the official exchange them for larger values. The man chatted away as he made stacks. He agreed continuing to Irkutsk was the best plan, and many Chinese were heading the same way. "Buryat!" yelled a man from a corner of the office.

This is how Aaron met Dashi. When Aaron ever wondered about the power of his G.., he remembered how Dashi was sent to him when he needed help the most. Within the hour, the two were working their way out of the Irbit Market, headed toward Irkutsk, two thousand miles away.

Warm, inside the felt tent, before sleep, Aaron wrote by candlelight:

Awareness -

- *Desire and obtaining - are 2 different things. Growing into and taking - we must study to improve*
- *I am going to see my foter*
- *My foter used to say it was he who should have had all of Lord Muravyov's wealth*
- *With all his money he would have made a better world*

Part Two

Courage - January, 1830

Fear

What many of us experience is low-level anxiety,
the gnawing feeling that things aren't right. This anxiety
permeates today's society.

We try to stave off anxiety through a variety of primate
behaviors. Most of us see this in others but fail
to see it in ourselves.

These acts of anxiety defiance are not acts of courage.

Don't confuse the two.

Courage is the antidote for fear.

Gratitude soothes the pain of an anxious person.

Yesterday at the livery, Aaron tried selling the third horse. He did not want the extra mouth to feed and, in the end, gave the horse away. Smartly, he had bought extra bags of horse feed, additional bags of charcoal, and tools like ones he had seen taken by Anton. The Zamov's badges hung from the front harnesses.

Dashi was Buryat, from the eastern side of Lake Baikal. When he spoke, he leaned forward and almost barked his Russian. Aaron heard him mumble under his breath in his native language, one Aaron was intent on learning. He had time.

Irkutsk was on the western side of Lake Baikal, almost two thousand miles away. With a full lifetime of travel experience in this environment, Dashi propelled them forward at a brisk pace. The roads were perfect; it was the best time of year to travel. February and most of March lay ahead. They would drag the sleigh as far as it would go, hopefully, all the way to Irkutsk.

"They left me," Dashi said with anger. "Rotten Chinese," he spat. "I drive them all the way to Irbit. They had no clue where to go. I set them up, sell all their chai bricks, I make them rich." He spat again and muttered under his breath. Dashi had maybe two kopeks that he could rub together. He had seen Aaron's cloth-wrapped coins hidden in the pail. Aaron knew and left it at that.

"Vi azoy ton ir zogn hela in deyn shprakh?" Aaron asked. Dashi shook his head. "How do you say hello in your language?"

Dashi opened his eyes as he faced Aaron. "Yes." Dashi nodded. "Mende."

"Mende, Dashi." Aaron smiled. "You teach me more. We have time. I pay you a ruble now and another if I can speak to your family and friends when we get to the eastern side of Lake Baikal." Aaron smiled proudly at his bargaining.

Dashi was wide-eyed at this young man and, henceforth, rarely kept his mumbling to himself. He spoke aloud about the beautiful eastern sunrises, the health he bestowed on the horses, and the blessings he made crossing frozen rivers. The Buryat repeated his phrases until the young man got them right.

Dashi also held the horse's reins unless he needed a break. His skills with the horses were far above anything Aaron had ever seen. He spoke their language. For Dashi, their care was effortless. More than once, on the most brutal of cold Russian nights, he crawled them into the tent to not only keep them warm but to keep himself and Aaron alive. The miles flew by.

"Bahra's legs never grew straight." Aaron began one of his stories to see how Dashi would engage. "Often, his father would call him the weak one and leave him when he traveled the caravan routes for eastern delights. You know what it means to leave another behind?" It was a question Dashi took as needing a resounding, Amen! "But you probably don't know what it means to be called the weak one and left behind?" Aaron watched for a reaction, for Dashi to show he was considering such a thought.

"Most of us consider two choices. Either we succumb to the label of being weak or fight to show we are strong. Right?" Aaron enjoyed seeing Dashi's brain at work. He was going to enjoy the miles with this man. "What would you do?"

"Never let it happen in the first place. Never show weakness. Once you do, your enemies will peck and peck until even the strongest crumble." Dashi had heard this his whole life.

"True, true. I've seen it." Aaron took this further. "I say, don't let your enemy define you. Don't let your father use your crippled legs as the reason to leave you behind. We all have weaknesses, but most of us hide our shortcomings. You are a powerful man, but you have no means to get home."

Aaron let the words sit before he added, "So you sell your skills with horses and languages and point out others' lack of experience going east of Lake Baikal." Aaron chuckled, "You sold me."

Dashi would not push this sore point.

"Most of us wear our weakness, though we think our medals or fancy clothing or enormous homes hide the pain." Aaron had heard Rabbi Hulstein talk about humility a hundred times.

"I'm learning. I can watch others, see what they are trying to hide and try to use this when I engage, but I don't know myself. My rabbi said, 'You are growing too fast. I don't know you besides being the talkative son of Joseph.' He taught my father." Aaron realized Rabbi Hulstein knew more about him than he had realized.

Dashi let Aaron talk. They had a long road ahead.

...

Omsk provided much needed rest and resupplies. The horses revived in the livery and the men filled themselves at the tables. Aaron met Jews openly speaking Yiddish. Officials would pass by and not harass them, as if they were no longer in Russia. *'Oy, kvell!'*

From them Aaron learned of the unrest back home. War was brewing as Polish Independence had been declared. These Jews declared their lives in Omsk a blessing, which nearly caused Aaron's jaw to hit the floor.

Dashi did not have the same experience. He was told to leave at several shops until Aaron started paying for their food in advance. Dashi's demure surprised Aaron, as it was usually he who looked down to avoid conflict.

Dashi was ready to leave in three days. "The road is good. We travel fast and get to Irkutsk before snows melt."

In Tomsk, ten days later, they had similar, if not more pronounced, experiences. Jews lived openly throughout the city. Aaron attended services, discussed the coming war in old Poland, opinions about travel to Israel, and the road east. With his synagogue donation, he probably could have gotten more. Though more Indigenous men filled the streets, Aaron and Dashi received a room at the back, a clear sign they weren't welcome in the inn.

March brought a fresh set of storms, which held them down for four days in a small village outside of Achinsk. Dashi rarely left the barn.

Aaron had learned to pray when he was under threat or attack. The last thing he would do was fight. Fighting is what they wanted. Never would he show his enemies his fear, despite its abundance. Dashi was aloof, head down. He could be yelled at, pushed down, and he would pop right back up, the same expression as before.

"Don't fight the wind, don't curse at the cold. These things are. It is I who can become." More strange sayings came from Dashi the further east they traveled.

East of Krasnoyarsk, they hit their first dry patch. It was the second week of March. They were five hundred miles from Irkutsk. For half of the day, the runners slid across the dirt and rocks, giving an illusion they could do this forever. Then a crack appeared in a rail and Dashi stopped and unhitched the horses. Not only did he buttress the crack, he took the rest of the day to cut, shape, and replace both runners, which had worn severely.

No snow did not mean warmer temperatures.

By midday, snow and ice had again covered the rough road. Dashi's spirits returned.

These lands were scarred by summer forest fires. Miles of blackened spindles reflected destructive infernos. Against the white snows, the blackened tree trunks created an eerie environment. And then healthy trees, as if a mighty hand stopped the carnage. Aaron had heard of Siberian fires, as big as entire European countries. He never wanted to experience one and was glad Siberian winds blew east, not to Lutsk.

In two weeks, they felt Irkutsk was around the corner.

"We didn't see one moose." Dashi shook his head for emphasis. "There are too many people out here." He said this like they had to push through hordes of travelers. There had been people, many walking their way. People whom Aaron believed were exiles like Lord Muravyov and others like his father and brother. Many looked hauntingly at their sleigh, for walking in was not the same as gliding across snow.

Aaron called to many, wanting to hear the name Nerchinsk. Many did not answer, and the names he heard were unfamiliar. Within the next exile group, as he looked into eyes filled with dark despair, Aaron recalled the story of Golem, the defender of Prague's Jews. Did these people not need a defender?

To Dashi, these people were a darkness.

"You think they are all like your father, 'noble in their cause'. Most are common criminals and some are plain murderers. Would you not want the man who killed your Samuel to be exiled to the mines of Nerchinsk?"

Aaron did not know how to respond. Several times he had recalled seeing the waitress kneeling next to the murder's body, frozen in the stocks. He had wanted to tell Anton she was as guilty. When he finally decided, Anton was gone.

More importantly, Aaron asked, "What is so bad about Nerchinsk?"

Now, it was Dashi who didn't know how to respond. How could he explain the misery and death surrounding those mines? How could he express his belief in such misery for murders without cursing Aaron's father? "You will see, being a miner is not for everyone." Dashi shook his head at his own words.

Dashi realized he cared.

He saw himself taking Aaron all the way to Nerchinsk. What would his wife say?

…

In the vibrant Jewish quarter of Irkutsk, Aaron ran into Feivel from Lutsk. At first, Aaron didn't know what to think. Feivel was shaking him in a bear hug, rattling his teeth. "Aaron!" Feivel screamed. "You've escaped!"

Aaron did not reflect the smile exploding on Feivel's face.

"I thought," and Aaron corrected himself, "we thought you were dead."

Why was Feivel shaking him down to his bones? He should be dead or worse.

"I escaped cantonist school, myself and four others. Honest!" said Feivel who was still having difficulty understanding what had happened. Months ago, soldiers captured him fleeing down the Dnieper. His sentence was a Siberian cantonist school, Russian Orthodoxy forced upon him, the soldier's death laid before him. Why was he in an Irkutsk yeshiva? It didn't matter. The story only made Feivel's smile and happiness all the grander.

Irkutsk, in the spring, proved to be magical. Not only had Feivel come back from the dead, he introduced Aaron to his yeshiva and Rabbi Fershster. During the first weeks of April, observing Passover gave Aaron an out-of-body experience. Rabbi Fershster and his Irkutsk yeshiva would continue for years, a bright spot in the otherwise dystopian world for young Russian-Jewish men.

Aaron and Dashi spent nights apart for the first time in weeks. Friends and one of his uncles took Dashi under their wings. All the same, by the second week of April, Aaron was relieved when Dashi responded to his request to move on.

Aaron had traded for, even added additional rubles to, a newer cart and two horses. To him, he got the sturdy cart and robust horses at a decent price because he was a good trader. Dashi immediately took the cart and horses to his friends and traded for what he claimed to be, "... one that won't fall apart ten miles out of Irkutsk...." with expletives added here and there.

Dashi knew where they were going. Supplies, especially metal tools, were in short order. People east of Lake Baikal traveled for days to trade in Irkutsk. They had room in the wagon, they could make money trading. Aaron agreed. In time, his modest investment would return nearly tenfold. Aaron was learning an important lesson.

From under Samuel's wing, Aaron had flown. He was directing his life, taking care of his life, relating closely with others without support. In short order, his travels from Irbit had crossed him over into adulthood. Aaron was too close to see it. He was engaged; he was living the moments with little time to worry. Dashi had traveled with many. He knew he was stubborn, if not angry at times. People accused him of being difficult, a compliment for any Buryat man. This young man was different. Dashi began to strategize how he would explain such to his wife. A bag of rubles would help.

As Irkutsk faded, Aaron knew and also did not know this would be the last of the proper cities he would see for a long time. True, he would see stone forts and stone city halls, but no longer would citizens live in stone homes. The societies would not have the resources to build such. Aaron's destiny was to travel thousands of miles, tens of thousands. Cities would rarely be part of his itinerary. It would be a testament to his ability to adapt, a skill he honed during these early years.

Kyakhta was out of their way. Dashi had begun his journey there, the Chai Gateway into Russia. He knew Aaron was learning Buryat, but to be sure and earn the additional ruble, a promise he had not forgotten, this detour could make the difference. The Buryat People controlled the border town, something the Russians encouraged. The Buryat were used to harass the Chinese when the Chinese withheld trade. For such a faraway town, Kyakhta had a real impact on the rest of Russia and its countless samovars.

"How much money do you have?" Dashi knew chai, knew how to grade chai bricks. He also knew how to tend the bricks to ensure their quality as they traveled.

Aaron was not used to talking about money, much less having money to talk about. He had hidden his coins in varied spots, fairly sure Dashi did not know them all. Aaron showed him what he wanted Dashi to see, the pail of cloth-wrapped rubles and the coin bag hanging from his belt. An honest answer would be two hundred eighty-two rubles and sixty kopeks. Keep the one hundred fifty hidden and call the one hundred thirty, a generous statement.

"Why?" As confused as Aaron could be, he knew keeping his cards close was always a good move.

"Kyakhta, it is the Chai Gateway. You won't find good quality, less expensive chai anywhere else. And Buryat control the town." Dashi looked at Aaron to see if he understood.

Back in Irkutsk, Aaron had invested twenty-five rubles, a sizable sum in metal tools. Now Dashi was asking for more.

"You know I have about one hundred between the pail and my belt bag." Aaron paused, watched Dashi's reaction. "One-hundred thirty-two and a few kopeks." Dashi's calculating mind was not masked. "I know I owe you a ruble if I can talk with your people. I'll also give you 25% of the profits when we sell all the tools. I'll give you the same when we sell the chai. Is this a deal?"

Dashi's calculations stopped. He pulled on the reins and stopped the cart. The horses looked at Dashi for an explanation. One was slow to form. Dashi had lived through countless trades, but only as a Buryat. He had never benefited from the profits. Was this a trap?

Aaron sat there. Dashi looked him up and down. Why did Aaron tell him how much money he had? What was the point of him paying for him to stay in taverns, feed him, learn his language?

"That'll do," Dashi answered in Buryat, and Aaron understood. "Twenty-five rubles."

"The bricks are like coins. A brick is a year's worth of work. We'll get the dark ones, not the fermented chai. I'll find you a full crate in Kyakhta for twenty-five." Dashi spoke, but his mind was calculating. The same crate of twelve bricks at Irbit had sold for hundreds more. *'What was 25% of two hundred?'*

When the wooden box thudded into the cart, Aaron was a bit surprised by the size. Inside were hard-pressed bricks with royal Chinese seals. In Kyakhta, Aaron had seen Buryat making milk tea with small pieces of chai bricks. He didn't think twenty-five rubles would buy so much.

Verkhne-Udinsk (Ulan-Ude) was the capital of the Buryat people. On this side of Lake Baikal, the Buryat were not Russian Orthodox like in Irkutsk. Colorful flags appeared, as did stone markers, some with a new style of writing. In Verkhne-Udinsk, men rode ponies, making their cart horses look like another species. Few Western Russians walked the streets. Aaron could feel the Eastern influence.

A bit out of town, Dashi stopped next to a small shed with a blanket for a door. A woman came around from the back, wiping her hands on her apron. She placed her hands on her hips, gave a sigh, turned, and walked quickly back around. Dashi hopped down and raced after her. Moving quickly, the woman came back, Dashi gaining on her. Aaron sat there as he could hear them embracing out back.

"Tuyana, this is Aaron." Dashi said this almost with a smile, something everyone noted. "He will pay me a ruble if you two can talk."

"My husband is horse droppings," Tuyana said flatly, but with a twinkle in her eyes.

"He smells like it," replied Aaron. A big smile spread across Dashi's face.

They continued their greetings outside. The light-green growths reminded Aaron of the fields outside of Lutsk. The corral and barn out-back were almost as tidy as the shed Tuyana and Dashi inhabited. Toq, their six-month old son, was asleep in Temyulen's arms. Tuyana's mom stayed with her when Dashi was away.

"You bring back treats for your mom," which was not a question. Temyulen was already looking through the cart, not happy. The extra bags of horse grain and charcoal were for their further travels. Dashi had not thought of bringing home anything except coins, and these were too few.

Aaron pulled forth a palm-sized brick of chai he had bought on his own in Kyakhta. He gave a little bow as he placed this in Temyulen's hands. Dashi looked at him, clearly indicating he had paid too much for the trinket. However, Dashi's mother-in-law stopped complaining.

Later, Dashi gave a slow retelling of his travels. By the end, Tuyana and Temyulen saw a miracle had taken place: Aaron had returned Dashi. The fact Aaron had paid to learn the language, paid for Dashi's meals and travel nights inside, all this would play to Dashi's advantage. It was time to celebrate.

Life on the edge of the Buryat capital was a holiday, yes, a holiday. Aaron didn't know what he was experiencing. It is hard for a person like him to have such a perspective. He slept in the barn, took his meals around the one small table sitting on the shed's dirt floor. He talked with Tuyana and Temyulen, who told him stories of days gone by.

They let him watch Toq and soon learned he was a natural with kids. He went on walks into Verkhne-Udinsk and bought items Dashi recommended. Verkhne-Udinsk's market sold much, including livestock, which entertained Aaron for hours. The jingle hanging from Aaron's belt may have been a larger contributing factor than he let on. He could buy almost anything at the market, a comforting feeling he let fill him more than once.

Aaron got his head shaved. He sat outside and watched the village shoppers as his hair blew away. He could understand most of what was being spoken. Buryat greetings, hagglings, and exclamations created another significant factor to his aura. The play unfolding around him was far enough removed for the drama of life to pop. Everyone leaned forward, talked as if they were going to whisper, which they didn't. While they hugged a slapping type of hug, once they finished their exchanges, men would sit for hours not saying a word next to what seemed to be their best friends. Chai was everywhere, brewed with butter and a pinch of salt, and served in bowls. Purveyors of this chai walked around and filled empty bowls.

One morning, "You need real travel clothes." Dashi exclaimed with a bit of attitude. He was looking at Aaron's long coat, torn and frayed, his boots that nearly gave him frozen toes, and that hat. "Where we are going, you don't need to look like a learned man." By the end of the week, Aaron looked more Asian, not like a Buryat, but not like he was walking the streets of Lutsk.

…

The June evenings provided hours of sitting around and a plan was developing. Trading a few of his goods had provided enough action to entice Aaron for more. Dashi explained how trading chai would be best. "We'll go back to Kyakhta before we head on to Nerchinsk. How much can you purchase?" They both knew how much Aaron had in his bag of coins.

With little caution, "Would we be able to sell seventy-five rubles' worth? Where we are going, is that not closer to China?" Aaron knew his geography skills were not great.

"Well, yes. Closer, but they do not trade. Kyakhta is the only chai market and the Buryat control the trade. Buryat control is good for us. We take it east and make many people happy." Dashi had a way of calculating and talking at the same time. Aaron understood.

"You will stay in Nerchinsk until we sell all the chai?" Aaron was trying to envision his future. His beard was growing. It was a bit longer, thicker. He stroked and tugged on the hairs when he thought.

"We have a business deal that comes once in a lifetime. Together, we could sell enough to set a man up for years." Aaron saw how little money they spent. Doubling what he spent on the trade items would give Dashi a coin bag of confidence.

Something was happening to Aaron. In the evenings, he would sit with Dashi and think about little. Their talk about trade would excite him. He understood he was sitting atop a goldmine and needed to use it wisely. Then Aaron would recall Rabbi Hulstein and a feeling of shame would envelop him like a cloud: for his lack of thinking, for his lack of studies. Then Aaron would recall his moter's pleas to make her proud and to deliver her message to his foter. Was he a failure? His thoughts were so useless, so he worked at thinking less. He gave his beard a tug at that thought.

One evening, a group of Russian exiles, destined for deeper Siberia, stopped in front of Dashi and Aaron. The weathered and worn group mumbled amongst themselves and sent one over. The Russian pleaded for food and water. He spoke slowly and with gestures. Aaron realized this man saw him as a local. Dashi gave a chuckle.

When he returned, Dashi had a cloth bag filled with meat pies, most of what Aaron had bought that morning. In good Russian and with his Buryat bark, up close and personal, "Go! Keep moving. My neighbors will not take it lightly if they learn I have fed you. If you stop again, they will beat you. Go!" Dashi pushed the man.

"You would have talked all night with these men. You would see they are not murderers and your noble cause would rise. You would have gone into town and bought more pies. You are doing well to let go of those lies." He had said this while standing over him. Dashi sat back down next to Aaron.

Aaron's confused thinking became exacerbated. Like with his anger while working for Yegorov, he latched onto an answer for his feelings. It was time to go.

Despite all the changes in his life, Aaron continued with his mussar journal. Tonight was:

Courage -
- *Scary*
- *The courage to be faithfully silent*
- *The courage to be held and protected*
- *The courage to stand in front of many*
- *Courage to wait*

Strength - July 15th, 1830

Strength

The power to achieve through resistance, resisting fatigue.

The old sailor treaded water all day.

He could outlast the younger because he had learned to resist. Our culture needs this.

In our world, the ability to resist fatigue is sadly engaged with doing more or despair.

How does one teach strength?

How does one learn without spending time with oneself?

The Zamov badges still hung from the front harnesses. Frequently, soldiers questioned Aaron about Zamov and hinted at bribes. Then the code of commerce would kick in even this far into the Russian Empire.

Today, the soldier vigorously demanded how they had Zamov badges.

"We work for Zamov of Lutsk. We have traveled from Irbit for chai. Zamov trusts we make him money." Aaron could see his words did not sit well.

"You?" The soldier's face grew angry. He pulled back the tarp and looked at the crates, boxes, and bags. The soldier raised an eyebrow at the four crates of chai, dug through boxes of metal tools, bags of charcoal, horse grain, and supplies. "You're going the wrong way." A truth Aaron did not know how to explain.

"You know the exiled Lord Muravyov of Lutsk? He has ordered supplies. Zamov delivers and will become the new lord of Lutsk." Aaron had no idea how those words came out of his mouth.

"You are taking these to Nerchinsk?" The soldier dropped his anger. He turned and turned back. "Bless you."

"But where is Samuel?" asked with a bit of sadness, a sadness only deepened as the soldier learned of Samuel's death. "The road ends for us all." The soldier lingered.

Zamov had proved loyal to the Empire during the Polish Revolt. A blessing for Aaron.

As they rode closer to Nerchinsk, the rolling hills were not what Aaron had pictured. Images of rugged mountains had filled his thoughts ever since the Urals. These hills were weathered in a northern way, bleak. All the same, this mid-July offered warm, long, summer days. Dashi knew his way despite the numerous roads, many abandoned since the border changes with China.

Katorgas, Siberian prisons, dotted their way since Irkutsk. Seen from a distance, most looked like logging camps. Nerchinsk's reputation preceded it.

Soldiers stopped them a mile before Nerchinsk.

"Zamov? Polish? Show me your papers." Aaron had not thought this through. Dashi had become accustomed to such harassment. They sat waiting for the soldiers to look through their wares.

"You are heading towards Nerchinsk. What business do you have here?" More soldiers came over to their cart.

"We are delivering for Zamov, to Lord Muravyov," Aaron said with as little emotion as possible. Dashi sat still.

"What makes you think you can ride right into a Katorga?" The lead soldier's tone shifted.

"The commerce code has delivered us this far. I have traveled for more than a year." Aaron's flat words surprised him.

"You are blessed not to be back there." The soldier said. Others nodded.

Before the soldier continued, Dashi extended a wrapped package. "You can find us with Lord Muravyov and he will give you more." Dashi looked down while he spoke.

The soldier slowly unwrapped the piece of chai brick, the piece easily got his attention. "We'll be visiting. We have to prepare for the cold months," the soldier said as he walked away.

While soldiers were everywhere, so were prisoners. Guards patrolled the prison, yet there were no walls. A roll call had ended. A unit of prisoners were straggling back to their barracks: crude timber hovels housing too many prisoners. Squads of soldiers were escorting teams of prisoners in other directions, and more were coming into camp. The long summer days provided plenty of work.

Under a Russian flag, Dashi stopped their cart. They had seen only a few other horses. Carts were being pulled by prisoner teams, animals were too valuable. Dashi waited, head down. Aaron hopped down and an older soldier greeted him. "What brings a Zamov cart to Nerchinsk?"

"I am delivering to Lord Muravyov." Aaron saw the disconnect in the old man's eyes. "Not these. They're going to Chita, the village further east." Again, words came out of Aaron's mouth that he did not control.

"Hmph. Wait here, enjoy the view," he said with a chuckle. Dashi sat in the cart. Both looked around at life imprisoned.

"Is this what you expected?" Dashi had a good question.

"I don't think so. The Kiev prison was stone, at least two stories. The iron bars and gates made it look impenetrable. This? Why don't the prisoners walk away?"

"Don't even think such!" Dashi shook his head. "All quickly learn commands are given only once. You won't get another." Dashi spoke while watching soldiers beat a prisoner. "Life here is cheap. There is a cost to keeping a prisoner alive. If they don't work, it is good business to let them die. All die horribly."

Aaron could see death on every prisoner's face. A sunken look failing to radiate the human spirit.

"Where is the mine?" Aaron saw huts and prisoners but no mining.

"Up the valley. Can't you smell it?" Dashi wrinkled his nose. Aaron smelled fires, an unusual smell in July. Dashi continued, "They dig up the ore and crush it. The prisoners do all this. They crush it into a powder. Then they smelt the ore in the furnaces. I'm not sure what part of the process is worse." Aaron looked around with more understanding.

The older soldier returned. "Follow me."

They left the cart and wove through groups of prisoners and crude structures. They were climbing a slight hill. A wooden sign nailed to a post read: 'Welcome to the rest of your life'. Underneath was scrawled, 'Dang,' with a sad cartoon face. The older soldier went into a low building. Inside, Aaron saw rooms, which surprised him though the inner doors were removed. Windows were vertical slits without glass.

Another soldier approached and the older one returned down the hill. Standing, with an air of anticipation, was an indistinguishable prisoner. "Lord Muravyov?" Aaron asked.

"Yes." His chin went a little higher at the sight of the youth. "To whom am I speaking?" The words rang with elevated tones.

"Lord Muravyov, I am Aaron, Joseph's youngest." He couldn't believe he had finally made it.

"Aaron." He looked at the young man. "Excuse me. I forget myself. I don't remember the last time I had a visitor." He spread his arms as if behind him was a bountiful table of delectable treats. "Aaron. I would never have guessed it was you."

"Lord Muravyov, it is an honor to stand before you. I have heard a thousand stories about you, but we have never met. It has taken me more than a year of travel. I did not know it would be so far when I started." Truer words, Aaron had rarely spoken. "Where is my father?" Aaron could feel the rise of uncontrollable emotions.

"Joseph." Lord Muravyov looked at the soldier by the door. "Joseph, your tato. He, he is near. He is not well, Aaron." Lord Muravyov looked at Aaron deeply. In an instant, he conveyed much.

In a small room, on what resembled a bed, lay Joseph. He was under-neath layers of blankets. With sunken eyes and cheeks, raspy breath, Aaron knew this man was not for long. Aaron failed to connect. *'This is my father?'* Aaron took a hand and held it tight. The hand, stiff, cold, bony, couldn't be his father's. *'I have traveled for a year. For what?'* The withered man stirred.

"Foter." "Foter." "Foter!" Aaron's words grew louder. No response.

"The white plague has him. He has not spoken for days. He has had nothing to eat. I give him sips of water. Nothing today. He hardly moves." Upon hearing 'the white plague,' Dashi quietly left the room.

Aaron looked at the dying old man. The breathing became more agitated. The smell of urine and mold dug deep into Aaron. Death, the smell of death, was stronger. Aaron could smell it on himself.

"He has been sick since we arrived. Never one to complain, Joseph failed to get up for work a couple of weeks ago. He would have been shot. I still have some influence." Lord Muravyov left the room.

Aaron bent closer. Was this his father? The smells, the sunken face, the white skin, nothing reminded Aaron of his father. He kissed the cheeks of this man. Aaron walked out into the July evening air.

Death, plague death, scared Dashi. He walked back to what he knew. With a piece of chai, he purchased stalls and feed for their horses. He gave them a good rub. He had a team of prisoners bring their supplies up to Lord Muravyov's.

"You will stay with me. I will appreciate your help." Lord Muravyov's sadness struck Aaron.

From their position on the hill, Aaron absorbed the camp below and felt the smoke from furnaces up the valley. A log lay along the front house wall and Lord Muravyov sat down. Aaron joined him.

"It is good to see a free young man." Lord Muravyov attempted a smile. "I am tired, old before my time."

Aaron watched a haggard group of prisoners line up for roll call. They stood, waiting.

"I could have lived with the others back in town," Lord Muravyov explained. "Your tato's loyalty meant everything to me. They would not let him leave this camp. He was not the one convicted." He pulled on his clean-shaven face.

The prisoners continued to wait. Lord Muravyov was in no hurry to explain.

Dashi watched the camp life below. He, too, sat down.

The log, the light breeze, the camp life, the summer evening sun, it all had a simple freshness angrily wrenched away by the horrific human experience below.

The prisoners continued to wait.

"Androv." Lord Muravyov called to the soldier by the door. "Inform the cook we have visitors." Turning to Aaron, "I don't assume you have any delicacies you want to share?"

"Of course," replied Aaron, who hadn't thought ahead. Dashi was waiting with a bag of their better food supplies. He handed it to Lord Muravyov.

"You are more than generous. This will make for a fine meal tonight and for many more." His words gave a nod to his harsh conditions.

"Aaron. Your supplies need to be stored here, away from prying eyes and hands." Dashi spoke, making sure their host heard his deference.

"Thank you," answered Aaron. Turning to Lord Muravyov, "A corner of a room would suffice. Do you trust your guards?"

"There is a price for everything. The greater the wealth, the greater the cost." Lord Muravyov chuckled and continued, "Look around. You can see how much I have to protect." There was nothing.

A raven soared across the valley. A squad of soldiers marched through the hovels. The prisoners continued to stand for roll call.

An hour later, they had finished their meager meal sitting outside. Dashi took the wooden bowls back to the cook. He returned and joined them on the log.

The pieces were coming together, not in the way either had predicted. For Aaron, he failed to plan for what would follow informing his father about mother and Estle moving to Israel. Would he and his father hitch up the horses and go visit them for Shabbat dinner? Aaron was not one to think ahead. Sadly, he also didn't realize his brother was nowhere to be seen. Aaron sat as if the weight of his long journey had finally caught up.

Lord Muravyov sat like he had sat for many a night, happy not to be watching his dying friend. The weight of his failed life stabbed deep into his soul, something Joseph represented visually. What now? Is this his fate? To die in a Siberian Katorga prison camp? Lord Muravyov's fall had been mighty.

"When my tato died, I was older than you. What are you twenty?" Lord Muravyov explained. "I joined the Army with a great commission thoroughly approved by my mama. It cost a fortune. I would one day be a great general. We all wanted the coming war. I did not understand war and almost got captured at Austerlitz." He paused. "I did not understand?" He gave a chuckle. "I met your tato when we rebuilt the Russian Army. Ha!" He slapped his knee. "I knew some things. The moment I met your tato, I understood he was a great man. We are Russian, but we are of many tongues. Your tato knew them all."

"As a kid, Camille, she was my governess, she taught me everything in French. I spoke it everywhere to the pride of my family. I was a spirited youth encouraged by my tato." Lord Muravyov got lost in memories of his father. Aaron and Dashi listened and watched the drama below. Colors splashed the evening sky.

"When Napoleon invaded Russia, we weren't as ready as we were hopeful for a coming change." Lord Muravyov told stories and then explained how Joseph and he, in time, were wolves upon the dying French. "The anger, the passion, gave us strength for our long stay in France. We did not think we would get infected, but the poison of 'Liberty' is strong. In a sense, I was poisoned for years." Lord Muravyov struggled with the word poisoned. He sensed, no, he knew this could be the fulcrum for his monumental failure of a life. Fanciful ideas had poisoned his whole life. A physical sharp pain froze his memories. He did all he could to sit and stare ahead. Why was this his life?

Aaron listened, captivated by soldiers' uniforms and army stories. He also had not been listening. Slowly, his mind developed a vision of Nerchinsk as a cemetery, a hole dug out of suffering for suffering men to lie. He could feel the pull of depression and death. Inside was a dying, suffering man, his father. Lord Muravyov, too, was not long for this world, whatever influence he still wielded. Aaron's youth screamed for him to run.

The fourth morning was foggy. Aaron's father had died during the night after a bout of ragged breathing. Lit by the light of one candle, soothing cool cloths, and prayers, the death scene would embed in Aaron's physical memory. He would judge future deaths by his father's.

As he sat on the log and sipped a cool cup of water, Aaron remembered it was his duty to recite the Kaddish. His forgetfulness shocked him. This was his father! Lord Muravyov and Dashi gave him space.

Earlier, Lord Muravyov shocked Aaron when he explained Joshua, Aaron's brother, was not in Nerchinsk. The fact Aaron had forgotten his brother was another sign something wasn't right. When Lord Muravyov shared he had paid for Joshua to have rank in the Russian Navy, a bill that could be repaid, Aaron heard nothing.

Dashi waited, and waited, before interjecting, "Of course." He added the obvious question, "The Russian Navy? Do tell us more. We are miles from any ocean."

"Ah, yes, the Russian Navy. They came through not long after Joshua had arrived, well maybe a month or two. A captain heard Joshua's language skills. These captains go everywhere. He almost took Joshua before I interceded." Lord Muravyov continued, "Joshua should be a first mate by now."

Aaron and Dashi buried Joseph before the next morning's fog had burned away. Aaron had spent the day before in a fog of his own. The three sat on the log and watched the Sun warm the Earth.

"Why was the Russian Navy here?" Aaron had heard some of their conversations.

Lord Muravyov gave a start, "Ah. They were going east. Russia may have given the Amur to the Chinese, but that does not mean we will not go where we want." He paused and thought. "The Russian American Company only takes navy officers." There was a time when Lord Muravyov thought he could escape to Russia's far reaches.

Later, Dashi caught Aaron alone. "I am sorry for your father's death." Dashi shared, though his passing was also a relief from suffering. Aaron nodded his appreciation.

"I do not know what to do. I don't want to go back, I cannot." Aaron looked to Dashi as the father he had become.

"You cannot stay here." Aaron easily agreed. "We will not make the money we could elsewhere if we sell your trade here in Nerchinsk." Dashi thought and then realized he must be clear. "I am not your servant." His words surprised him. "I do this to make your difficult time easier. But you do better... partner." Dashi kept leaning forward, though his words wanted him to recoil.

The words woke Aaron quickly. "Ye. You are my partner." Aaron looked him in the eye. "We have a deal. After the expenses, you get 25% of the profits." Aaron paused. With a bit of passion, he stated, "You stay till the goods are sold?"

Dashi nodded in agreement. He had made his peace. He knew he too had fallen into unbecoming behaviors, ones Aaron saw but did not judge.

As the day ended, sitting on the log, Dashi sat in the middle. "How far is America?" He asked Lord Muravyov with an inquiring tone.

"You have a month on the lazy Amur, it's difficult dealing with the Chinese." Lord Muravyov followed the map in his head. "One has to cross the Sea of Okhotsk. The sail from Okhotsk to New Archangel is a month through the islands, two months if the weather is bad." He was proud of his geography skills.

"What does it take to become a Russian Navy officer?" Dashi was on a roll.

"You make a joke, my Buryat friend." Lord Muravyov included a little laugh.

But Aaron sensed the story unfolding. "I need a future. Joshua needs a bruder. I could join him in Russia-America."

Lord Muravyov hadn't felt this pull for his influence in a long time. He relished the moment and dreaded its end. "Colonel Sokolov's office is at the center of camp. He will need to be influenced. Your chai bricks have caused a bit of a stir."

…

Colonel Sokolov allowed himself to be influenced because he was intrigued by men like Lord Muravyov. But with everything, there was a limit. "So this young man gets a commission. What makes you think he can get to Okhotsk down the Amur? I would not take on such a journey." Then again, in his head, he could already taste the chai during the coming winter.

Aaron weighed the advice, considered his alternatives. He would not, for he could not, go back to Lutsk much less travel to Safed. This Siberia was not for him. Russia had found a perfect location for its katorga camps.

Dashi thought he could sense Aaron's dilemma. "You don't know any Chinese. If I come, I must bring my family." Such a grand twist had not crossed Aaron's mind. "My wife knows some Chukchi, the people of the East. You will always trade better when you can speak their language."

Aaron was lost in his thinking, he may well become a naval officer. He felt the wind was blowing destiny his way, an adventurous destiny. Now it was from the bow of a ship.

Lord Muravyov gave Aaron two surprising items, both from his foter. First was his mussar journal. Joseph had been dictating to Lord Muravyov, working with him until the end. The other was a letter, his tzava'ot, he had written when he knew death was near. It was a letter, "for my zin if they are to become better men than I."

One evening, Aaron read the letter.

Zin,

You live in a world desperate for redemption, in great need of healing. I have tried to provide and know I have failed in countless ways. May the words of Rabbi Hulstein make up for the years I missed.

You must start by redeeming yourself. If the world is to be healed, you must first be healed. These are daunting tasks, ones I failed though I gave my all.

Once you have mastery of yourself, you can attempt to change others and change the world. There is no better way to live than to serve the needed redemption and healing.

You will rarely know who you truly are without a partner. Through the love of a wife, I learned my beliefs were rarely seen by all and nearly always less important than a fat chicken on Shabbat. Temper your expectations by going inward.

I have learned much from my mussar work. You must have a daily practice. Do not wander the desert wasting your time. Study for your sake.

I have tried to know which way the wind blows. I have come close. There is no better way to know the unseen than by studying. A good study partner is almost as good as a wife.

Money is a tool. Do not think it is anything more. A shovel is a shovel even if it is made of gold, though a gold shovel can buy you ten men to do the work.

My saba, your great saba, enjoyed owning vast fields of wheat. May you one day have the time to study like you own all the fields you can see.

Care for all you have or give it away.

The journey is quick.

Don't waste your time.

The end comes for us all,

Your loving foter,

Joseph

Aaron recorded notes on 'strength' for his daily mussar entry:

- *May I always have strength to study*
- *Strength to do what is right*
  - *What is right is a dance between body and brain by a graceful heart*
- *Strength for what is*

Anger - Fall, 1830

*Consider anger as a dangerous tool, not as
a common emotion.*

*Formerly understood for its universally destructive
nature, it has been trivialized.*

*Daily, people get angry and fail to understand they
are wrecking their world.*

*Understanding anger will provide a better path forward
when dealing with such people, including yourself.*

*They live in a damaged world and expect others
are living similarly.*

Live a bountifully rich life.

It could take a month for Dashi to return. He promised to be quick.
No one wanted to sail the Alaskan islands to New Archangel during winter.
Dashi knew his deal depended on it.

Colonel Sokolov saw the boxes of chai and realized the 'gift horse' that
lived at his camp: a newly commissioned officer needed training. The young
man needed his wisdom. He had Aaron join his officers for their morning
review. They saw his lack of leadership skills despite his shiny new uniform.
Regardless, they needed the fresh blood. Colonel Sokolov was wise to step in
and shield his new officer from the tough men.

"I can train you, teach you what it means to be an officer. You'll have to
teach the soldiers how to follow your commands. I figure on four traveling
with you down the Amur." The colonel was proud of this forward-thinking.

He expected a snap response to his offer of multiple soldiers joining his journey.

Aaron did not have an ounce of military behavior. He did know to keep his mouth shut, but salutes were not in his bones. The colonel's offer was not understood.

"That's, 'Yes Sir!' when spoken to, young man. And stand up straight." Colonel Sokolov shook his head. "Listen, I can send four soldiers with you down the Amur. You'll need the help despite whatever your Buryat friend says." He looked at the young man, trying to stand at attention. "It will cost you. Half now and half when you get to Okhotsk."

"Yes, Sir!" Aaron looked straight ahead.

"This is a deal, not a command. You agree and I'll get you trained to lead these men. You don't want to show up in Okhotsk not knowing how to lead men."

"Yes, sir." Aaron looked at the colonel in his eyes. "I appreciate your help."

"For a brick of chai, half now and half when you make Okhotsk. The soldiers will get half a brick when they return. So, it is they who get to choose the four who will travel and behave as all will share the chai this winter." Colonel Sokolov paused. "Let this be your first lesson, motivate your soldiers. Things are easy when they keep themselves in line."

"Yes, I can imagine self-directed soldiers are much easier. Thank you." Aaron had relaxed and picked up a small rock from the colonel's desk.

"That's 'Yes, Sir!' And put that down!" The colonel growled his words. "Don't make me regret this deal. Dismissed."

"Yes, Sir!" Aaron added, "Dismissed!" with an air of authority.

"K Chertu." muttered the colonel.

The training filled Aaron's days. Most of his work involved escorting groups of prisoners. His squad changed daily based on the soldiers' trust in their comrades. While he was getting the work completed, he was not learning to lead soldiers.

"I learned the hard way." Lord Muravyov began one evening on their sitting log.

"I don't know what I'm learning," Aaron replied with a sigh.

"When you are a leader, you're constantly being watched. The men will forgive your harshness, and mistakes in judgment. What they never forgive is cowardice. Does this make sense?" Lord Muravyov could see Aaron working to digest those ideas.

"At Austerlitz, we were routed. I stood with my men as chaos swirled, every man for himself." Lord Muravyov recalled the terror in men's eyes. "The men looked to me for strength and all I could say was, 'Retreat.' None who survived wanted to be under my command."

"That sounds awful. What else could an officer do?" Aaron never wanted combat. He would talk with Colonel Sokolov.

"You never know when the challenge will arise. The best you can do is realize it at the moment and not expect a disaster to be anything else. Struggle with all your might to survive. A disaster destroys everything. It doesn't care who is an officer or not."

Aaron knew to keep his mouth shut.

The idea that this eighteen-year-old could be seen as an officer was a tribute to Aaron's hard-won independence. He was touted as a twenty-one-year-old, a good age for an officer. Colonel Sokolov saw Aaron's intelligence and his proper manners. What was lacking could be improved during the next weeks and travels to Okhotsk. It was Aaron who had the negative internal dialog, causing him to mistrust and stumble.

"You must protect yourself, Aaron. Joshua was much older than you and understood he must never expose himself around others. You are a Jew. Russia does not allow Jews in the military besides on the front lines. As an officer, you will be shot if they learn who you are. You are circumcised. No?"

Aaron had not realized his circumcision was such the clear announcement of his religion. But more so, Lord Muravyov's intimate reference to his brother caused Aaron's confusion. "You knew my brother well, to talk of such things."

"Let me be clear. You let someone see you without clothes and you will be shot. Ok?" Lord Muravyov looked for recognition in Aaron's eyes. "Joshua, what a mensch. Isn't that what you say? Why, he is easily ten years older than you, understood his responsibilities. He went with the Russian-American Company because your father did not want to see his son whither away in a place like this. There are real business possibilities across the water."

"I want to set up a store. I learned a lot in Irbit."

"I imagine you did." Lord Muravyov looked across the valley. "You are an officer in the Russian Navy. You are not a merchant."

Together, the two watched the activity below, the ravens soared across the valley, and stars popped out amid the colorful Siberian evening sky. The view from the log, sunrise and sunset, gave a good account of the human struggle surrounding Aaron.

...

"You want to be a merchant!" Colonel Sokolov's yelling stirred the secretary in the other room. Aaron stood with a blank look, unphased. *'What a strange young man!'* thought Colonel Sokolov. "I've got you training to be an officer, not a merchant." His anger was a good reflection of how powerfully his morning chai had brought him into the day. Now, this insolent trouble of a man wanted more.

"Can I be an officer and a merchant?" Aaron's question now made a little sense and Colonel Sokolov calmed down. There was a price for everything.

"Merchants need money. You must have more than the little jingle I hear from your coin bag." He watched the young man squirm. He waited.

Aaron thought and then responded, "I'll give you five now and five when the Russian Navy agrees with what you write down. The soldiers can bring it back."

"Hmph." Colonel Sokolov was not going to let on that he liked this idea. "Ten now and five later."

"Six."

"Eight, or I won't write anything." The colonel almost laughed at the thought of eight rubles for no skin off of his back. He didn't expect to receive the five.

When Dashi returned, Aaron was grateful not to see Temyulen. During the past weeks, he had learned a grandmother like her was not one to take directions. Tuyana and Toq would follow Dashi. They looked fresh, like they were out on a picnic, instead of having completed a fast five-hundred mile journey.

This would be the end of Aaron's journey by cart. Samuel would have been sick. The Shilka River flowed 250 miles before it joined the Argun and together made the mighty Amur, the 10th longest in the world. A few miles south of Nerchinsk, they would purchase a riverboat, which would take them nearly 2000 miles to the Pacific Ocean. The Amur River was known both for its fast canyons and lazy braided sections. Not one of them had traveled this river. Since the Treaty of Nerchinsk, the Chinese had controlled the mighty river and only Dashi knew a bit of their language.

"All the best for finding your brother." Lord Muravyov was visibly sad to see Aaron go. The past weeks had restored his spirits and, importantly, given him a vision of the future. He was being left behind and this reminded him that he needed people. There were other Decembrists with whom he would connect. He would move away from the camp and into the city of Nerchinsk. He still held influence.

"The Russian-American Company has a great territory. He could be anywhere." Lord Muravyov shared stories. Russian-American Company boats were going as far as the Baja of California, as well as Kauai, looking for product. "They all come back to New Archangel. If you can't find him, I would wait there." He wanted to give something to Aaron, something of value. His life had pivoted around his father more than Aaron would ever know. In the end, he found including him in his daily prayers was the best he could do.

The soldiers brought their supplies to the Shilka River in a large wagon. Their crates were added to the trade goods and extra supplies Aaron and Dashi had purchased. Small boats were common, as the river was not easy to navigate. Aaron purchased a larger flat-bottom barge as their numbers and supplies demanded it. At the end of the day, he got the barge for an extra ten rubles and the small fortune he had made selling his cart and horses in Nerchinsk.

"You're lucky the water is high," said the barge salesman.

"Do share your advice. We're going all the way." Aaron had enthusiasm and his military uniform.

"You've never floated this river? I'd strap a pole on the front. It'll give you a heads-up when you're losing the channel." The riverman watched

Aaron. "In fact, take several poles. You'll need them for getting off the sandbars." He then chuckled and said, "These soldiers will learn to hate you by the end." Aaron took his advice. In time, he learned how heavy the barge was.

...

In the fall of 1830 China was gripped by internal struggles and devastating trade from foreign powers. The British had spread opium across the country like any typical drug dealer. Aaron had heard, Dashi too, about the addictive drug and lucrative trade. Steering clear, they brought silver from the Nerchinsk mine to bribe their way down the river. Aaron had fifty small silver bars imprinted with the Czar's crest for a touch of quality. He only used ten down the Amur.

Oh, there were plenty of problems with the Chinese, or more accurate, the Indigenous people of the Amur. Their barge, with little tent shelter, attracted a lot of attention. Silver helped with the officials, but the people wanted food. This was not farmland. At first, the people would trade fish for flour. Later, small boats would sneak up so they could steal. The soldiers were shocked but were told to only use clubs, not their guns. One soldier had to stand guard at all times. This became crucial when they ran aground.

The murky Amur became braided in many areas. The sandbars snagged the barge despite their constant attention to the river depth. True, the poles became key for moving the heavy barge back to the current. But when they were stuck, they were easy pickings if they were not attentive to the locals.

Nights were the worst. The long summer days had been replaced by dark nights. Night duty allowed for guns, and a string around their camp with metal pieces proved priceless more than once.

At numerous bends in the river, Aaron thought the whole adventure would be undone. The barge had his life wrapped up in so many ways: his bricks of chai, his metal trade wares, the soldiers for whom he felt responsible, his partnership with Dashi, his journals.

Aaron had begun to read from his father's mussar journal. He was struck by how small his father wrote and how his spirit bled through his words.

Anger:

- *The stories these men tell are horrendous. Few are here for any reason besides the arbitrary thoughts of a Russian noble. It is hard not to imagine Muravyov rubbing shoulders with these pigs. They are the scourge of our great empire, we must purge ourselves of these useless swine. They are of no value to our future.*
- *Am I the convict? I toil like them all while Muravyov sits on his log. Today, I saw a man beaten to death. He failed to move a boulder and was deemed less than the cost of his food. His body was dragged by three men to a ditch they had outside the mine. They keep the ditch open, knowing more will daily die - or - be killed.*
- *The cabbage larvae have become a treat. When did I get so low that rotting food and the worms growing within are seen as a delicacy? No soldier who fought for Mother Russia should ever have to experience this hell.*

September flowed into October and the frosts grew into snows. Being on the river in October required fires, both a danger and a blessing. The tent had become a wooden structure, demanded by the wide-river winds. For most, illness was a seeping condition. They believed it came from the cold and damp, while their sedentary life, poor food, and lack of quality sleep played as large a role. The end could not have come any later.

Fuyori, was the Manchu village at the mouth of the Amur. It became apparent a Chinese boat needed to be hired for their sail to Okhotsk, a Russian port north along the coast. Forty silver bars and their river barge proved to be a powerful sales pitch. In short order, they found themselves sailing north along the Sea of Okhotsk.

…

Okhotsk was the Russian-American Company's main port on the Asian side of the Pacific. These were the last days of the poorly built town.

"A new second mate, and you come with soldiers." The Russian-American Company director in Okhotsk reread the letter from Colonel Sokolov. The company's Okhotsk warehouses were plentiful, the director's office was in shambles. Colonel Sokolov's office had been organized. The soldiers made note.

"It says here you are also classified as a merchant." He raised his eyebrows at the young second mate. "You have a brother also with the company." The director plopped into his desk chair, eyes on Aaron. "I recommend the rest of you leave. Go get some food and rest." He spoke without taking his eyes off of Aaron.

"You must take life lightly to sign up for such an adventure." He eyed Aaron for a reaction. "The soldiers will have to stay. There are never enough to protect the Czar's valuable interests. This, Colonel Sokolov, will understand." He continued to watch for a reaction from Aaron.

Aaron stood at attention with his mouth shut. He listened and also didn't listen to this director's babble. He had become used to giving the orders and was slow to pivot.

"I imagine you had a 'deal' with the Colonel. You can pay me and I'll compensate him. You don't want to start in the company with a debt hanging over your head." The director had seen the crates come off of the Chinese boat.

The Russian-American Company map had captured Aaron's attention. It took Aaron a moment or two or three to orientate himself to the Pacific theater. He knew he was not good at geography, but maps always caught his attention.

The director was obviously not his captain. Yes, he would have to pay this man a bribe. Since joining the Russian Navy and the Russian-American Company, Aaron had experienced countless men demanding bribes. Aaron's mind calculated as he pretended to read the map.

Repeatedly, Aaron counted his supplies with Dashi as a reminder of their deal. His rubles were a different matter. Aaron took the coins hidden in his travel bag and spent 75 rubles on supplies, the barge, and silver bars. Of the remaining twenty-five, he kept half hidden in his travel bag and mixed the rest into the bag hanging from his belt. Those in the belt coin bag he knew Dashi had tallied to the last kopek. In a sense, this was comforting to Aaron.

"We sail in five days. Kind of perfect timing." Aaron smiled as he shared the news with Dashi and Tuyana. The soldiers had a table to themselves in the small shop.

Tuyana was as cool as her mother was aggressive. During their sail here, she had worked hard to pick up Chinese and help with communication. At

Okhotsk, she connected with several Chukchi and learned of the challenges they would face on their next adventure.

"We know we're not going back to Nerchinsk," one of the soldiers called from his table. "We still want our payment." Relaxed, enjoying food and drink around a table, they looked like they were on holiday.

The soldiers had provided legitimacy to his endeavor. He was not keen on losing them now. "Yes. We have done well, thanks to you." Aaron smiled wide and added, "Figure out a way to come to New Archangel and I'll give you more." His words had a mixed reaction.

"Not interested," was the first response.

"It's not us you need to convince. The director controls our fate."

"So, if I can get one of you to sail, who would like to come along?" Aaron had ideas for engaging the director.

The next day, he met with the director. Their chai crates had been opened, the director knew how much he had. Even a 5% tax would be costly. Aaron started the negotiation by asking for help. "If you can find my brother, I'll make it worth your while." He knew there must be ship manifests somewhere in the mess.

"I haven't seen that much chai in a long time." The director let his words settle in. "Your brother is on the Ches'ma. He sailed for Kauai last April. He should be back in New Archangel by November. You'll see him in a month." The director was being genial this morning.

He walked over to the company map. "You came down the Amur. Not smart." His finger was tracing the river. "Less stupid people have caused wars because of their ignorant actions." He let those words settle.

"The soldiers come with me to New Archangel." He wanted the director's shock to happen early. Aaron knew his asks were going to cost him. "What do you want for one?"

The older man was less inclined to deal with this newly commissioned officer. He undeniably had connections backing his adventure.

"At the least, a quarter-brick goes to the colonel. You've got requests for soldiers, ship manifests, special shipments to New Archangel. You're looking at three bricks. You haven't met Captain Orlov of the Saratov. He will need some."

It was a reach, Aaron knew it. "I appreciate knowing the Ches'ma sails back to New Archangel. I'll deal with Captain Orlov in good time. I'll give you two bricks and I expect the colonel to get his share." His offer was low.

"Two and a half. You know this is a good deal on four crates of chai."

In five days Bogdan, the one soldier the director allowed, joined them aboard the Saratov for New Archangel. Captain Orlov was ashore, leaving the three-masted ship to first mate Kuznetsov. He eyed Aaron, his newly commissioned second mate, with an air of authority. He saw Dashi and Tuyana with Toq as a pleasant surprise. With Bogdan, he was quick to give orders.

"We have rights to trade and can make a pleasant journey worth your efforts." Aaron's words took the day to trickle into Kuznetsov's mind. The same words received warm approval from the captain.

Captain Orlov enjoyed his evening drink and pleasant conversation. Because of a presence needed on deck or because of his first mate's lack of talent, the captain nightly requested Aaron. The slight was a bitter pill for the first mate.

Their evening talks dove deep into Lord Muravyov's adventures, as well as the war in old Poland. Aaron knew to come with topics and questions for such a captain. His natural tendency was to ask questions like Rabbi Hulstein, but he knew they needed a new structure.

"You've got watch," Kuznetsov ordered. "The winds are shifting south, signs it should rain by morning." His evening questions about sailing to Hawaii would have to wait. Aaron walked the deck.

His First Watch should have ended at midnight. His duty rolled into the Middle Watch, which ended at 4 A.M. That crew switched but he did not. By eight bells for the start of the morning watch, 8 A. M., Aaron was ready for a hot cup of chai and sleep. No one came to relieve him, and the wind and rain began. Aaron was not an experienced sailor but knew not having a third mate did not allow the boatswain to take over.

By four bells of the Forenoon Watch, 10 A.M., first mate Kuznetsov came on deck with a frown. "These Aleutian storms can get real nasty. Unalaska is too far if this gets worse." He gave no mention of his failure to relieve, something all sailors witnessed. He gave orders to sail closer to the islands. Aaron was more than tired, he was embittered, but he knew he had duty in just a couple of hours.

The Aleutians are a string of volcanoes. Through breaks in the clouds, those on duty could see illuminated snow caps on conical mounts. In a couple of hours, the blue skies grew larger and the low-hanging clouds moved on. One after the next, like beacons, volcanoes marked the way to Alaska.

By four bells of Afternoon Watch, 2 P.M., Captain Orlov emerged and smiled at the blue sky. "Mt. Pogromni is sending up ash. I don't think too many men from Lutsk have ever seen an erupting volcano." He walked out to the bow, rising and dipping in the cold water. Ocean spray blew back on deck.

Mt. Pogromni was a sight, smoke spewing forth as if it were slow steam from a kettle. The volcano also marked the beginning of the mainland, which they followed to Kodiak Island.

Their October crossing had gone better than imagined. Aaron's first experience as a second mate was one he did not want to repeat.

Docked at Kodiak, Aaron stayed in his berth reading his journal entries on anger. He had watched the crew handle multiple issues under dangerous circumstances during the crossing. They provided rich insights from which he hoped to grow.

Anger -

- *Rises like waves under mighty winds*
- *Drop yours if you have dreams*
- *Expect another is always watching*
- *Causing another to get red from anger is spilling their blood*
- *First mate Kuznetsov knows too little, no need to get angry*
- *On occasions, anger can be used to pivot a point into position*

Modesty - Winter, 1830-31

Sometimes,
I'm not sure if people are trying
to confuse others, reduce human potential,
are truly lazy, or are something in between.

But expecting children to sit up straight, clean
their plates, watch their words, make their beds was
never meant as punishment.

These expectations build a better person, one we
all want to be around.

Modesty reduces the sharp edges between friends.

And a vain friend is, to put it bluntly, weak.

New Archangel (Sitka) had its own beauty and its own volcano. As the center of the Russian-American Company across the Pacific, the port town had a wide range of people: sailors, soldiers, laborers, merchants; Alaska Natives from the Aleutians, Kodiak, and the mainland around Fort St. George and Fort St. Nicholas, as well as the neighboring Tlingit people, currently at peace. New immigrants were arriving, including Finns from Europe in addition to the Americans and British who jumped their northern sailing ships. In 1830, American and British ships would appear to the delight of New Archangel residents. For Aaron, this would prove profitable.

Baron von Wrangell was the new governor of the Russian-American Company. His drive to improve infrastructure and investments excited the people. He wanted bridges, roads, and governmental buildings. He sent out missionaries and, in time, Russian Orthodox churches created a network throughout southern Alaska.

Dashi, Tuyana, and Toq looked upon the new world as the young, adventurous family they were. Dashi could feel Tuyana's expectation for success, as well as her consistent support for his work with Aaron. The family had been the fun extras during the crossing. Toq gave the sailors endless hours of joy.

Bogdan proved to be a silent, patient man. From a small village west of Tomsk, there he was rejected by his peers because of his meekness. His permission to join Aaron had partially been because the director did not see a future for the small man in this dangerous world. Personally, Bogdan was proud of his success and expected his future to prove quite profitable.

The unloading of the Saratov did not excite the town's people. Aaron paid off Captain Orlov with additions that allowed him freedom from sailing duties unless the captain was in 'serious' need. A sail to Fort Ross and back actually sounded grand to Aaron, as long as Kuznetsov was elsewhere.

"You're young. A career in the Navy is not a terrible choice. But it looks like you've got some backers who want returns on their investments." Captain Orlov was eyeing the crates of chai. "You may not find the buyers here for your chai. I'll be in touch." The captain would spend the winter in the fort drinking and telling stories to all who would listen.

"That's two rubles port tax on your merchandise." A burly harbormaster spoke as he handed Aaron a receipt. He paid with kopeks despite the two-ruble coin in his hand.

"Your man and wife will have to live north of town. There are more local folks there and the Tlingit have their village about another 10 miles out." A rough, hairy hand tugged on a robust beard. "Things are good right now. Don't go stirring up any trouble with the locals and you'll fit right in."

"Any word on the Ches'ma? I have a brother, first mate, on the ship."

"I don't think it will be back anytime soon. The salt in Kauai comes slowly. Those sailors will have to work all winter if you get my meaning." The cheeks blushed a bit accompanied by a big but hidden smile. "The captain said as much when he heard how much salt he was expected to gather. Who wouldn't want a winter in paradise!" Aaron had no idea what he was talking about.

Dashi overheard much of their conversation about living out of town, and the following about attending church. The harbormaster continued,

"The last governor's mistress and kids still attend St Michael's. He left them behind so the priest could ridicule his name every week. That fool is going to burn."

Aaron was hungry, mentally elsewhere, and looked around to hire a porter. In time their supplies were stored and they asked for a place to eat and talk.

Sitting around a small table but still swaying as if at sea, Aaron stated, "We need a shop. If we all live there, at the shop, things will go better. It'll be safer." Dashi agreed. Tuyana and Toq were in their own world. Bogdan was glad to be under Aaron's leadership and not under the fort commander.

"We can't live in town. You and Bogdan will be outsiders if you live too north of town." Dashi had seen such divisions throughout Russia.

"Maybe we can find a place in between?" Tuyana rarely spoke. Her suggestion made sense and proved to be a grand idea.

Their place needed much work. New Archangel had gone through many upheavals in its thirty years. The Tlingit uprising had caused much destruction and then a lot of rebuilding. This structure was in the middle and no one else was ready to live as an in-between. The good foundation gave them something with which they could work.

Local Tlingit people came by within a day. Men looked through their wares while Bogdan looked to Aaron for direction. No one understood the words spoken by the other.

Aaron took a stick and hit a man's hand, which had taken a shovelhead. The Tlingit men reacted as one. Aaron froze, stuck up his hands. Slowly, he bent and placed the shovelhead back in the sack. And slowly he cracked open a crate. Dramatically, he pulled out a quarter chai brick and smiled. "We need to present this to their leader if we don't want to have constant trouble." Through a mixture of head nods, hand motions, and lots of misunderstood words, Aaron and Dashi followed the men to their village.

Aaron kept his aloof cool despite repeated threats. Dashi worked to understand their language, though it didn't take much to comprehend their initial refusal to everything. They took the chai brick with little acknowledgment. Then a few days later, a group of six Tlingit men knocked on their door.

'Naadkym wanted more tea.' or so Aaron thought. The men looked inside at the beginnings of their shop. Aaron had seen them approaching and welcomed them inside. Dashi walked to the backdoor and Bogdan walked outside to the front, to set a tone.

Tables of ax heads, shovelheads, and pick heads, were separated from a crate of tea. On the other side were four bolts of colored cloth and metal cookware Aaron had bought as a joke before leaving Okhotsk. The metal plates had already rusted despite being oiled.

Cold, damp, rain 'every-other-day' weather made the old but warm building quite cozy with eight men inside. The laughter of Toq in the back made a young man grin.

Aaron picked up an 'eighth-of-a-brick' and gave it to a marginally Russian-speaking Tlingit man. "What else do you like?" Aaron spread his arms and used his hands. His engaging market skills were with him for life.

The man picked up an ax head and showed it to another. He lifted and smelled the colorful cloth and handed it to another. Aaron took another bolt of cloth and unrolled six feet. Inside, the cloth still smelled like new.

"What are you wanting?" Aaron asked, as a skilled servant.

Dashi did his best to interpret. "They want food." Aaron looked for more from Dashi. "Naadkym wants food and tea." The Tlingit men looked into Aaron's eyes for understanding.

"Of course. When we get food, flour, turnips, or anything else, Dashi will come and let you know. In fact, he should accompany you back to learn more." Aaron and Dashi had talked earlier about the importance of learning their language.

At the end of November, an American crew found their way to Aaron's door. They were searching for furs. They bought the crate of tea Aaron had on display and another. The sailors could make a fortune selling it to the British, who were expanding beyond Fort Vancouver. Hudson Bay Company trappers were everywhere. The few rubles they had were nowhere near enough. Aaron didn't know how to exchange for dollars. A Tlingit man translated the English to Dashi who had learned the basics of the Tlingit language.

"Tell them we want food, barrels of it." Aaron added, "Try to sell each tea crate for supplies equal to 200 rubles." Dashi turned and spoke with his Tlingit interpreter. The Tlingit man recognized the importance of his role.

"He wants an ax head for his work and I would give it to him." Aaron knew Dashi had become close with him and several other Tlingit men. Aaron agreed to the ax head and handed it over with a nod.

"They have barrels of fish, oil, and flour." Dashi's news came with a smile. "How much do you want?"

At the dock, Aaron inspected the twenty barrels of flour, eight barrels of corn meal, two barrels of sugar, and two of tallow. The sailors were so pleased they moved the barrels back to Aaron's shop. The whole town took note, as did the harbormaster. Despite the tax of ten rubles, it was acceptable as Aaron got an invite to dinner with Governor Wrangel.

…

"Officer Aaron. I heard you came to us from Nerchinsk, such a dismal place." At the sight of the governor's long sideburns, Aaron ran his hands over his beard. "I've heard rumors about you. It is good to finally meet you." His handshake was strong for a short man.

"I had delivered supplies to Lord Muravyov from his home in old Poland." Governor Wrangel raised his bushy eyebrows. "Colonel Sokolov talked me into a navy commission." Aaron added, "My brother was commissioned two years earlier."

"Ah, yes. First mate Katz. It does sound Jewish, but I've never been to that part of Russia. Nor do I desire to. I imagine Colonel Sokolov knew you would be sent back if you didn't join the navy." The governor waited for an answer.

Aaron knew to keep the focus on his positives. "Lord Muravyov used his connections to ask for our family's help. We have had much success trading in the East. Colonel Sokolov benefited from our visit. We look forward to Joshua returning to the family business." Aaron wanted the Governor to know his merchant license had real value.

"And as a token of my appreciation for doing business, let this barrel of flour make your winter all the more pleasant." Bogdan rolled the barrel around the corner. *Were the bribes ever going to end?*

The Winter Holidays in New Archangel were extra sweet with Aaron's supplies. He had to make a false bottom to the sugar and tallow barrels so though they would run out, the next day he would have more. When he tallied up his profits, Dashi happened to walk around the corner.

"Over two hundred. It's what I calculated." Dashi was shrewd. Aaron appreciated this.

"We've got two more crates of - tea." Aaron mused at the word. "And at least twelve more barrels of flour and two of corn meal. It's way over two hundred." Aaron burst into a wide smile. He stood and handed Dashi his share. "You're my partner. We did this." It was a moment, then Aaron turned. "And take these." He handed Dashi more coins, five. "Give them to Bogdan as you see fit. We want him happy." Dashi understood.

Dashi walked to the back of the shop where they had created two rooms. Tuyana was playing with Toq. The fifty rubles looked like a pile of treasure. "Plenty more to come." Dashi smiled and waited for her to realize what had happened.

Dashi spent days at a time with the Tlingit people. They did not need food this winter like the people of New Archangel, but the gifts of flour went a long way. Dough, fried in tallow, Naadkym could not get enough. A man named Gushklin spent a lot of time with Dashi. It was rare to see the two apart. Several of Dashi's coins ended up with Gushklin, and Aaron received an earful when he visited town.

Aaron needed to correct such a wrong. "What Dashi does with his coin is his choice. He's also smart, as Gushklin makes Naadkym happy. If you like how things are, compared to how they were, I would welcome and encourage Gushklin's coins." Aaron pulled on his beard for a final emphasis. The other men at the table agreed with Aaron. Most had heard about the large ransoms paid to return captives after the uprising. Gushklin's coins were specks of sand compared to those amounts.

Grandfather Frost brought many gifts. Aaron received a new fur hat, his first Christmas gift ever. Dashi received new boots, something Tuyana and Aaron had worked on for two months. The one cobbler in New Archangel made more money than Aaron. The beginning of January needed festivities, as the snows and then rains were constant.

Whether it was the weather or whether it was not, Aaron felt turning nineteen years old to be a burden of boredom. In less than three months, he had successfully established himself in New Archangel. He was physically healthy, his friends were happy, and he was connected to the community. He felt more than depressed.

What he knew, he couldn't put into words; his travels had given him purpose. As if it were the greatest adventure ever, his daily passages had provided a mountain of adventure. He had nurtured an internal drive from traversing thousands of miles. Here, in New Archangel, his drive was told to stop, and it proved more difficult than he knew.

Dashi saw the agitation gnawing at Aaron, making him irritable, if not mean. Arguments over merchandise came quick with little reasoning. Later, Aaron would apologize only to have them happen again.

Tuyana was pregnant, her first trimester was hidden from others. Dashi's over the moon euphoria had not gone unnoticed by his new friend Gushklin and even Naadkym who congratulated him. His time with the Tlingit people had created close relationships and his own market, making Aaron jealous. Aaron's brain, like in the past, looked for a reason for his frustration, his pain. He grasped at many things and came up empty as he was not seeing the bigger picture.

One notebook for sale in his store found its way into his bedside stack with a pencil as a bookmark. He was doing impulsive things, including writing. Descriptive stories about his travels poured forth like rain off the roof. His and his father's journals provided rich material that fueled a stilted path forward.

Aaron struggled to see the connections between his studies and his current predicament; stuck in New Archangel for the winter.

"... the winds east of Irbit came from an empty land. They roared across miles, caring not for the life striving to add light to these dark lands. Order is found in small, barely protected crevices like the one I found beneath reindeer hides on the sleigh. Our horses were gifts from G... They were beacons. They were rays of light in this wasteland, transporting me to a better, a healthier, and more orderly place. A life allowing me to flourish and prosper through my studies."

"... Silence. Days are blank in my journal, Foter had whole weeks. Silence, like the story of people who wandered off into the wilderness. We all long for the sound of pages being turned, of pencils scratching paper, of students debating the word. A life *without is a life adrift with no rudder. Aimlessness creates silence. To be silent, aimless, adrift, and wasteful is shameful."*

Days turned into weeks and word from the Ches'ma came to New Archangel. Sailors reported the ship's hulls were nearly full and their sail home had more than likely begun. Aaron's mind struggled with images of his older brother. Did he know Aaron was in New Archangel? Would Joshua accept him, help him, love him? Would Joshua approve of his studies? Joshua was an ordained rabbi.

'How can I tell Joshua our foter is dead? That I forget to say the Kaddish and it has not been a year? Will he understand why I came here? Why our moter is in Safed? Why Estle is in Safed?'

His journal filled with conversations that spilled off of the pages. Bogdan was nearby most of the time. The soldier created an air of authority, an air of order. When Dashi was around, the shop echoed with their talk, hours of talk. When he was gone visiting Gushklin, the drip of water drove Aaron a bit mad. Towering spruce trees never ceased to have one more drip of water to drop.

"Do you have a brother?" Increasingly, Aaron's paperless conversations were directed at Bogdan.

"I have several," Bogdan responded, wary of Aaron's questioning.

"You know my brother is older, ten years older. He is first mate on the Ches'ma, which is due back any day." Bogdan could feel Aaron's anxiety.

"How do I tell my older brother our father is gone? I haven't seen my brother in years." It was a question not needing an answer, though Bogdan knew more than Aaron.

During his time off, Bogdan gravitated to other military men. Time at the pub provided him a story or two about the older brother, a first mate who was fair, one not to have his orders questioned, but more humane than most. Some of his tongue lashings were said to hurt more than the rod. The 'Pole', as many called him, behind his back.

In a sense, the two were definitely brothers.

"He will need a week to transfer trade from the Ches'ma, time to readjust to New Archangel. I say, give him time." Bogdan knew pathways to success if one listened.

Passover appeared on the horizon and then the Ches'ma. Months had turned the rain into snows and then rain again. April had days when migrating water birds filled the skies and gave Aaron a renewed sense of purpose. The empty lands were being filled.

He watched his brother before saying hello. A taller-than-average, fast-moving, ever-watching first mate. His mouth moved as much as his feet, giving sailors a briskness to their work.

"Hello bruder."

Joshua stood erect and slowly turned. His gaze was sharp, then softened, and then came back. "Aaron." He embraced his brother in a familiar bear hug.

Joshua introduced him to his second mate. The shorter man eyed Joshua with a look Aaron understood. They left him in charge and walked the dock, Joshua's arm on Aaron's shoulder. Their exclamations of 'oys and joys' were interrupted by laborers calling out to Joshua for directions with the shipment.

"Stop! I can't believe you are here!" Joshua held Aaron's shoulders and inspected him as a first mate does. "You've become a man, Aaron."

"I'm a second mate."

"You don't wear a uniform!"

"No. When I paid my commission, I also paid for merchant privileges."

"What is this 'merchant privileges'?" Joshua made a face. "I've never heard of such a thing. We all work for the Czar." Joshua pondered. "Did you inherit a hundred rubles when our foter died?" He was being serious.

"No, foter only gave me his mussar journal. In fact, it was Lord Muravyov who gave the journal and foter's tzava'ot, his final letter." Joshua worked to recall what Aaron was describing. Old brain images took a bit to bring forward.

To confuse him more, Aaron added, "I have way more than a hundred if you are in need."

Joshua was quick to compose, "My younger bruder, the rich man, the good life." He was proper to say it, but Joshua could see a sadness in his brother's eyes.

They spent the day together meeting Joshua's connections around New

Archangel. He received an invitation to dine with the captain, Aaron too. All the more so when Captain Gusev heard he was the 'merchant second mate' who had made Christmas.

"Captain Orlov left a note about you. You have powerful support back home. Nonetheless, we do have the right to call upon your service." That work was done, now, time for enjoyment. Captain Gusev knew best to let a port call be a port of call.

A day later, Aaron had not shaken Joshua's words. 'The Good Life' clung to him like a weight only he could see. He replayed the morning in Irbit when Anton gave him his first fortune, 'Go somewhere and make a good life'. Was this not a good life? Now with his brother, his shop, his savings, his friendships, was this not good? No.

He could feel it wasn't good. Many times a day he saw he wasn't right, something wasn't right. Despite his constant obsession with a cause, he had nothing to blame. This was the good life. It wasn't good for him.

Aaron knew he couldn't stay in New Archangel for another year, though the winter was over. He realized the beauty of being a second mate was having another to blame. He needed time away from blaming himself for everything, when all everyone else saw was success. Where was Kuznetsov? Where were Captain Orlov and the Saratov?

"You're doing what?" Joshua was more upset than Aaron had predicted. "You've got everything! You're making more money than I'll ever see and you're choosing to join Captain Orlov's trip to Ft. Ross." Joshua wanted to say more but he took a few breaths and held his tongue. He shook his head and muttered.

Aaron tried to hold on to his aloofness. "I know you know. You don't say anything, but you watch me, judge me. I'm not happy. Something has changed. I can't." Aaron spoke plainly, though his anger was rising.

Later, Aaron explained to Dashi he was leaving him in charge, that they would trade in Ft. Ross, but don't count on any investment return. He wished a healthy year for all, and then Aaron realized something which brought him relief. His few moments of pleasure had been his regular talks with Dashi. Their habit of debating life, of Dashi teaching him the Buryat way, of their mutual respect for their lives, he was going to miss their talks.

He was going to miss Bogdan's simple plodding movement through life. The pain radiated from a spot he now understood. Aaron realized he missed his haver, an open wound that had yet to heal.

"I want a school." Aaron said it aloud for himself as much as for those who stood around the shop.

Dashi looked to Tuyana and realized now was not the time to tell Aaron. Bogdan knew Tuyana was expecting. For all his smarts, Aaron struggled to keep up with basic awareness. Even later when he heard Samar was born, Aaron failed to understand the significance of Dashi's growing family.

Like he had done countless times before, today before sleep he recorded his thoughts about 'Modesty' in his mussar journal:

- *I am modest because I know to also be humble. I am modest and humble because I know I am made from dust*
- *My dust could no longer hold my happiness inside. I leaked happiness, and it was painful*
- *I still leak happiness but I now have a name for it*
- *I have a name for it but I do not say. I don't think it is modest not to say. It is selfish*

The Ever Changing World - The 1830s

It wasn't only Aaron who tried to find himself during the 1830s. Numerous social issues confounded humans, the least of which was the prolific consumption of hard liquor. Cheaper than milk or tea, whiskey was consumed at levels that confounded all. In hindsight, it was a world reeling from oppressive laws, restrictive thought, and celebration of classism for which most needed the numbing effects of alcohol. What they did invent honored their need to break out and connect: the railroad, the telegraph, and the camera.

How does one explain the Opium Wars? Is there a way to spin the Indian Removal Act without accepting national efforts at genocide? Did Darwin's insights into evolution make sense to anyone?

The people immersed themselves in stories to spin their oppression into freedom. Victor Hugo's Quasimodo, however his hunchback story ended, he had his day in the sun. Charles Dickens' Oliver gave readers so many twists, success was inevitable. It felt right.

It is the decade the United Kingdom ended slavery. Not a bad act for a universally acknowledged drunken ten years. Hong Kong fell to the British, who saw their rising star to include a port in Southeast Alaska. The decade ended with Queen Victoria picking up the mantle and leading the British into their worldly position.

Siberia continued to be a pathway to ironically glorious possibilities for convicted criminals. But, it would take another two decades before steam-powered ships and rails could make inroads into the rich lands of this foreboding Asian corner.

Russians expanded further into their Alaskan Territory, improving their infrastructure, founding new forts and trading posts. Surprisingly, their use of alcohol in Alaska had not taken hold as it had by other Europeans in North America. It was seen as unhealthy and the priests held strong sway over the Russian-American Company. Only in the Southeast did alcohol become a problem. Most blamed the English and American traders.

For Zelde, Estle, Nathan, and their children, Safed was no easy street. Right after their arrival, the Egyptians conquered Safed from the Ottomans, bringing what most Jews hoped for: religious toleration. While religious freedom was possible, fighting between local tribes and amongst themselves did not produce a land of milk and honey. A devastating earthquake nearly ended the Jewish habitation of Safed. What Zelde had hoped for was torn between the violence of the land and the people.

Across the world Zelde's youngest son also reflected on the tenuous nature of life. "The fighting has stopped in old Poland. The people have been defeated." Aaron's words reflected his lack of understanding steeped in empathy.

"War is never good for people." Dashi watched the young man work through his thoughts.

"The sailor said an epidemic of cholera has devastated those still alive." Aaron worried without comprehending.

Dashi attempted to soothe. "War and epidemics go together. People are fragile. We strive to be strong. If your friends were strong, they survived." Dashi patted Aaron's shoulder.

"If you live a strong life, healthy and pure, the evils of the world will move on. It is the way of the land." Dashi had seen this a hundred times.

"Nerchinsk was not good for my father." Aaron said.

"It is a death pit for all." Dashi waited. "You might say your father should have died on the battlefield?"

Aaron had visualized his battlefield death a thousand times. No, such a death was no better. Disease was no better. Being strong was no cure.

Aaron knew not how he was going to die but yearned for his painful passing to be blessed by the love and strength of another. No one should die alone.

Gratitude - 1831 to 1833

Like a salve upon a burn, like a cool breeze when stuck in a hot room, like a day of rain after weeks of drought, gratitude soothes the human spirit.

How many times do we rush faster, ruminate more, or plot vengeful acts instead of basking in the glory that is ours.

This is not new.

Social norms guide our steps like roads, going only to established places.

We are so much more.

Take a minute to find the hidden treasures lying right beside you.

Feel better.

All of us embark on new adventures, on new ways to improve ourselves. Aaron was no different, though his path looked different. He wanted to blame others, learn to not blame himself. He fought with Kuznetsov, with Captain Orlov, with everyone on the Saratov. He was put on bread and water rations and finally threatened with losing his commission.

Not everyone can pull themselves together. It is a simplistic method for weeding out the weak. In the end, Aaron was able to balance his needs or at least cull them to more acceptable behaviors. Culling was on everyone's mind as they sailed for Ft. Ross.

Furs had expanded the Russian-American Company, but the animals were harder to find. North of Ft. Ross, a competition line with the British had been declared, though Russians would continue to trade south for another decade. Seal furs were replacing otter pelts, beaver pelts were working their way towards importance.

Ft. Ross was a vibrant Russian post 80 miles north of San Francisco. Farming, with the first west coast windmill, was actively engaged. Russian work included shipbuilding, trading and ranching within the surrounding 'ranchos'. People from the breadth of the Empire were a sight for Aaron's sore eyes. He heard and spoke languages he had almost forgotten. At a shop selling chai, Aaron engaged a Lithuanian who danced between Russian, German, and Lithuanian. When Aaron added Polish, the man paused and shook his head.

"Don't talk like that," he said in German. "The language is dead to Russians. It is best if you don't remember how to speak it." He added a bit more with his bushy eyebrows.

The June day was nearly perfect. Aaron didn't have an ounce of trouble keeping his happiness inside. He found a crate outside the Lithuanian's shop and sat in the sun. He realized his shop in New Archangel was out of town and lacked the traffic he enjoyed watching. Eventually, the Lithuanian sat next to him.

"Why does a second mate have time to sit around?" It was a good question.

"You've ever been to Irbit?" Aaron wanted more conversational control.

"It is rare for anyone in my family not to have been there at least a half-dozen times. We have sold chai in Kaunas for a hundred years. Our new shop and warehouse is across the river from Napoleon's Hill, where I fought the French both times. You should come visit."

After a good chuckle, Aaron began to share that his rabbi was Lithuanian, from Vilnius, but caught himself. "He taught ethics in Lutsk. My father was passionate about us learning from Mechlenberg, my brother, and I." The cover barely worked. "My father was a Decembrist exile." Maybe this would change the subject.

"Terrible. The Czar kills his brother, *bless Czar Alexander,* and only a few care. Exiles pay for all our failures." The man looked at Aaron to ensure this officer would keep his treasonous words private. "We all want a better world and must talk about how to build it without the threat of exile." He nodded his head with a bit of vigor. "No one should be sent to Siberia to die."

It had not been an entire year, but Aaron had stopped saying the Kaddish. His father had been absent for years, so the merchant's words found little on which to stick. "It is a cemetery where suffering men dig their own graves. A horse is worth more than a man. You die in a million different ways, but for each, it is a horrible death." The man nodded his head in agreement.

"Irbit was where I learned to love winter." The merchant talked about filling his vozok with crates of chai bricks and speeding home. "Many times we brought our wares to trade. Twenty years ago, there was always something new being invented." Irbit was a long way away. Something they could both safely talk about.

"I'm here because British tea goes all the way around the world before it gets here. One can hardly call it tea." Aaron figured as such. What he saw in the merchant's shop reminded him of the chai he saw in Kyakhta.

"I thought it would be tea," Aaron paused as he said the English word, "but what they want in New Archangel is food. Wheat. Is there wheat here?"

The Lithuanian turned and looked directly at Aaron. "It is June. The winter wheat should be at the mill. I don't know if the ranchos here are producing enough to be sold. If not here, then in San Francisco or further south, you can find all you want." The merchant continued to look at Aaron as he spoke.

He was not like other merchants. His Lithuanian culture reminded Aaron so much of home. "When will you go back home? Kaunas?"

"I'm in no hurry. When I go home, I know what my life will be. Here, every day is an adventure. A fortune could be waiting around the corner. Like I met you. Then I go north with wheat and learn how much the people will pay. You don't have the entire area covered. We provide a service. I enjoy this work."

"The Indigenous people love fried dough." The Lithuanian agreed.

Captain Orlov loaded 30 barrels of wheat onto the Saratov. Aaron paid the captain one ruble a barrel to load his five on board. Each cost him double what he got from the Americans, but that is how things go. Lard was cheap, he got three though it was something he didn't want to handle.

He had a growing crate of reading material. At different shops, from different people, he purchased pamphlets, magazines, and books. At the first shop, he sparred with the owner over authors and ideas, rekindling his love of study. He purchased more than 15 items, trying to get the merchant to provide details for each. It ended poorly when he offended the Russian. His excitement for Benjamin Franklin's book had elicited 'Savages', and Aaron got the door. Others did not enjoy Aaron's intrusive banter, either.

On board, Aaron now kept his comments to himself, showed up on time, did extra watches without complaint, and blossomed his detached character to the point he looked slick like the duck having water run off his back. When not in his hammock, he was in the galley, helping the cook during his time off.

Mid-July and they were sailing for the Farallon Islands and seal furs. Captain Orlov was in no rush. Russians had been going there for years. These remote islands, just west of San Francisco, were an easy place to be ashore. Aaron recalled what he had heard of Hawaii and felt it must be like this. Well, when the wind stopped blowing. What his body memory recalled were the hot summer days in Lutsk: cloudless days which made the wheat grow and the river the best place to be. Paradise?

Captain Orlov was tempted to sail for San Francisco but instead went back to Ft. Ross. His concern was not for making money. He was concerned about another winter in New Archangel. The captain of the Ches'ma had not been reprimanded for last winter's slow voyage. Captain Orlov was not alone thinking the new governor was lax with his captains.

Aaron was told to take five sailors to a rancho and find them work for the winter. If there was none, then they were to travel inland hunting and trapping till spring. What they made would be split with the captain. Sailors acted like they had done this before.

It would be a much warmer winter, less rain but rainy, and not so enclosed by mountains and towering trees. Rancho Eropa was a Russian farm that watched the Sun set across the Pacific. Aaron romanticized waking Russian farms to a Sun he had already enjoyed. He had time to think as he spent his days herding goats.

After milking the five nannies, he took the herd out to pasture. The hills along the coast had fewer trees, making it easier to shepherd the animals. He brought the goat herd in at night. Plenty of creatures wanted one for dinner. Three weeks into his duties Aaron got a dog, 'Shep'.

Aaron had not grown up with dogs. He understood milking animals and chickens, even a cat made sense to him. Dogs were an animal that most in his community shied away from. Shep was big, furry, and always hungry. Any food Aaron had had to be split with Shep, probably why the second mate ended up with the large dog. But Shep knew to not run around. He stood by the goats, by Aaron, or where he was told to stay. He came when called. For many who knew dogs, Aaron had a 'good dog'.

During the second milking, Shep would stand patiently waiting for Aaron. The goats didn't mind Shep but didn't interact with him, as some are apt to do. Shep enjoyed the warm goat's milk, as did a cat that snuck around.

When Shep did bark, it was so rare everyone took notice. Foxes were the most common hunter lurking in the shadows but were too small to cause concern. Coyotes were a threat and would send one forward while the pack waited in the brush. Shep sat much of the time and rang the alarm when there was an intruder.

The books came in handy. A winter herding goats probably shrank Aaron's tongue, definitely reduced his agitation. At night, the goat butter lamps provided a warm atmosphere and the pungent aroma permeated all his belongings. When he wore the inherited sheep vest, he smelled and looked like he had been a goat herder his whole life.

He reread his few chapters of 'Eugene Onegin' by Pushkin enough to feel Lensky's death to be his own, shot by his former friend. Then he would become the protagonist, flirting through life with the wealth inherited from his uncle. Literary friends were passe and easily disposed of. Shep would listen to him read passages aloud and sometimes provide a sigh at the appropriate moment.

When one of the Rancho Eropa sailors visited and heard the second mate conversing at length with Shep, within a week the first mate paid a visit. Aaron was not amused.

"I'm fine, Sir. Doing my work, making sure my sailors are doing theirs,

Sir." Aaron stayed at attention despite Kuznetsov's rummaging through his belongings, mostly lifting books and throwing them across the sleeping pallet once he had read the title.

"You need to regain your sailors' respect. They're talking about you as if you're headed for an asylum." Kuznetsov leafed through one of the readers containing a chapter from 'Eugene Onegin'.

"You'll like that one, Sir. Take it. I've read it many times. Sir." Aaron continued to stand at attention. His eyes were looking at the corners of his little shed. Shep watched the whole thing as aloof as Aaron.

"Let's go see your men."

During January, Aaron turned twenty. His height, his words, his manners, his education put him a few years ahead in most minds.

The rhythms of human lives are far easier to see in others than in ourselves. We call out their ups and downs, fast times and stoppages, yet expect differently for ourselves. The hand of destiny guides us all.

Farmers know to tend to their breeding animals. Not only are the conditions watched, but which male mates with which female is highly debated. In time, their care builds a strong herd. A young farm animal, like a colt or filly, needs a careful introduction to the world of work which can make or break the creature. The wise farmer accepts all this and adjusts the lives around him. It's called husbandry.

Aaron understood this and how it applied to the leadership of his sailors. He saw their years of neglect and missed opportunities. What he struggled to understand was his personal husbandry, his missed proper guidance. Others saw him bent from a childhood filled with extra freedoms but lacking a father. The search for wisdom, the need to debate, were these not his quest for a secure male figure? The common sailor could see this. But like a little imp whispering in his ear, Aaron could not twist himself enough to see. Searching for wisdom that should have been innate, Aaron was tumbling forward, knowing something wasn't right.

He also did not care. If he had learned anything, it had been the unwavering pride a sailor had in himself kept him alive in the worst of conditions. The dwelling upon failures, or his childhood failures, would do no one any good. Was this the weight upon Aaron's shoulders, an endless questioning?

Should he not go proudly forth at each new dawn?

People talk so they can think and influence the imps incessantly debating in their ears. Yet, all these efforts fall short when the person is awoken at night, without support, victim to the incessant negative goblin.

Was he rudderless? His aloof character, an attempt to disregard those endless internal debates. No, Aaron understood his patterns enough and where they led him, he was not a mindless victim. He had been schooled and educated far more than most.

The fact Aaron was not driven to drink was a bit of a mystery. The rancho men gathered in the evenings, promising to pay the barkeep once they got paid. Aaron had visited enough, but the rude talk left him feeling worse. Shep watched Aaron during these outings after the goats were safely in for the night.

At the first signs of spring, Captain Orlov sent word to gather on the Saratov. He was not going to push his luck with the governor. His holds filled with the last items. He was proud of the pelts he was bringing, feeling secure with the amount of food.

Hours of ship duties were balanced with his books and Shep by his side. Aaron had tried to leave him, only to return and pay a small fortune for the large, hairy pup. The dog became everyone's best mate. They had a safe passage home.

This time with youthful energy Aaron shared, "I want to start a school." At Ft. Ross there had been scores of children. Bogdan was used to Aaron's emotions. Dashi looked at him as if he was daft. Hadn't they gone through this before?

"There are scores of Tlingit boys, but they don't want to learn Russian," said Dashi. "If you are interested, I'll show you a different kind of school. Maybe you'll like it."

…

Aaron wished he could be more like Shep. After the initial posturing by the village dogs, and a clear display by the Alpha male, which Shep took in stride, all were off playing. Aaron didn't know how to get past the hatred burning in several eyes. His aloof posturing could take him only so far. He needed another gear to get past and into the play he saw Shep enjoying.

Dashi had easily done such. "You are one peculiar Russian." The obvious comment didn't help. Also, Aaron had no desire to be a Russian.

"You need to understand these kids are learning." Dashi knew Aaron was smart, educated, and wanted to be around learners. This would not be successful if it had to fit within Aaron's ideals. "There are no tables, no chairs, no books."

"What are those boys over there learning?" Aaron didn't mean for it to come across as half sarcastic.

"They're making cordage. You know how to make rope." Aaron nodded. He saw boys watching an older man pull fibers. "They take the inside bark fibers." The boys had fists full of fibers that they twisted and braided, each to their own ability. The older man continued with his own small cord.

Aaron watched an older girl work her own pile of fibers. She raised her head to call to a sibling running in and out of the plank longhouse.

"Come." Dashi walked closer, picking up some of the girl's small cord. He felt it for its strength and its ability to stay tight despite his twisting.

"You, an annoying man, Dashi." The girl laughed, continuing to braid.

"You learned well. Who taught you?"

"Not you! Auntie taught me the big cord. Grandpa there, he teaches us all how to make the small for nets."

They walked over to the older man who was looking unimpressed. Endless material to make the cordage allowed for the boys' mistakes.

"What am I supposed to see? They don't want to learn to read and they already have teachers for what they are expected to learn." Aaron was a bit frustrated with Dashi.

Dashi ignored Aaron. "Grandpa. Tell us a story." Dashi probably had heard the story before. He smiled. 'This is a setup.' thought Aaron.

"Long ago, my grandpa's grandpa didn't have the food we have today. Winter forced the village people to eat mushrooms and shellfish gathered from the rocks. They were a rough bunch, not many smiles. They didn't live with the land as much as they picked at it." Aaron laughed to himself when he heard, 'not many smiles'.

"My grandpa's grandpa spent much time on the rocks. He watched the birds, the crabs, the shellfish, and the tides as they came and went, pulling seaweed up and back. There, he built rock walls at low tide and tried to catch food in his enclosures. He wasn't smart. In a roughly made basket, he collected small shellfish and went home.

Mother Spider lived in the corner of his longhouse. She was a big mom with a web that had captured much. He was jealous and asked her why he didn't have the ability to make webs like her. She laughed at him and called him a bad name - something she would throw out of her web as it was nasty." Here Grandpa spit.

"So, my grandpa's grandpa was not worth much. Even a spider saw him as rotten. I bet you were thinking this spider would teach him how to make nets. Ha! My grandpa's grandpa was nasty. He was not a fine specimen. His hair was not brushed, his clothes were not clean, his words showed he did not think. My grandpa's grandpa died never knowing a full winter belly. He hadn't evolved to the level of a spider."

He paused and looked at Aaron. To Dashi, he asked, "What makes this man your partner?"

Dashi thought, pausing before his words, "He let me sleep in his people's longhouse. No one else would allow this, though the snows and winds were cold enough to freeze the whole bay."

Grandpa shuddered at the thought.

He continued his point, "That may be nice, but why partner?"

Dashi looked elsewhere. His words came from far away. "He shared his victories. There was no reason to share, and he has never not shared." Dashi paused again, "Why Am I - his partner? I often ask the same question?" Dashi looked at Aaron.

After a moment, Aaron responded in Buryat. "I became a man, a successful man leaving Irbit. Your strength was the example I needed. I never would have made it to Nerchinsk. I would never have seen my father."

Grandpa understood this exchange. He didn't need the words.

"You become what you aim for." Grandpa wasn't done.

"Some take their time, their whole life, to become a spider." He shook his head.

"I don't see the point. Such a waste. I wanted to be a sea lion when I was young, like young-young. I lay around in the sun, ignored all my chores.

147

I dove deep into the waters for the biggest of crabs, the biggest of shellfish. I roared. I was a sea lion able to fight for my spot on the rocks." He filled with the strong memory.

"One day, my grandma, she was a short woman, she came to my rock. She was fast. I didn't listen. She hit me on the head with a stick, sent me home, poking me with the sharp end every time I slowed. In the longhouse she cut my hair and put a big wrap on my wound, calling me a sick sea lion, 'careful everyone it smells'. If I complained, she threw hot coals at me or picked up the stick. I had more chores than anyone else. Yet, every night she came to my pallet and told me to become a healthy sea lion, stronger than the strongest. It took me a week to understand she meant it, and wasn't messing with me." Grandpa paused and looked around.

The boys had been listening. One commented to another under his breath. Aaron thought he heard, "stinky sea lion," and Dashi confirmed it with a fake kick at the disrespect.

"I became more than a sea lion, and I felt this when I was still young. My grandma made sure of it. One day, these youngsters will feel more than something too. I don't know what."

Back at the shop, Aaron chewed on his experience. He didn't know how to make rope. He felt threatened most of the time in the village. The fact he understood half of Grandpa's story was noteworthy for Aaron. He could hardly speak the language besides rudimentary trade phrases. What had he learned?

He watched Dashi busy himself around the shop. Toq and then Tuyana carrying Samar popped in. Dashi went to his new daughter and backed away, seeing she was asleep. Tuyana smiled and went back to their room. Aaron saw but didn't understand as his mind wrestled elsewhere.

Were Dashi and he partners because their partnership was the right thing? What had he become when he was young? What had Dashi become? Were these not the point of Grandpa's story?

"I bet you wanted to be a horse when you were young."

"Who didn't!" All of Dashi's friends had wanted to be horses. "I ran everywhere. I could run all day. I watched my father give them so much attention I had little choice." His father had two dozen horses. One mare ruled them all. Dashi would watch the way the stallion gave her space to guide the herd. She was relentless. The stallion had to pay attention.

"I don't know what I wanted to be?" Aaron was perplexed.

Dashi looked bewildered. "You! All you talk about is Rabbi Hulstein said this or Rabbi Mechlenberg had you do that. You wanted to be a rabbi!"

The words surprised Aaron. Had he not wanted to be an animal? He thought hard and came up short. No, he had not, and he felt jipped. Today, he wanted to be a watchful raven. Why had being an animal not come in his youth?

"You tell as many stories. This is why I thought you would enjoy seeing their school."

"I never became more than a rabbi." Aaron was more perplexed.

"At the time you became the rabbi, you were meant to be. How many stories have you shared with me?" Dashi waited. "Most of your stories are not a lesson as much as they are a path for the listener. You always end with, 'Your answer reveals more about yourself'. Isn't this what Grandpa did for us?"

Aaron felt Dashi was right, yet felt almost upside down. "Why don't my stories talk about becoming more than the world around us?"

Dashi didn't have a quick answer. He thought about the rules Aaron was supposed to follow. Did they have nothing to do with becoming more than his world? He recalled Aaron's words, "All the time you say you're made in the image of your G... This sounds a bit more than the world around you since your G… made everything."

"You listen closer to my stories than I." Aaron was lucky to have such insight into his dilemma.

"Yep. The school you want is for yourself." Dashi went onward with his busy work.

If Dashi was correct, what was he supposed to do? Go hang out with people who saw him as an enemy?

Later in the week, "Don't you miss Rabbi Hulstein?" Joshua was visiting, enjoying shopping almost for free. He never thought about the yeshiva or Lutsk.

"Not much. You?" As much as their lives had been separate for years, being an older brother had not been lost.

"Lately, all the time. Stay, we'll have some tea. Let me tell you a story."

Aaron had no clue what he was going to share, but he wanted to feel the excitement of a story's insights.

"An exile wandered for years. He had been banished for his extreme religious practices despite the official's clear order to stop." Aaron had to pause, as the next part had not yet formed.

"During his wanderings, he continued his worship and in time, far from home, he found others with whom he could share. Things were different, yet the same. Over the years more joined, some with their own twists, and the community grew. One day, a wealthy patron approached our exile who was now a wise elder. 'Why are there so many wise men?' The exile thought for a bit and responded, 'We have so many rich members because we have so many wise elders. If we lose our wise men, we will lose our rich patrons.' The patron gave generously to the extent the exile had money to travel. So, after fifty years, he returned to his homeland. What do you think surprised him most?"

Joshua tried to think, but nothing came to mind. "I don't know. His synagogue was now painted blue. Or maybe the prayers were now mostly in Russian, not ancient Hebrew." He liked this idea.

"Maybe. The story continues with our exile entering his old synagogue and being approached by a young student. 'Elder, look what I've found.' The student showed a simple idea backed by Talmudic references. It was about boarding heifers who were ready to give birth. The exile didn't know what to say. The young student exclaimed, 'Isn't it clear! And to think, I found this on my own!' The young student practically skipped away, leaving our exile to ponder what he had witnessed." Aaron stopped for Joshua to catch up.

"Then an elderly man walked up, 'Are you not Dagan, who was exiled years ago?' The man looked into the face of our exile. 'Why have you returned? We don't want trouble.' Our exile saw his friend Simon behind all those years. 'Simon, you can't fool me. You called me back because you wanted me to see you do know how to teach. The boy is right. It is all about the joy of learning."

Dashi heard the end of the story.

Joshua responded, "Yep. You like this story. I get it, but I never had the passion you have. I did what foter told me to do." Joshua was uncharacteristically sad.

"You're a rabbi! You learned from Rabbi Hulstein for ten more years than I. If I had your luxury, I would be the happiest man on Earth!" Aaron knew he was being the younger, dramatic brother.

Joshua replied, "It doesn't take much to lose something that doesn't work for you. Following orders, giving orders, has provided me with a life. I don't have the money that you have. I don't see things being any different for me." Bogdan appeared to nod his head while standing guard. Aaron knew he had boasted. This had all started because of his troubles.

"You don't get to live in a fantasy world when you have only two kopeks to keep you warm." Joshua reached into his pocket and pulled out his few coins.

"Well," Dashi joined the talk. "I had less when my fantasy became my reality." He let his words sink in. He and Joshua were still figuring out how they ranked. "I was ready for my fantasy because I had nothing else to lose."

While the two sparred for top dog, Bogdan reflected on being part of this family. He absorbed the nuances, never truly questioning the facts: these two were Jews, hiding and lying as officers in the Russian Navy. This fanciful life never troubled Bogdan. He went to sleep every night, exchanging stories with Aaron and then listening to him scribble in his journal or flipping pages. The few stories Dashi had shared about Aaron's fortune were agreeable and didn't align with the corruption stories others told in town. Everything he saw pointed to a thoughtful, generous but still quite young man. Keenly attentive when he buried his rubles, Bogdan would allow himself a moment of emotions. One day, all this glittering and clinking would transform his life.

During the winter, Grandpa died. Aaron had visited him until he could no longer tell stories. The stories Grandpa shared, the conversations allowed Aaron to be somewhat accepted by the community and satisfy his need for learning.

Aaron gave much for the totem which would be erected beside the longhouse. The process allowed hours of storytelling around the large spruce. First the cutting, the limbing, the hauling, and the designing. Aaron thought he had a knack for telling Grandpa's stories. Did they listen?

"Frog, he was a mess. His mother didn't want him coming around anymore. It was his loud mouth that bothered all of his brothers and sisters. 'Go make your racket elsewhere. See if they like it!' Frog gave them space, though it hurt his heart. He spent hours high on a limb where he could see the bay. His loud mouth scared all the timid creatures, and they ran over the ridge till his hullabaloo was no more. Frog didn't enjoy being alone. He missed his family, but he couldn't stop creating such a clamor. 'Why?' he would ask himself when the pain of loneliness was unbearable. He spent the night cold, out on a limb, overexposed. Soon Owl soundlessly carried him away. But before the silent hunter could tear him apart, Frog let out a shocking ululation. 'Good grief!' Yelled the owl and let go of the green goblin. Down Frog fell, and there he lay till morning. By sunrise, he had thought enough about his dilemma and felt he had a way forward. Back to his home he hopped until he was close enough to hear their laughter. There he stayed. He lived within earshot, even saw some of his family, but back home he did not go. His blaring was truly maddening. He understood. But it was so for anyone. His commotion was a shield for his family, who soon came to realize his gift. Frog lived out his days protecting his family, who honored his work by visiting for as long as they could."

Hopefully, they had been listening. On the other hand, Aaron had gone on and on without getting a look from the carvers.

"A Roon," as they called him. "What is 'goblin'?" Several looked at him now.

"Well, I can't imagine you don't have at least one lurking somewhere." Herschel had been his first story with goblins. The wicked creatures were relentless until you taught them there was no point. They liked riddles, and you needed to show them you were smarter to stop their evil pursuits.

"What do you call evil spirits that cause problems?" Aaron's words caused a stir.

An older carver was quick to reply, so all heard, "Don't mention the Kushtaka unless you have plenty of spirit to protect us." The carver heads nodded in agreement.

It was a month later when Aaron heard his first story about Kushtaka. An elderly woman, tending a fire, mumbled the following.

"This fire is made of Kushtaka bones. I roast them because I killed it. May they all hear and know to stay away lest they die and get their bones roasted, too. My mothers have always had Kushtaka bone ash.

Kushtaka came from mountains far to the East. It would sit in its cave and eat children stolen from villages below. Its call would excite the young-sters who would wander, looking for its sweet source. Many times, Kushtaka would catch them looking deep into a pool of water by a mountain stream. It fooled them all. Kushtaka grew fat.

Don't be the fool who gets caught looking into a deep pool of water.

The people left their village. There was no point in working so hard when Kushtaka stole their young ones. Far away they went. Kushtaka had to eat deer. It grew skinny.

Skinny Kushtaka was a hungry Kushtaka and able to move like the wind through the trees and across the water. Deer only kept it alive. It needed the spirit of children to fatten for winter.

I knew all this because I could see Kushtaka in my mind." *I will keep the bone ash of this Kushtaka and use it to track the others. I will always be ready for the next.*

"Around our village, there are many pools of water. I lured deer to each and watched as Kushtaka killed and pulled them to its new lair. The mouth of its cave was small and easily missed if you didn't see Kushtaka sneak inside. Being close to a Kushtaka was dangerous, but I kept my spirit strong with my mother's bag of Kushtaka bone ash.

I caught the Kushtaka with a forked stick pinning its head to the ground. The wicked creature thrashed its tail, hitting me like a bear. If I let go I would have died, but hold it, is all I could do. So there we stayed. I had its head pinned to the ground and every so often it got an angle on me with its tail. Eventually, Kushtaka stopped thrashing. I kept watch.

Day turned into night and Kushtaka grew stronger instead of weaker. The little devil spoke about my children and my dying husband and all the horrible things it would do to them. I cried much that night because of my desperate position. As dawn slowly crawled over the mountains, I saw Kushtaka was not looking too good and its suffering gave me hope. Then I looked at my hands and realized I was not looking good. We both grew strength from the other.

No one likes a Kushtaka, and it likes being detested. Being hated by everyone, the Kushtaka could hate everyone back. Rotten to the core is what it was. An evil that needed to be destroyed. This insight gave me fresh energy. I remembered my mother's bag of bone ash and I saw the Kushtaka take fright.

With renewed strength, I held Kushtaka to the ground and opened the bag. I took a pinch of ash to my mouth and Kushtaka wailed. When I swallowed, the creature twisted like it was being burnt alive. I took another pinch.

When I awoke, I was looking at my body. My face was in agony and my body twisted. My clothes had been torn and my hands were a bloody mess. I tried to stand, but I couldn't move. I was pinned to the ground at my neck. I cried, knowing this wasn't right. How could this be?

Laughter from the cave froze me silent. Slowly, a small Kushtaka emerged into the light. It looked closely at my body, old and damaged, and then it looked into my eyes, turning its head this way and that to get a good look. Then it moved away like the wind.

Slowly, my broken body awoke. I watched myself sit and get its bearing. I understood, grabbed the dead creature, and walked back to our village. I knew to burn the Kushtaka would be to burn myself. I still don't live within my body. I am of the wind."

Aaron didn't know what to make of what he had heard. The old woman's hands were gnarled, her eyes were dark and vacant. The others walked away, and no one talked about what they had experienced.

After talking with Bogdan, Aaron wrote before bed,

Gratitude -

- *This moment is worry-free*
- *My roof does not leak*
- *The water birds are returning*
- *My life has a focus for learning, a true blessing*

Wisdom - 1833 to 1836

Wisdom,

is one of the more difficult treasures to obtain.

Yet, when freely given, many turn the other way.

Our repetitive lives need those skips in our songs to pop us out of doing the same thing, once again.

Our learned lessons can burn shamefully, distract us for hours, or be some of the best stories to tell.

Turning twenty-one was not a pronounced birthday for Aaron. At his yeshiva, he had anticipated twenty-seven as the year of adulthood, like every other youth there. Graduating as a rabbi was basic entry into his community. A younger man wasn't mature enough to be a husband, a belief also held by Aaron. Of course, not every Jew attended his yeshiva, but this didn't matter. Aaron's community, his family, didn't see any other life besides his youth spent at the yeshiva. Joshua had achieved this only to then leave for Nerchinsk. All had expected him to marry Adiela, even her family talked with Aaron as family, but this never came to be. Joshua was a prime match for the few single women of New Archangel.

Spring brought life and fresh business adventures to New Archangel. Governor Wrangell created new objectives as sea otter pelts were gone. Explorations of the Interior were conducted, the Yukon River being a major focus. Fort St. Michael was built as a launching point for the mighty river. The mouth of this waterway was so twisted that an overland route needed to be identified. Indigenous people commonly discussed an overland route starting near Fort St. Michael. Joshua was scheduled to go.

"The Chirikov is set to sail in a week. I've talked with the captain, Rudakov, and he's agreed to have you as his first mate." Joshua paused. "I need you to do this for me." He paused again. "I don't ask for much." Joshua was almost begging. Aaron let the energy sit, taking note of the rare moment.

"What? It is spring and Captain Orlov will call me any day. And where is the Chirikov sailing? Hawaii?" Aaron was laying it on thick. He should gain much from this exchange.

"Captain Rudakov is doing Orlov a favor." Joshua, like the other officers, had heard about Aaron's bread and water rations. "We're resupplying Fort St. Michael and then looking for an overland route to the Yukon. Traveling upriver is a slow slog. If all goes well, I've heard rumor, you will run the trading post there." Joshua had done some homework.

Aaron reflected on the information. He had heard the rumors and discussed with Dashi the wisdom of such an adventure. "Why can't you go?"

Joshua quieted and contemplated his next words. "I've become attached." He looked for his brother's response. "Now is not the time to leave. Captain Petrov has given me leave if you can sail with him on the Chirikov." Joshua was attentive to his precipice.

"Oh, do tell! At the very least, I'm going to get a juicy story out of this deal." They both knew such a statement was a joke.

When Governor Wrangell took over two years earlier, the old governor, Chistyakov, had left behind his Indigenous wife and three children. Officers frequented Ms. Artemev's home, supporting her single parenting adventure. Joshua had done his share and in the process met one of her maids, Miss Vera Antov, sixteen, born in New Archangel, having a Russian father and Tlingit mother. Joshua was thirty-one and ready for a family.

Later, Aaron brought Dashi up to speed to gain his advice on the shifting landscape. "Do we ask Joshua to join our business?" Aaron felt like exploring the possibilities of change.

"Joshua, no. He does not want this life. He wants your money." What Dashi was thinking about was how small his room was now with Samar in the family. He needed to build another room.

Aaron felt there was a middle ground. He knew his brother to be of solid character, not long from being the captain of his own ship. Was he not their future supplier of goods, possibly finding them new connections and markets? "Once he enjoys the money, he'll change his tune."

Before he sailed, Aason didn't expect any business prospects when he sailed on the Chirikov. When Captain Rudakov sailed into Fort St. George on the Kenai Peninsula, Aaron was shown the turnips growing in the surrounding fields. Rudakov knew the food source was being underdeveloped and Aaron could make something of it. They struck a deal using Aaron's capital. Time and again, Aaron's capital proved to be a pivotal tool. On their return journey, they would pick up their investment.

Fort St. Michael was further than Aaron had imagined. After a stormy passage around Unalaska, they sailed and sailed for the little island. North of the Yukon Delta, Fort St. Michael was the border between the three local Indigenous groups: Yup'ik, Inupiaq, and Athabascan. Aaron was not great at mental maps, but he understood these people had vast lands to roam. What would these people need?

The island was a construction zone. Their supplies were stored in a crude shed. A winter here would be dismal for these soldiers. When the wind shifted, Aaron could feel the Arctic nipping at his exposed skin.

What became clear was the difficulty of sailing up the Yukon River. Favorable winds did blow, but the river twisted south for miles. Other explorers reported friendly relations and good hunting for as far as they could go, maybe two hundred miles. Beaver pelts were secured at twenty to thirty for an iron kettle, not poor deals. Aaron squirmed, thinking about his days in Kazan with Yegorov and Samuel. Kazan was two lifetimes ago.

The expedition inland proved far more arduous than Aaron had expected. After a short sail north, the crew debarked at a sluggish river. For the next ten days, Aaron dragged his body through cold swamplands, fighting clouds of mosquitoes which drove him mad. These were not the evils of the Siberian Steppe. These enemies knew how to devour a man, both physically and mentally. It was common for the men to submerge themselves in water and cake themselves with mud, anything to relieve themselves from the torment. The hills were a welcome sight, but they never saw the Yukon River. Their guide had both experienced and watched the expedition with distaste, and he was done. Though the language difference was a barrier, all understood travel in winter was preferred. Aaron agreed.

The Chirikov sailed into New Archangel with one hundred and thirty crates of turnips. Aaron paid Captain Rudakov as he had paid the farmers around Fort St. George. His capital rose and fell with the seasons. It would rise again as winter set in.

What some knew others wanted to ignore. Devastation from a plague was a specter looming over any port town, anywhere in the world. Routinely, ships were turned away because of illnesses. The feeling for the Winter of 1834-35 was ripe.

Priests began to vaccinate against the disease. The Indigenous people were wary but saw the locals lining up for what looked to be a death ritual, and they lived. Across Russia-America, people grew ill. The plague seeped into the country despite their efforts. Fewer ships, fewer opportunities to acquire more supplies, Aaron knew to ration how much people could buy.

...

Before the winter holidays, Aaron's older bruder, Joshua, married Miss Vera Antov at the Russian Orthodox Church. For the past year, Joshua had attended services every Sunday. He asked repeatedly for Aaron to join him to the point Dashi knew to intervene. When Joshua told Aaron he would be married in the church, Aaron had a visceral reaction.

"What will moter say! I can't imagine what foter would do if he were still alive."

"But he is not. Moter is ten thousand miles away, and I doubt I will see her anytime soon." Joshua added, "There is no way we can think about exposing ourselves, even for a wedding. Why do you think I'm marrying a young Indigenous woman? I doubt she has ever seen a Russian penis!" Joshua had spent far more time thinking about parts of his Judaism than Aaron realized.

"How can you let go of all your learning!" Aaron was confounded.

"I don't believe everything the priest says like I didn't believe all Rabbi Mechlenberg said we should do. If there is one thing I believe it is Rabbi Hulstein would understand!" Joshua was not one to be swayed.

"You need to explain what will happen because I don't want the celebrations to come off socially wrong." Aaron smiled and gave his older brother a long and strong bear hug.

Joshua and Vera wore their crowns all day as they paraded around town and finally to their reception. Her parents had extorted an extra large ransom from Joshua, paid by Aaron, as she was the most sought-after bachelorette in town. The priests also appreciated the generous donation.

For many, the party was talked about for years. People came from far and wide, including a few Americans. Aaron had enough pastries, food, and cake to feed everyone for two days. Dashi, despite his personal beliefs, brought ten people from the village. In a rare twist, alcohol was removed from the party and only a few complained. Bogdan watched over all as he had rank with the common soldiers.

It was about two weeks later that Vera had the first signs. Smallpox created a fear not only of contagion but, for the sick, of being excluded from loved ones as they died. The fever, the pains, the general sickness erupted in two weeks with boils, which made the sick recoil in horror. The cries of pain, both from the sick and loved ones who cared for them, could be heard throughout New Archangel.

Joshua cared for her every need. Aaron would leave food at the door, messages of encouragement, and news. Within two months, half of the town had become infected. The caregivers were nearly all the next victims. Miraculously, Joshua and the priests were spared, a fact that did not go unnoticed. Prayers of healing became as important as the presence of one of the priests.

The sickness spread like a slow-moving wave. By the summer of 1835, hundreds had been infected. Nearly eighty people died in New Archangel and several thousand throughout Russia-America. Vera had struggled for weeks. She emerged weakened and with a new appreciation for her husband. Friends, sailors, and family members had died during those harsh months. The sickness was ebbing so that when winter began, most felt safe. Then Dashi fell ill and Aaron's world took a major turn.

When his boils appeared, Dashi wrapped his arms, legs, and hands so he could not see the pustules. He rarely mixed his anger with any other emotion besides fear for his family. Daily he would hide from the light only to demand to see, from a distance, his wife and children.

"I will not make it." Dashi's words shocked Aaron. "Did you hear me?"

"Why do you say that? You are the strongest man I know. Illness does not take the mighty. You can't leave now. We have too much to do when spring comes around. We have piles of money to make." Aaron felt Dashi was sharing an odd weak moment.

"I don't sleep anymore. I'm constantly dreaming. Imagine seeing your father, there, across the room, telling you to get it done and move on. I screamed at mine. He laughed and said not to be foolish." Dashi was scaring Aaron.

"You know what I'm talking about! Promise me! You must take care of my Tuyana, my Toq, my precious Samar, who is so full of words I believe she has your gift for languages." Dashi laughed, thinking silly thoughts.

Aaron did not follow Dashi's logic. The sickness took many, but those were the very young or old. Taking care of a widow was never a thought to have crossed his mind. His studies had countless lessons about widows, but Tuyana was family. Aaron froze at the thought of a family widow.

"Don't be a weak book boy! Promise me. I cannot live through another night unless I know my family will be cared for." Dashi's desperation woke Aaron.

"Of course. Know Tuyana, Toq, and Samar will have the best of lives. They will be the envy of everyone and all Buryats. You must not stress yourself like this. Focus on your healing so you can run with your children and laugh with your wife. These sad words you've shared will be kept here. Rest and heal yourself." Aaron was exhausted. Dashi whimpered 'thank you,' and fell asleep. He never regained his voice and died five days later.

The hours Aaron spent with Dashi were a reaction to the shortness he gave his father. He knew Dashi at a depth he never knew the man who died in Nerchinsk. The candlelit nights filled with moans, then ragged breathing, giving Aaron meaningful depth to a loved one's passing.

Aaron spent days wandering in his mind, recalling their friendship, a bond he couldn't let go. He ripped his clothes, he covered his head with ashes, and he moaned for his loss. When he knew not what to do, he would again recite the Kaddish.

Tuyana cried the cry of an Indigenous woman far from home and family. Bogdan, Joshua, and Vera cared for the children.

"You have mourned for six days." Joshua said. "Gather your strength for one more and then move on with your life." He tried to be as caring as possible, but left the room before Aaron could turn on him.

All winter the specter of death hung over New Archangel. Crews could not disembark, trade became sparse, and supplies ran dangerously low. Spring launched high expectations. The new Governor, Kupreyanov, prioritized food production and continued trade expansion.

"I'm resupplying Fort St. Michael. Then I'll lead a marking of the Yukon portage." Joshua checked on Aaron and Tuyana nearly every day. Spring energy was in his bones.

Aaron recalled the clouds of mosquitoes. "We saw little good from summer travel. Consider waiting for everything to freeze."

"The new governor wants new dots on his map. He wants larger numbers in his reports." Joshua waited for Aaron's attention. "You know his wife has started a girl's school. A school for Tlingit girls." Joshua looked for a reaction.

Aaron did not provide. That passion had left long ago. Dashi's children tired him. Unlike the excitement of stories and self-discovery, being a parent was a defeating experience of seeing your boundaries overrun by miniature barbarians. The little excitement he enjoyed was teaching different ways of saying the same word. Between Tuyana and himself, Toq and Samar flitted between Buryat, Russian, Tlingit, French, and German on any given day. Recently Aaron had been dabbling in American, 'Howdee'.

Joshua was well positioned in the Russian Navy for a governor like Kupreyanov. He was past his mid-career mark and going strong. Most saw his promotion to captain as next-in-line. Captains like Rudakov were fine with their routine voyages, others were ready to move on. This was no longer the navy these captains had joined twenty-five years ago.

As they sailed for Fort St. Michael, Joshua and Rudakov discussed options. Joshua would surely make captain by next spring. Captain Burov and Poda would not last another winter, or they would go mad.

The captain also pried into Aaron's business dealings as if he weren't a part of the system. For his minor involvement, the Fort St. George investment was noticeably elevating his usually mundane captain lifestyle. This spring of 1836 Aaron invested double in the adventure and Rudakov wanted more. Joshua would let Aaron know.

Fort St. Michael was growing, much busier than Joshua had imagined.

Additionally, fifty miles across the bay, a new post marked the beginning of the Yukon portage, Unalakleet. At first, Joshua didn't understand Aaron's warning. They had already cleared a mile of trail, and built a new bridge over a side river. Then all travel came to a halt. A bog, with a mind of its own, swallowed everything, including two donkeys. It was not as much a swamp as it was a monster bent on devouring them. As if they needed another reason to change course, clouds of mosquitoes descended like a fog and decimated their minds, bodies, and spirits. There was little to do but return to the new trading post.

Joshua wrote Aaron a note about their Fort St. George investment and Rudakov's interest in more payment. He added few details to his portage work besides, 'I'll spend a winter here setting the route.' Vera and he would have to be apart, implying Aaron or Tuyana would need to look after her. There was no note for his young wife.

Aaron spent much of his time at the Tlingit village. Tuyana enjoyed running the shop and would invite Vera, especially once she learned of Joshua's extension. If Aaron was to be in charge of the kids, it was easier with playful peers. Work had become a slow game. His capital was needed when it was need-ed. He had become the object of many a financial pitch. His aloof character was stiffened by his sadness and sixty extra pounds. Fried bread was his staple and a treat he shared with all.

Freeze-up came early for Joshua, much earlier than for Aaron. Before he headed up the trail, a group of Athabascan men arrived in Unalakleet. They came to look, nothing to trade. After a few payments, Joshua hired four to help with the trail. The difference dumbfounded the Russians. Not only did they start by a different route, they walked thirty miles a day, donkeys included. These were not the guides from Aaron's expedition. These men took them down well-worn paths. They expressed, without using words, the coming ease of travel when snows allowed for dog sleds.

The Yukon River was impressive. Floating islands of freshly formed river ice landed on shores, bunching and crunching. It would take another month before Joshua trusted travel on the behemoth. The group blazed away, widening the paths, recording on maps. Forty miles north along the waterway, they found a fish camp. The site would become their trading post. Snows deepened. The Athabascan men parted ways, but not before Joshua hired them to return to

Unalakleet with dog sleds.

These were not the hills and valleys of Nerchinsk, but they were not dissimilar. During winter, the grinding winds rounded the hilltops and smoothed the ice. Birch trees swayed with the eeriness of a German folktale, and black spruce silhouetted against long sunsets as twisted souls stuck in an endless struggle. Animal tracks were studied with awe. Their stories were as personal as any spirit that could survive in such lands.

"We will be back later this winter." Joshua felt a victory unlike any before. This was a special spot. They spent two days digging pits and cutting logs. They crossed the hills before the snows became too deep for travel.

They returned on snow hardened by snowshoes. It became clear their passage was not the only one. Crates of iron pots and tools were lashed to dog sleds that flew over the land. Aaron's investments stretched far from his shop in New Archangel.

The Russians, who had to walk, repeatedly requested that Joshua hire a team for their return. There were a few unnerved by the dogs. The powerful beasts could stare for hours, not unlike their wild relatives. At night they would howl, and fights were as bloody as the reprisals by the dog handlers. Joshua had not grown up with dogs and did not attempt to intervene.

They stored the crates in their earlier diggings. To their guides, they promised generous rewards if the supplies were not touched. A lone guide ferried men back to the coast. Joshua thought several times about staying all winter along the river.

Spring was one of the best times of year to travel, and Joshua returned to the trading post site in March of 1837. The cached supplies were gone, the cut logs were missing. Joshua, a seasoned first-mate, for an odd reason was not concerned by the substantial loss. He also sensed Aaron would understand. Joshua had a deep feeling about this place. There, on the banks of the mighty Yukon, he understood he was home.

…

Aaron turned twenty-five during January of 1837. His youthful spirit was missing. In its stead was a heavy sadness blocking his passions, his zest for learning, his hunger for forward movement. Tuyana gave him space. When he returned that spring, Joshua, along with Vera, would visit as long as tempers stayed cool. Shep also may have gained more than a few pounds. Their pace to the Tlingit village would have lacked any excitement had it not been for the children.

Sitting, watching the children play, Aaron heard the following story.

"Beaver built a dam across a mountain stream. The summer had been a dry one, the water was a trickle. When the fall rains came, in great sheets of water, a wave blew through Beaver's dam. His beaver lodge stood lonely and exposed. The family had to move.

Up the stream, up another stream, up and up they climbed. Eventually, a wall of ice blocked their path. Beaver stared at the rock, the dirt, the ice, and the water flowing from underneath. His family returned downstream. He fell asleep burrowed into an ice crevice. Dreams shook him all night.

A dreamy beaver told him he was done. You are no longer a beaver, as you cannot provide. You are now fish food, lucky you. Enjoy moving like leaves in the wind. Have fun being consumed by a thousand bites. Frozen, Beaver stayed in his crevice for the winter. Then spring rains washed him out and down the stream. Raven watched the whole thing.

Eventually, Beaver fed a fish, then two until Eagle swooped down and flew him away, high into a tree. He liked the view. Maybe one day he would be a tree." The storyteller stopped, sat silently.

"Why would anyone want to be a tree?"

"You can't control what the Great Creator makes you. You can only control the spirit that you bring to your being."

Aaron pondered such lack of control. Spirit? You are commanded to do so much more than spirit.

"Watch the kids. Watch your dog. They have not forgotten who they are."

Aaron was offended and left. Shep slowly followed.

He read for hours before putting pencil to paper.

Wisdom -

- *I've learned it is normal to lose yourself, but don't go far*
- *Blaming others is useful, as constantly blaming yourself is maddening*
- *Focussing on pain doesn't make it go away. You get calloused, able to hold*

those moments when you used to run

- *I don't understand women and need more courage before I ask Joshua*
- *I don't want to lose another. I have a sadness that oozes across my life*

Family - 1836 to 1867

*The rhythms of life, the currents, the ups and downs,
create patterns worth following.*

*We know our youth, our virile adulthood, our
working years, our golden years are not set in stone,
but we share our experience as gospel.*

Why wait till you are twenty-seven to begin adulthood?

Happy family or unhappy family in their own unhappy way.

Humans yearn for predictable, successful social interactions. When engagements fail or look to fail, it is quite human for construction to begin. People build shielding walls, lots of walls which paradoxically keep their pain in more than suffering out.

Healthy social exchanges start with oneself. When internal interactions stop being predictable, it is nearly impossible to move down a good path. Successful social interactions extend to one's family, making routines or rituals key for peaceful households. Thus, the individual adjusts to or struggles with their social exchanges.

The expanse of Russia-America allowed for new ways in new lands. While feeling unencumbered, these pioneers still fell under the canopy of the Russian Orthodox Church. Priests expanded with the Company and lingered in villages spreading their beliefs. The clergy frequented the shop and considered Aaron destined for Tuyana. In private, they would debate the pros and cons of a Pole raising Buryat children. Their primary concern lay in Aaron's lack of church attendance. They needed more predictable exchanges before they could trust his intentions.

"You should attend services this weekend." Father Ilya was taller than most and looked hard upon Aaron.

"I'm not a believer. My papa wanted us to learn ethics before religion." Aaron had shared a similar story more than once.

"Still, you are out here," Father Ilya looked around and pointed to the backroom, "and we want to know all is well. Visit us. You can attend Saturday evening services and then stay for dinner." The offer included the implied need for a donation.

Other priests had not been so forward. "I can send an offering, but I won't be attending." Aaron's words were clear.

For the priest, the words failed. "You must hear the gossip. A child born under this roof would not be kindly looked upon by this community." His words were blunt.

Like the night he struggled to agree to Dashi's dying needs, he failed to see Tuyana sexually. He looked at the priest with honest surprise. The look did not go unnoticed though it didn't matter.

"I see. I had not heard. I will, we will see you Saturday evening. Tell your cooks I'll have two loaves and two pies to share."

The priest looked triumphant. "Splendid! I will see you soon and expect this to be the first of many. Have a blessed day."

After Aaron's family had attended, the priests had much to discuss. Several wondered if Bogdan was not the best route to pursue, as he obviously had a religious upbringing. Tuyana proved a delight, connecting with many for easy follow-ups. The children failed to grasp the holiness of the church and would need much to curb their upbringing.

For Aaron, the dinner was a surprise. Once the religious control dropped, he found himself engaged in pleasant conversations with congregants. He had forgotten how two hours of robust dialogue could revive one's spirit. He walked home thinking of next weekend's dinner.

Upon his return from Fort St. Michael, Joshua had discussed his plans for trading on the Yukon with everyone except his young wife, Vera. When she found out, she made clear that his departure during their honeymoon year was not acceptable and another, never. One could see the gears in Joshua's brain turning as he worked the fact Vera would be giving the orders. Joshua's education had not predicted such. Vera was fifteen years the younger.

Life routines settled for our characters in New Archangel. While others were pushing expansion, Aaron and Joshua enjoyed the summer and winter of 1837 living the simple life.

Trade stayed consistent. Aaron had his regulars. Losing the Yukon supplies reduced his desire for risk. He was slowly smiling his way to a healthier life and didn't need additional worries. In a real sense, he was growing fond of the children. Toq was seven and Samar was turning four. These ages allowed for a good bit of fun. Tuyana received his support, and it is hard not to become attached to the person you serve. Their weekly dinners at the church slowly bent them into what others already saw them as, a family.

When Bogdan conveyed his joining Joshua for trading on the Yukon, it was again the priests who saw the writing on the wall. With Bogdan gone, the remaining two adults would bond once and for all.

Joshua was more excited than Aaron could remember. "Aaron, you'll not be disappointed. Bogdan will always be with the supplies, and the trading post will be completed before any items are brought over the hills."

"To be clear, Joshua, I'm not wanting to expand into the fur business." Aaron was surprised by how little business sense his brother had. "I don't see much profit because a fur merchant doesn't need much capital to start trading. I buy whole shipments to leverage my position. Figure out our angle and this adventure may prove profitable." Despite the poor prospects, Aaron began to acquire crates of iron pots and tools. What did the Indigenous people of the Interior want?

Joshua planned on transporting supplies to Fort St. Michael during the coming summer. He would do a quick trip to the trading post site at freeze-up, cut logs, and dig pits. Joshua would spend the winter in Fort St. Michael. Aaron agreed to hire others to build the trading post and transfer the goods. Joshua would cross over to the Yukon in the spring and if all went as planned, they would be doing business by the summer of 1839.

When Tuyana realized the coming life changes, she spent more time in town. She and Vera met to discuss options, Vera's as well as her own. There were excellent prospects for both. Vera would have a child come summer. If Joshua could stay on land, such would be best. She did not look happily upon months without her Navy husband. If staying on land meant a remote cabin at the edge of the Russian Empire, so be it. Both knew a payment for Joshua's career change would be needed. Aaron was one not to deny his brother, but both felt there must be a limit.

"I still don't see them as brothers. I don't think if the tables turned, Joshua would be as generous as Aaron." Vera's makeup was thick, hiding scars from her smallpox. Her long dark hair fooled some into thinking she and Tuyana were sisters.

"Yes. He rarely says no." Tuyana thought about how he played with the children, losing himself in their games. "He's still young at heart, despite all of his adventures." She had heard much, including the discipline he received at sea. "Dashi told me some about their father. He died at a Katorga camp. Did you know?" Vera nodded, though she didn't understand. "The man lived by his convictions."

Vera nodded, then shook her head. "You've seen these camps? What is a Katorga?" Vera enjoyed having an older friend who didn't mind her questions. She truly relished their time together sipping tea and discussing life. This would be one of their last afternoons before she left for Fort St. Michael. She sat up straight and focused on Tuyana's words.

"One day." Tuyana took a moment in her memories. "You will have to travel with Joshua to see the breadth of Mother Russia." She would too, as she had never been west of Irkutsk. "So Kartorgas. There are a few people who don't follow the laws. Some are locked up. Then some have done much worse but are not killed for their crimes. Many of these men are sent east to cut trees or mine for silver in camps. Their father was connected to one of these men. He was quite wealthy, but not one to follow the Czar's rules."

"I've heard some of this story." Vera sipped her tea and thought about how long it would take to see all of Russia.

Tuyana sipped her tea and thought about how she was bound to Aaron. Dashi had begun that. Her daughter, Samar, would never remember Dashi. For his whole life, Toq had known Aaron as a caregiver, almost like a father. Tuyana often thought fondly of the younger brother. It was his own beliefs that were the biggest obstacle to their bonding. The Saturday dinners were slowly pulling down his walls, and the priests were clearly on the side of them being together.

When the summer of 1838 ended, Aaron was quite pleased with the house he had built. The in-town wooden home had wooden shingles and four real glass windows. The same carpenters had expanded his out-of-town shop to include a bigger kitchen, eating area, and large room at the back. They had expected the backroom to be storage but were surprised when they were asked to build long benches and tables. Two glass windows also went into the backroom.

Toq was seven, and it was time he received an education. The few boys in town either worked with their fathers or went to the church school. Priests did the best they could, not what Aaron wanted. Aaron's schooling in Lutsk had such depth he couldn't replicate it anytime soon, but he wanted to try. He gathered readers, paper, and pencils from traders and acquired a large piece of slate for a wall.

Tuyana enjoyed their new in-town home, as the walk had become tedious. She understood the home to be theirs and was surprised when Aaron continued to live in the out-of-town shop's backroom. Saturdays he spent in town after their social church dinner, but slept in his own room. Some of this had to do with protecting their trade items since Bogdan had left in the spring with Joshua and pregnant Vera. Some of it.

No news came from Fort St. Michael. Each ship was pried for information and, more than once, Tuyana had asked Aaron to ask around about Vera and her newborn. She would have to wait.

Gushklin saw her as a customer when she entered their out-of-town store one September morning. The kids were with Aaron and she was moving fast, picking up a few items for the in-town home.

"Those are nice. Also, take some turnips. They will be gone by this afternoon." His voice barked the Russian almost like Dashi.

Tuyana looked at the Tlingit man behind the shop counter. He was not marked by smallpox scars, handsome, strong. "I will take a bag of them. I'd take more if I had a cart."

"Which way are you going? I know a village cart will be here later." She could feel Gushklin's questioning.

"I'm Buryat, central Russian. I live in town. Where is Aaron?" Tuyana got back to business.

"Ah, you must be the children's mother." This caught her by surprise. "Aaron has gone up to the village with the kids. He wants more students to give Toq a better school experience." Gushklin laughed. He didn't think many would want to learn. It would be the fry bread that would bring them in. Which it did.

"Then you know, I pick up these items because Aaron wants them for his home in town." Tuyana didn't receive the expected approval.

"Hmmm. If Aaron had wanted something, he would have let me know." Then Gushklin smiled and added, "Let's make some lunch." His change in tone turned Tuyana, and she warmed.

When Aaron walked in, Tuyana's glow sold him. Her spirited smile, her excitement at seeing him, pushed him over the edge. He knew she would be his wife. Before him lay destiny like few other moments in his life. There she was, his wife, his partner. She was bonded to him.

Or so he thought. Like much of life, few things are ever black and white. Tuyana's flushed face was from embarrassment. Her flirtation with Gushklin would be fodder when they argued. Over the years, Tuyana would not understand Aaron's struggle, she knew he felt her love. Aaron rationalized his insecurity as failing to wait and learn more about women. In his mind, he committed before completing his education.

…

Personal struggles ride on human shoulders like little imps. Driven towards mayhem, martyrdom, or mundane existence, the internal dialogues are rarely correctly interpreted: repetitive, simple stories. Humans feel an epic struggle is unfolding, while most see another's complex as childish behavior. Blessed are the people who have true heroic adventure stories. Most are wrestling with a muddy puddle.

Thus a haver, a study partner becomes one of life's cherished gifts. Aaron's journal work repeatedly reminded him of the importance of reflective work. People would leave him one way or another. He would always appreciate human reflections, but his constant companion was his journal. Written in privacy and in Hebrew script, thank you Rabbi Hulstein.

He knew others looked at his journals. His personal worries, angers, and passions were thus kept private, but caused several to ruminate. Tuyana, like Samuel, would press to learn his narratives. Neither would learn to read the script nor understand.

These worries were but little swirls within the great waters of life. The bigger currents were already set in motion. Aaron would trade and teach for years, taking breaks to visit his brother and his family in what soon became known as the village of Nulato. A team of boys filled Joshua and Vera's lives. It was an ever-growing household and names became a challenge. Isaac was the first and, for Aaron, destined to run the business.

Letter from Joshua dated March 23, 1848.

Dearest Bruder,

The days are busy as is our business. One would think on the edge of the Empire, little would happen. Any visitor here would be surprised. Between locals, far from home traveling Russians, and others (mostly English and Americans), we rarely have a free day. Winter is as busy if not busier than summer. Everyone wants our attention, even if it is to tell us how they struggled to get here. The dog teams out back howl their songs of sorrow. Oh, how brave these travelers are. I joke.

I sell them a beaver pelt's worth of grub before they finish their first story. Most know to bring a bundle if they are going to set foot in our shop. I've gotten a few to share nuggets of gold, but not more than a few. I also get baskets full of dried salmon. At this time of the year, they are one of the most valuable items we sell.

Earlier this month, Father Netsvetov visited. He is causing a stir down at Ikogmiute (Russian Mission) and seems to be always on the move. We've talked before, but on this visit, we settled into a couple of days of long discussions.

First, he has heard of you. He returned to Atka, on the Aleutians, on a ship after yours back in 1829. In a sense, he has followed your career. He has a younger brother in the Navy. His mother was an Aleut and his father was a merchant for the Company. He wants to know when he is going to meet you.

Second, he cornered Vera for two hours once he learned she was Russian-Tlingit. It seems he is doing a brisk business with the Yup'ik. Marrying more than fifty is what I've heard. He was more than pleased to know we married in the Church and ended up leading a service in our shop. You know me, I just follow orders. The boys enjoyed playing with him in his long robes.

Thirdly, he wrestles with his demons in a way that made me think of Rabbi Hulestein. I know, I rarely think about our yeshiva, but Father Netsvetov spoke endlessly about suffering to the point I wondered if he wasn't Jewish! His dilemmas would captivate you, his ideas of suffering, of free will, and grace. He grew up in Atka and attended seminary in Irkutsk. He spent several years wanting to be a monk, but the Church needed him. Few are the priests in this part of the Empire.

Point is we had an in-depth visit. Most folks move on when their bill gets close to their pile of pelts. Father Netsvetov tipped generously. Like I've said before, the Church has more money than our Czar.

The boys are everywhere and nowhere when we need them. Our dog team has given them free rein over the lands. The good news is I haven't chopped wood in over two years. Isaac is one strong young lad.

Do visit us soon. We all miss you.

Your devoted bruder,

Joshua

…

The fireside chats and stories in the Tlingit village were Aaron's continuing education. Rarely did he not bring gifts to soften the hard life of elders. Aaron consciously labored with the Indigenous acceptance of life's harsh realities. He wrestled, as he was supposed to do, with his Jewish questioning and sacredness for life. He developed his mantra, 'Why the struggle?' while never letting go of the rope.

He and Tuyana were blessed with a beautiful boy and then girl. Both died from illness before they were five. He adopted Toq and Samar who grew into confident, intelligent, and business-savvy Russian-Buryats in the Americas. They were the interest of many locals who applauded Toq's acceptance into the Navy. Samar grew into a beauty.

When word of German Jews settling in New Archangel, even a future Jewish Governor, reached Aaron's ears, he questioned nearly everything. He knew their business dealings would exceed his capital and reach. They were not coming to escape but to supplant him. What in the world had shifted so that Jews could announce they were coming while so many, like himself, had to live in hiding? They could openly worship, a concept that gave Aaron a giggle when he thought of Father Ilya. The real question was, would he join?

But it wasn't only the German Jews, the Hudson Bay Company was traveling the Yukon. They had set up Fort Yukon a thousand miles upriver, and it challenged Joshua's river trade. He and Vera had already seen a drop in their exchanges. When the British merchants visited Nulato, the dance they played proved prophetic.

The Russian-American Company toiled to exert their dominance. Explorations of the Interior tried to connect routes to Cook Inlet or the Yukon to Yakutat. Detailed coastal maps made travel safer and defined the grandness of Russia-America. Yet all knew, the days of easy money were over, a transition was underway.

…

The massacre of Nulato never made sense. All were lost. Some blamed the Hudson Bay Company for their sales of liquor. Others said it was a long standing feud between Yukon and Koyukuk men. Aaron and Tuyana mourned for days. Father Ilya provided comfort, unlike the German merchants.

"We will rebuild the trading post." Aaron eyed Tuyana.

"Ahh." She had a wave of thoughts, least of which was the loss of Vera's family.

"I've been told this is a priority that brings soldiers. They'll have the post rebuilt by the time we cross in spring." Aaron was looking at twenty years in New Archangel lost to larger merchants. The Interior offered little prospects for wealth compared to what he had acquired. His brother Joshua had done fine, that would be fine with Aaron.

He sat around a village fire explaining his coming move. The elders nodded. They had seen many changes and never felt permanence was practical. They did question the characters of Interior people where cold was at another level. Joshua had expressed similar thoughts many times.

"Bring good stoves and saws. The People will thank you. Your wife will thank you." Heads nodded in agreement.

The Nulato Trading Post bubbled under Aaron's guidance. For years

Tuyana was the trading face, Aaron the tea drinking partner by the stove. Samar became the focus of a whole river. The British, the Russians, and the Indigenous people talked about the princess. All the talk made Samar ever more indignant. She wanted an intelligent partner, not some seeker of fortune. Tuyana backed her every day.

Tadzee was a Koyukuk River man who melted her heart. The two enjoyed their little spot on the Yukon so much Tuyana and Aaron decided it was time to give them space. They needed to start a family, and Tadzee's extended family had already joined them in Nulato. Tuyana and Aaron were seen a bit as outsiders. Go figure. Talk of Tuyana's home, Aaron's Lutsk, and Safed filled their nightly chats. Aaron had many Russian coins to spend.

Father Netsvetov's visit proved timely. He had stayed many times during other spring travels. Out back, his dog team seemed better mannered compared to the others. This year, storms had kept many hunkered down, so when the snows stopped, the store was abuzz. The Russian Orthodox priest hung around the back, where he did most of his work. He enjoyed the tea from the store's endless samovar.

This visit he talked much with Tuyana about being Buryat. Father Netsvetov went on and on about Irkutsk Buryats before he learned she was from the eastern shores of Lake Baikal.

"I do wonder how much Eastern Philosophies filtered into Alaska's Aleutian Islands. My mother was one to keep her life expectations in check." The priest leaned against the log wall.

"I must say, I appreciate you Alaskan Russian priests. You don't seem too jealous of other religions." Like many, Tuyana balanced her traditional upbringing and Russian Orthodox practice.

"The Aleuts, your mother, they survived a vile bunch of men." Aaron spoke, knowing Father Netsvetov had experienced things on Atka that had deeply challenged him.

"Yes, yes." Father Netsvetov went internal with his memories, yet still clung to his original idea. "Personally, I find solace in knowing to let go. When I visualize my mother, my healing is even stronger."

"I struggle to let go." Aaron recalled his thoughts and experiences with

Tlingit views of spirit. "I know I am meant to wrestle, though it muddies my insides."

"We have wrestled with visiting Mother Russia a thousand times." Tuyana was animated. "I believe I will go mad if we don't decide soon."

"I found peace at the Irkutsk Seminary. For whatever reason, I can't find the same elsewhere." Father Netsvetov spoke with conviction and with sadness. "You should go now while you can. Every spring that I travel, I feel new aches and pains."

The peace following the Crimean War solidified their decision to go. Samar could run the store as well as her mom. Ships at Fort St. Michael sailed for Petropavlovsk, Kamchatsky, which had survived a siege during the Crimean War. From there, a European ship would take them through the Strait of Malacca, around India, and up the Red Sea to start their land journey to Safed. At well over 10,000 miles, Aqaba would take nearly a year of sailing. Aaron smirked, thinking about all the mosquitoes he would be missing.

Older, and hopefully a bit wiser, Aaron knew he was not the same man who traveled in his youth. Gone was the drive, the passion, the 'high' he achieved from a successful day of moving forward. In its place, Aaron watched, mostly others, including Tuyana. She had the travel bug. Besides her excited and lengthy descriptions of their progress, lists began to appear. As if she were doing an inventory check for their trading post, her updated travel lists were discussed and debated. Aaron could step back and see their play unfold, a drama worth watching.

Aaron's coins were much appreciated by each ship, by each port, by each person they met, and by those they knew from a lifetime before. Much of the journey filled their bags with ethereal moments, far more magnificent than the coins that disappeared. Then, Aaron's Safed family proved more difficult than he imagined.

"She is not Jewish!" His mother didn't talk to him for a week.

"She loves you, Aaron. She loves Tuyana. She doesn't understand what you have sacrificed. All she understands is her struggle: wars, pillaging, earthquakes. You would think the life she has now would melt her heart. There are grandkids and great-grandkids everywhere." Nearby lived Estle and Nathan's eight kids, four of whom had kids of their own.

The passage up the Dnieper made Aaron anxious. Passing Odessa and the Crimean War damage was humbling. Kiev had grown, showing no ill effects from the Polish Uprising now nearly thirty-five years earlier. Lutsk was nearly the same. The divided city still had thatch-roofed homes, the yeshiva still had tile. Smaller than he remembered, the yeshiva's new rabbi had but a few words for Aaron who not only did not wear the proper garments, he failed to have a demeanor that respected his rabbinic position.

"I don't need another minute here. We go west or east. If it is east, I vote for winter travel." Tuyana wanted to go back home. So east it was.

Leaving Irkutsk heightened her awareness. The hills around Verkhne-Udinsk brought her goosebumps. The reunion dinners and gifts were the talk of the town. Tuyana was lost to needy hands and hearts.

Travel on the Lena River proved much easier than the Amur. The Pacific crossing to Alaska was routine. The steamboats that plied the waters around New Archangel had yet to consider plying the Yukon. Their spring crossing to the Yukon in 1860 proved uneventful. Samar was happy to have help with her new baby.

In their store, Aaron had a favorite chair by the stove. The window or wall-mounted candle provided him with endless hours of light for reading and writing. His travels provided him with two new crates of books and much to write about. Samar and Tuyana gave him the area with reminders to keep his book stacks to a minimum.

As a bookmark Aaron's tzava'ot, his final letter, was not a mystery. His travels had prompted him to get his life in order, though at forty-eight he had plenty more living to do. Whether it was in The Sebastopol Sketches or Rudin, Aaron had written multiple versions of his final letter. The current one had many edits and additions written in the margins. Aaron had seen Tuyana reading it.

"Do you have any questions?" That's not how these letters worked, but he asked anyway.

"You got most of it." Tuyana smiled and then added, "You are a very loving man. Not all men trust others like you do. If you don't add it, I will."

Aaron's tzava'ot read:

To my family,

I spent my youth watching people, searching for answers. I grew wiser when I finally watched myself. Most adults gain understanding of complex life tasks. People cling to these learned skills even though they know they will require more energy and commitment than they are able to maintain. They fail, repeatedly. I do the same and expect so will you.

First, you are more than your unique qualities. I wrestled with 'being more' at many stages in my life. Surprisingly, it took years to understand this was normal behavior. Humans adapt and thrive. It is what we do. If you don't, it has less to do with your skills than the simple ability to wait for the correct path to reveal itself. It will be similar for you.

I did things my way, but I doubt if I could have done it any other. The more I saw how others lived, the more I realized my system was just as strange, but mine. Like a horse that always stops when it sees a child, I learned how to steer my uniqueness towards my life goals. In time, I learned to make better goals. You will get what you aim for, pay attention to what you want, and add space.

I am describing a possible foundational richness for your life. Being more than your learned skills is not a grandiose accomplishment, it is not something you build. What I want you to know is a richness that you tend and grow. It is wealth that comes from knowing yourself. You will experience this richness when you understand yourself.

Second, while you give space, engage life and learn the routines and rituals that unlock the levers of society. If you uniquely benefit people, you will be rewarded. Power that comes from following and meeting societal needs can go to your head. I found a life of service was a healthy road to travel.

I have felt fears, a sick child being one of the more powerful. Having another child get sick after one has died is a labyrinth from which there is no escape. Lessons like this taught me much, as there was little to fight. What will you learn from loss?

The North Lands are deceptive. Most think of it as a brutal fight against the cold. Once your behaviors are halfway reasonable, what the North teaches you is acceptance. I imagine all environments teach this, embracing what is. Find your routine, build your connections, and serve those around you.

179

Lastly, fill your life with people who reflect the beauty of the world. If you experience the sacredness of the world through human love, consider yourself lucky.

Each person is a universe unto themselves. If you cannot see another's beauty, go further. A person's universe is ever expanding and there are millions of us. That being said, surround yourself with good people. You'll know they are good when goodness fills your life. Look at me.

As I grow closer to death, I am surrounded by the most important people in my life. I have my faults, but when I rise, I live the life of a king. How blessed can an old man be!

Treasure the wisdom from those before us. Don't waste time wandering in deserts.

A good story is just as important as a warm cabin.

You are loved,

Aaron

...

Over the years, different explorers came through Nulato. A Russian-American Company man said Ft. Yukon was far, having kayaked up and back; Aaron couldn't believe such an adventure in such a small craft. American explorers went here and there looking for cable routes. The idea flummoxed Aaron, who couldn't imagine a cable going all the way back to Russia. Still, men trekked and talked about wild ideas in wildlands. Then one winter day the flag changed and another day an American riverboat pulled up to Nulato looking for cordwood to burn.

Part Three

Lieutenant Allen - 1867 to 1885

Lieutenant Allen was

Explorer of Alaska Interior-ish,
A bit
Lewis and Clark-ish.

Survived starvation with the help of
Indigenous Nation.

Found no USA hatred.

Two years earlier in 1867, the Alaska Commercial Company purchased the Russian-American Company. The special arrangement Aaron had with his former supplier was now looking to be altered by the present. It became clear this riverboat representative aboard the 'ACC Yukon' was not able nor interested in answering his burning questions. Time would tell as trade was now in their hands. The ACC territory included Fort Yukon, the former Hudson Bay Company trading post. What the company man needed was fuel, firewood for their upriver journey. Relationships were always a negotiation on the frontier.

In his maturing English, "Don't. We cut, you buy." Aaron knew the benefit of adding value to an item. These people were not interested, but they were far from home and not looking for a fight.

For the next four days, Aaron learned more.

"The ACC is here for the long haul. Ft. Michael has crates of items for you." The riverboat man looked around the log cabin, noticed a few things he wasn't used to seeing. "I'll be back in a couple of weeks. Maybe you'll trade me for some of this." He pointed at a pan of gold flakes.

Aaron listened and got the gist of his words. He also knew what he had. "No." He waved his hand. Instead of haggling now, he kept his focus on his need for a good relationship. This man, or another like him, could make the difference he needed to continue his store. "We trade. Talk more." Aaron pointed around his store.

The riverboat man was pleased and knew this Russian had much to offer. "Good. Keep learning your English. The Russians are gone." He waved his hand away. "Vamoosed." He frowned a bit, pretending to be sad. "You'll get it. You probably do fine talking with everyone else." In short order, he learned Aaron did.

Similar visits were repeated. Aaron and Tuyana's English improved, so did Samar's and her husband's. Improvements were not always a blessing.

The ACC store supply list made little sense to Aaron. How could he buy something without first seeing the item? More importantly, with whom was he trading? The rivermen became his gatekeepers in this new game. One paper bag of jellybeans set much into motion. Oats, grains, and flour could be bagged instead of needing baskets or large bolts of cloth to transport. The sweets sold out in a day. It was the liquor that cursed the land and was banned from their store.

During the early years, the Alaska Territory was run by the US military. One way to look at it was that this was the 'Reconstruction Era' and troops were used to keep folks in line. Near Sitka, a Tlingit name for New Archangel, the US Army and Navy attacked and destroyed several coastal villages. The conflicts climaxed with the bombardment, destruction of, and severe penalties for the Tlingit People of Angoon. This harsh treatment of Indigenous people was acknowledged in the 1884 Organic Act which set Alaska on a new path towards development and ultimately ANCSA. Word flowed north in the stories told by American fortune seekers.

Samar was upset, but not as much as Tuyana when changes forced Samar to leave. "Papa, we will not be back for a while. Tadzee must get away from these rivermen. He fights when he drinks their whiskey. These relations and drinking will not end well." Her husband had finally reappeared after a week. His family knew he needed to go up the Koyukuk, get away from these men. It was a pattern that repeated throughout his abbreviated life.

The shop would have been too quiet had it not been for Aaron's school. He held onto Samar's kids under the pretext he needed help making birch-bark canoes. Other children joined and their minds needed stories. Grandpa joined too.

He was Tadzee's grandpa, and he had trouble moving about. His body was twisted. A warm fire, a warm cup of tea, made the elder quite talkative. The kids needed lessons, and he was motivated.

"Never trust Raven. He doesn't want you to be happy. Stop thinking he's doing his song for you. Fools are everywhere. They want to think a fog on the river ice is a spirit. They want to think a hissing log on the fire is curses from past enemies. They want to think good people grow old while the spirits from the bad ones leave early. I'm here to tell you I'm old and not good."

The kids laughed.

"Seriously. I'm a wicked man. I'll steal your food and take your boots." His smile and ruffling of hair caused more silliness. The kids enjoyed it while their focus remained on their work.

"Don't trust Raven. He does not care about your good life. All your happiness and health, good food and clothes, he does not care. He'll take it if you let him." He stood and walked around the stove to other kids.

"Raven has two legs, like me. He struts around like a young chief, all proud of what he has done." Grandpa stuck his chin higher and flapped his arms like a bird.

"Grandpa, my grandma says she remembers when you were young and got stuck in a tree. She said you stayed there for three days and nearly died. That's why she won't let me climb trees." The kid didn't look up when she spoke, but the words squarely hit Grandpa.

"Hmph. Your grandma don't know. She too old to remember her days before your Eenaa'e." He did his awkward strut around the room.

"Raven can sit for days if needed. As patient as a rock, but as light as a snowflake. Raven can watch from afar. His eyes can see the fish in the muddy river or the caribou on the far hill." He strutted some more.

"I see too. My legs may be awkward, but my eyes see all. Bashinki, I know what you've got in your belt. You don't share because you're a bad chyaa tsal. If Chenashi knew what you had, she would not be a nice older sister." Chenashi punched her younger brother.

"I won't share!" He was loud for the little room. "She never shares!

Eenaa'e tells her to share, but she takes everything." He got another punch.

"I know." Grandpa waited for Bashinki to quiet. "You want to know where she hides everything?" The question drew the kids to a halt.

"Raven steals everything too. He takes my buttons. He takes the red ribbon for my parka. He takes my bootstraps and I've seen him take the shiny things off of soldier uniforms. Raven has a special spot for his things and he never shares." The kids nodded their heads as everyone had their own story.

"If you go to Raven's hiding spot, you must wear a mask. He will never forget your face and he will haunt you for years. He will make you pay twice for what you take." Grandpa strutted to his chair.

"I stole from Raven a long time ago. That is how I got my limp." He sat down and moaned a bit for effect. "Raven had stolen our only metal pot. My Eenaa'e was so angry she kicked me as if it were my fault. 'You get our pot! Don't come back until you do!' She could get real angry when she wanted to." He moaned some more.

"I watched Raven fly home one winter at sunset. I got about halfway to his roost, then could go no more. I spent the night and next day waiting. When he flew over, I followed again until the long sunset disappeared. I spent a second cold night buried in the snow. By the third evening, I was close enough I could hear them all gaggling about." Grandpa stood again and strutted his awkward bird walk, flapped his folded arms.

"'You one smelly bird.' 'No, you one smelly bird that don't know nothing.' Ravens could be so mean to one another. The one I wanted was nowhere to be seen. But there were piles of shiny stolen objects hanging everywhere. Soon the squawking black birds got to fighting and one flew after the other. Then they all took off to watch. There I was surrounded by hundreds of shiny objects. I began to climb the biggest tree. This is when Raven, the one who I had been chasing, perched itself just out of reach."

"'You silly boy. I know who you are. You get out of here now or I'll make sure I curse you for twenty years.' Raven was so mean when he talked. But I had had enough. Three days out in the cold had made me mad. With a leap of faith, I threw myself at Raven and caught him by the neck. Down we fell through branches, breaking sharp, and onto the ground, swallowing us whole. I dare not let go, but I could see nothing."

Some of the younger kids were watching Grandpa, not working. Grandpa enjoyed their attention.

"'You let me go or I'll peck your eyes out!' Raven screamed, so I squeezed harder. 'Hhmpp' was all he could say." Grandpa smiled at a younger boy.

"You one bad Raven. Give me my mama's pot or I'll bury you here till next spring! Raven didn't agree until I squeezed harder. 'Hhhpppp' was all I could hear." Grandpa sat back down.

"Slowly I eased my grip and Raven took some deep breaths. 'You one bad boy. You know I won't forget.' So I squeezed again and Raven could only say, 'Hhhh'." Grandpa stuck out his chin.

"You, the bad one. I get my pot back or I bury you forever. And I began to dig while I squeezed Raven tight. His air was running out, the bird began to let go. 'Wake up, you bad bird!' I eased, and he let out a sigh. 'You get your pot and you go!' Raven was breathing heavily. 'I don't want to see you again.' And to that, I agreed. But when I went to stand up, my leg was curved and wouldn't straighten." Grandpa showed his curved legs to the kids.

"Raven said, 'You die here, all because of some metal pot. And to think some animals call you the smart one.' Raven was such a bad bird. I managed to stand and saw all the treasures which had also fallen. I gathered them and then saw my mom's pot. I put all the treasures inside and began to go home. Not so easy." Grandpa pointed at his leg and laughed.

"I crawled, but I couldn't get away. Then Moose, who had been watching the whole thing, came over to help. He, too, had his troubles with Raven and saw the opportunity to get some revenge. I rode all the way home on his back. He gave me some advice. 'Raven can see everything, so don't act like anything is going on. You too busy, bad boy, and Raven want a piece of the fun.' I don't know if I ever followed Moose's advice. Raven still comes around, smart enough to stay out of reach."

Aaron thought about all the shiny things in his store. He thought about his piles of useless Russian rubles he had buried out back. He thought about the struggles shiny things caused and wondered why the stories never changed people's ways. This lesson was as old as time.

He looked at the canoe frame, the sheets of birch bark and pots of spruce pitch, birch tar, and moose fat bubbling on the stove. Aaron watched the children's faces and wondered if Rabbi Hulstein ever felt like he did now. He looked at the Latin alphabet on the wall and the few English books on a corner table. He mused about a slate-roofed school with scores of students.

Chenashi grabbed at Bashinki's belt. Out fell several jellybeans. He screamed, she grabbed. They wrestled. Grandpa had had enough.

Leaning against the front of his store, Aaron watched the mighty Yukon flow, day and moonlit night. Summer sun never stopped. Winter snows created a world of pinks and blues. Some news came upriver, news mostly came down. Aaron sat and talked for years with the spirits traveling these waters.

To say Aaron was a contemplative man would be an understatement. He spent most of his life waiting for people to come to him for things. Few who spent time with him felt he was present, as his spirit was usually elsewhere. But then again, he was the most present person most had ever known.

One of his favorite pastimes reflected this. Early in the winter, before the windows iced over, he would wait for the first nighttime snowfall. He would sit in his cabin with a lantern on the window sill, looking at his reflection against the dark windowpane. He could see a blurry image of himself, of the life he had built. Then swirls of night snow would be illuminated from his cabin window and he could see the chaos outside. Winds would shift to nothing, then again sheets of falling snow interrupting his life, distorting the image of himself. It was one of his more anticipated winter activities as he felt it illuminated his struggles to understand and see clearly.

...

Far away, on farmland so fine Aaron would have given pause, a boy grew up during America's Civil War. Henry Allen would mature with the echoes of this conflict and educate himself at West Point. Few places could be further from Nulato. By this time, America had entered its young adult phase. No longer was it squabbling and flapping about, the war had given the people direction: West.

Aaron discerned from the stories he heard that something was brewing. Traders and trappers, adventurers and miners were moving towards something big. Traveling religious men brought new energies perpendicular to the land, to the way of life Aaron knew. These weren't the Russian priests of yore: not wrong, but not right. The vastness of the land caused many to falter. Some years, the spring break-up was so violent the mighty river changed course. Lives could be washed away as easily as they could be frozen by the brutal winters. Summer steamships needed their wood, winter travelers needed their warmth. Aaron got his stories.

Few went unnoticed by the aging man. Long ago, he realized his life turned on stories. Stories brought people together. They left Aaron with endless internal dialogues. Was this not the way life was supposed to be? He used these stories to hypothesize and understand the world with which he struggled. This was who he was. He happened to also be a good merchant.

And fifty years of consistent mussar journaling had given him great depth to the common human traits: pride, courage, anger, humility, calmness, trust, and more. Strangely, he rarely voiced his learning. His wisdom was a labyrinth. He couldn't talk about courage without going to distant lands and to do such, he needed the others' patience. The wisdom was in his head, in his heart, not his mouth.

People intuited this. The hours they spent sitting with Aaron were vibrant exchanges, even when no words were spoken. He knew he wasn't like them, but he knew his youthful struggles had matured since his arrival in Nulato thirty years ago. Folks knew he was like them, and they also knew him as a conduit between worlds. Hours created a shared history of understanding.

The Americans were a common topic. Brashly exploring yet fearful to lose their youth, they were not the Russian patriarchs of old. Most did not learn the language as had their counterparts. There were Russian priests still working their parishes, some a few days downriver. New religions had new men wandering the lands. Men of Nulato considered their lack of understanding as a root cause to their wandering. Rootless was a slang word tossed around.

Raven paid little attention to these latest men until one day he did.

"I hear word about Americans, Army men who have come from the coast, from the other coast." Grandpa practically lived with Aaron and Tuyana.

Aaron had also heard the rumor. Summer was waning. Steamboats were making their last trips down from Fort Yukon. Boatmen liked to talk.

"I heard they went up the Koyukuk too. Young men do like to dash around." Grandpa was glad he no longer needed to wander.

What Grandpa and Aaron didn't know was that the Army was assessing the hostility of Alaska Native peoples towards America. A few years earlier the coastal Alaskan violence had caused reverberations and here came the US Army.

The young lieutenant from West Point was driving hard for the coast. His small troupe was suffering from poor diets and toils in harsh lands. Escape was imperative. They were new to Alaska, lucky to be alive. Understood by most as rootless, still capable of mischief.

Aaron's interest was sparked. He considered the stories such men would tell and hoped for ones more dynamic than the simple ones repeated by the new churchmen. Maybe stories of President Grant or word about gold in Juneau would get him to travel again. Aaron wanted to share his story, 'White Dog.' He could feel the Army man's presence along the river and looked upriver each morning for smoke from a breakfast fire. Raven did too.

The last ACC riverboat was filled with pelts, empty of trade goods. There was little reason to stop as they burned so little wood going downriver. Grandpa didn't get up. Aaron waved at the captain with his worn hat. His normally cropped hair was finger length. His beard, in need of a good comb. He looked like most along the river except for what others called his Russian manners. Aaron leaned backward when he stood. He bear-hugged, he used his hands for most of his talking; he barked his words and stared holes into you after uncomfortable questions. Aaron waved at the captain, looking a bit like most but also out of place, like a shiny object moved by Raven.

Sitting in a nearby spruce, Raven watched the steamboat move quickly by Nulato. No need for things to be easy, he had seen what was coming. Lt. Allen and Private Ficket, his last remaining soldier, were but a few hours behind, trying to catch this final riverboat. He still held a grudge against Grandpa and cackled thinking these army men could cause trouble.

"You've got to be kidding me!" The Army man screamed when he learned the steamboat had just left. Aaron stood leaning back, his merchant arms trying to guide the lieutenant to relax.

"Tea? Or is it coffee?" The barked words were understood and the emaciated man turned. "I may have some fresh pies." His words captured more than the man's attention.

Aaron disappeared and returned with two mugs, one for each. He motioned them to the store log. Grandpa scooted over. Tuyana appeared with blue enamel plates carrying large slices of fresh blueberry pie. A napkin, fork, and motherly smile melted the young men. After five minutes of silence, Raven drifted closer.

"I am indebted." And for such kind words, Private Fickett received another slice and refill.

Grandpa happily announced, "You look like a worn-thru patch on a blown-out boot." Raven turned his head, maybe the Army man would take offense.

"Ayyup." Lieutenant Allen refused to ask for seconds and received none. Tuyana smiled at his youth.

"I've heard about you." Private Fickett was beyond pleased by the second piece of pie. "Folks say you've lived here longer than most, a Russian from the Russian days." The words lingered for all. "Seems you would know what goes on around here." Lieutenant Allen slowly pulled a notebook from his jacket.

Aaron wanted a better lead into his story. He paused.

Grandpa stumbled in. "Few know more. Everyone wants a shiny thing." Raven listened for the answer.

The leader squinted a mean squint not unlike many a man Aaron had known.

Aaron pulled the talk back to the shore. "I know the area. Ask away."

Private Fickett looked at his officer. "You got another slice of pie?" Lieutenant Allen gave him a glare. "He's too proud to ask. He gets awfully snarky when he's hungry and he's been hungry for 1500 miles." Lieutenant Allen dropped his shaking head to keep from hitting Fickett.

"Come with me." Tuyana's warm words pulled the lieutenant inside. Golden lantern light illuminated their wares. The West Point man was a bit impressed.

Fickett's words were enlivened by the nourishments. "He means well and is not a bad officer. He's young."

"I've seen worse." Aaron replied while looking across the mighty river.

"We've got to get out of here." His words held emotion. "You may have this figured out. We'll die if winter catches us here." True words, Raven enjoyed this. "When is the next steamboat?" Fickett asked, almost expecting a posted schedule. The food and service had lulled him into a relaxed state.

"That may have been it." Grandpa enjoyed saying those words almost as much as he enjoyed the man's reaction.

"It's nearly 500 miles by boat to Ft. Michael. There are other ways to get there." Aaron didn't like Grandpa's energy when guns were lying around.

Lieutenant Allen sat inside and enjoyed his big slice of pie. It was sheer pleasure leaning his elbows on a table, sitting in a chair, looking around a kitchen that could have been his neighbor's in Kentucky. He watched Tuyana, noticed her features, and realized she was not from the area. He savored the crust and dunked a piece in his coffee as an indulgent act. Mindful, he swept the crumbs into his hand and dropped them back onto his plate.

Raven hopped around, impatient for something more dramatic.

"Have you heard the story, White Dog?" Aaron had waited for the lieutenant.

"The Iroquois 'White Dog' story? No. Why would I have heard this story? It's not like I sit around with folks telling stories."

"Huh. Well, it's my story folks like to tell. I mean, it happened to me, right here. The first spring riverboat pulled up, though going downriver it didn't need any wood. The captain approached me. He was in a twisted fit. His words were all garbled, but I got the gist, he was mad at this old man. Specifically, he was mad at the old man's dog. It was a little white dog. That's how the story got its name."

"Good grief. You're going to tell me the story."

"You kind of need to hear this."

"I'll be hanged! Go on."

"You see, this white dog was small, the last thing you would worry about. The old man came over and pleaded with me. He knew me as the 'Nulato Whitie' and felt I could help with his dog. Honestly, he tried to thrust the dog on me to the point I had to push back." Aaron watched the lieutenant for understanding.

He continued, "The dog was a demon. The captain wailed, 'He's caused so many problems!' The old man whined, 'He doesn't know our ways.' He looked at me with a mixture of pain and sadness. 'Maybe he'll follow you? You white.' The old man's blatant association caused me to push back again.

'Take this dog or both of 'em. I don't care!' The captain headed back to his boat.

'He needs to learn. He's not a bad dog.' The old man's eyes pleaded with me. There was a story far deeper than he could say. Then the kids came out.

So now I had a dog.

Long ago, I had a dog. 'Shep', was a great dog, and I'm not a dog person. 'Whitie' had big soft eyes which at first melted you, made you want to care for the little thing. Then he slunk away, and the problems began, little things. A shoelace broke, then a teacup. The front door hinge snapped, as did an ax handle."

"I knew the dog was no good." Grandpa's interjection stirred Raven. "I don't know anyone who would have kept a runt like that. When I looked, really looked at the dog, I didn't see its white fur. I saw the dark skin underneath. Ayyap." Grandpa looked around and spied Raven in the tree.

"The next morning, I caught the demon talking with camp robbers, those jays." Grandpa didn't take his eyes off Raven. "He was squawking like a bird. He was no dog."

"Tuyana saw him squawk like a bird too. She came and shared with me as well about an earlier dream." Aaron looked at Tuyana, who let him go on. "This is what I remember, 'Our daughter's husband was alive. His smile was broad and his cabin filled with wealth. Samar, our daughter, brought our grandson to Tuyana, a bundle of joy and love. The husband turned to his friends, a group around a fire, they drank the poison water. He turned white, but black inside.' Did I get it right?"

Tuyana nodded.

"Ok. I got it. Can we talk about this shortcut to Ft. Michael?"

Aaron put up a finger in protest.

"I understood and took the white dog out behind the store. I didn't need to hear anymore. When I raised my ax, I realized the handle was broken. The dog looked at me sideways like I was a fool. I heard him say, 'You know better.' That dog was no dog."

"White Ravens come every generation to break the world. Too much success makes people weak." Grandpa spoke to the men but kept his eyes upward.

"Ya. I let the dog go. All this happened this spring and summer."

"What kind of story is that?"

"Well, what does it mean to you?"

"Nothing. You had a runt of a dog. So what. I assume it got eaten by some coyote or wolf?"

"Yes. I hear you. Why do you think it was white?"

"What kind of question is that? It was white because it wasn't black." The Army man thought for a moment. "Ok, I've got a story." Aaron was surprised.

"Long ago people had it all, no need to toil. Nobody fought, people got along. You know why all was lost?" The Lieutenant looked at Aaron, who wasn't ready for another bible story. "I'll tell you, there wasn't enough! You all sit out here enjoying your fireside chats while millions of people fight for scraps to keep their kids alive. Nulato Whitie, you remind me of the thousands packed into the Lower East Side. I had a pickle man, like you. He always tried to tell me stories. You Russian? Right?"

The White Dog had never left. It would circle the village, break into cabins, smash holes in boats, and change into the wind, trees, and mist hanging over the water. This lieutenant could not stay. Even Raven understood this.

"I'll take you." This the Lieutenant heard and readily agreed.

That night as he lay unable to sleep, Aaron wallowed in the chaos of death. All the final moments of life that he witnessed were judged by his father's: his death rattle, his smell, the single flame, the burial the next day. A whole world collapsed. Dashi's death had been as painful as his kids. Both had torn him doubly through Tuyana. Aaron realized he was next in line for the reaper.

Keep moving.

...

"It's easier in the winter." Aaron was moving slow. He had not been feeling well, but these men needed to go. He had kissed his grandchildren, hugged Samar, and held Tuyana at length to get a view of the only woman he had ever known. She gave him a glare and then a twinkle, letting him know he was doing the right thing.

"These people don't seem too up-in-arms about America." Private Fickett was shouldering the most gear.

Aaron had to catch his breath. He was seventy-three. The path had a few leaves; the air smelled rich.

"America has been here for a good while. The last troubles weren't with America. The Koyukuk men killed all in Nulato, my brother included. Almost thirty-five years ago." He stood. "It's the poison drink that does all the killing. You want a calm country, get rid of the drink." Aaron was out of breath.

"There's no gettin' rid of whiskey." Honest, Fickett was.

"Why are you still here?" Lieutenant Allen had a bite to his words.

"Good question." Aaron had to think before he spoke, which was getting harder.

"You need a break?" Fickett could tell Aaron was not doing well.

"Ayyup." Aaron did appreciate. He pulled on his beard and leaned against an old birch, one he had repeatedly considered chopping. At the right angle, he could see the Yukon below. He had walked this, how many times?

"I went back to my home once. It wasn't my home anymore." He moved his head to see more of the river. "I may not have everything here, but I've got enough to continue to learn about myself." He looked at Fickett, who got it.

"I won't be back." Again, honest.

"Me neither. I do appreciate what a city as fine as San Francisco can offer." The Lieutenant moved forward, then stopped, turned, and looked at the two. "Really!"

"Grandpa Aaron ain't looking too good. I bet a good cup of tea will bring the life back to him." Fickett was already gathering wood.

They made the ridge before setting up camp for the night. Aaron explained the rest of the portage. The two army men got it.

Aaron sat with the men, chatted with them, but his spirit was a swirl of inescapable stories. These American Army men were not the Russian military he intimately knew. Why was he so concerned? Why did he so fear their presence that he pushed himself to rid them from his valley? In days gone by, was he similarly seen when he wore the Russian uniform? Was he feared by others? His head swirled with his heart.

That morning, Aaron threw another log on the fire as the two men descended to the Pacific. He was feverish, ached all over, but didn't let on how bad. Once they were gone, he crawled under his blanket, boots still on.

He was not doing well. This was a different kind of sickness. He could not get his breath, a strong pain in his leg made him immobile. Aaron felt the danger. As his fever rose and his breathing labored, he repeatedly prayed. Vivid visions flashed: the Lutsk yeshiva, the benches along the wall, the hooks with coats, the sycamore out back.

Aaron woke to a painful, cold darkness, scaring him deeply.

He was going to die here. Alone.

He yearned for a candle flame, a cool hand on his forehead, relief from this wretched pain.

In his delirium, he realized his story had led him to this exact moment. Each act, each decision, each choice he had made or not had brought him to this ridge overlooking his river, next to a crooked black spruce bent by many a winter.

This was his. This was his. He had done his best.

His life was a blessing.

He gave thanks for the oneness.

Years Roll By

In the years following Aaron's death, Alaska transitioned from an unwanted ice colony to a rich resource territory. In a sense, America reset the clock to how Russia began in Alaska. Like with the Alaskan fur seals which provided federal revenue when the national economy demanded such despite its harm.

Alaskans like Captain Healy became key for protecting the country's investment. The captain's character, both rough and compassionate, was decisive during these transitional years as he was essentially the federal government in western Alaska. Aboard the 'Bear' he enforced whaling and hunting regulations, as well as judicial and medical services for everyone along the coast.

Economic hard times made the Klondike gold rush an easy choice for many. Skagway and Alaska's Inside Passage provided launching points for many fortune seekers, especially along the iconic Chilkoot Trail. Eventually, Alaskan gold rushes brought men and women to the Interior. Nulato saw men race down the Yukon for the gold beaches of Nome. Then miners raced back to new places like Fairbanks.

It took years of fighting by Alaska Native people to win full citizenship rights and control of their land. While the Alaska territorial government granted women the right to vote seven years before the 19th Amendment, they passed literacy tests and Jim Crow laws to disenfranchise Alaska Native people. This oppression was further exacerbated by trauma from the Alaska Native boarding school system. It took the work of advocates like those in the Alaska Native Brotherhood & Sisterhood to end those policies and amplify Native voice throughout Alaska.

The Aarons grew and multiplied throughout the Interior. It didn't take long for many to move to the bigger Alaskan towns.

Alaska continued to be two-deviations from the norm. Whether it was the bounty of resources or the climate, these environments had a distinct way of developing a person: watchful, patient, enduring, and reliant on one's neighbor.

June 15, 2023

Mark Aaron had several helping him clean out his great auntie's Hall Street home: little, but packed. Here she had raised her boys, her grandkids, her neighbor's kids, any kid who needed love. She could be hollering one minute and squeezing you tight the next. Mark had spent many years in and out of this Fairbanks home.

Last month, the St. Matthews' pastor had called. Mark was the last of the Aarons living in Fairbanks, the others had moved on. Several were buried up on Birch Hill, or back in Nulato, a few were down in Arizona, and then, of course, Anchorage. These folks helping were from the church and they were a chatty bunch.

"Lookie here!" The woman exuded motherly love and joy at finding familiar things. "This jacket is skookum." She held a beaded, moose-hide jacket from which Mark could still smell the tanning smoke.

The goal was to save everything of value for a church yard sale. The home now belonged to Mark, and he didn't see much point in holding on to it. He had his own, this worn shell would be sold as-is.

He focused on the kitchen. Mark had boxes filled with plates, bowls, and glasses. Now the kitchenware needed to be boxed away.

"You got a weird box downstairs." A man wiped his brow and slowly put on his blue cap with a small white ribbon. Mark followed. He had always been spooked by the basement.

The room was a mess with piles upon piles, as if no one had thrown anything out for years. "Look at it, that's Chinese." They looked at a wooden crate weathered as if by ten thousand hands. Still, here and there, they could see faint red Chinese lettering. The man handed Mark a leather-bound notebook. "These books are written in freaky letters." There was a score of notebooks inside the pried-open crate. Mark looked at the notebook's handwritten passages, the pencil marks still crisp. If he could make any sense of these strange writings, they read right to left. Mark was a bit dumbfounded thinking his great-auntie Aaron had anything to do with these.

He pulled out another notebook similar to the first and the next. Then they were bound in cloth with the printed letters - ACC. Most of the remaining notebooks had the same letters. Then he found the little box.

Inside, he could hear coins rattling. The snug lid revealed a dozen shiny, small, gold coins. Mark lit up. Between his thumb and forefinger he could tell these weren't American, nor were they Chinese. They all had a similar style, though several had different engravings. "You've got yourself somethin." The man was impressed, but gave Mark some space.

"Let's get them upstairs and some better light." Mark was excited. At nearly $2000 an ounce, he began to calculate a small fortune.

Larson's was one of Fairbanks' oldest jewelers and was just down the street. Old man Larson was working and gave Mark his condolences. "Grandma Aaron was the best of a generation. We won't have folks like her anymore." He agreed they were gold, though the coins would need to be tested. The markings looked Russian, as did the box, cute and tight.

"You seen anything like this?"

Larson took the notebook.

"I have not." He turned pages. "Can't tell if this is gibberish or for real. These numbers look to be dates. 17-7-72. I don't know." Larson turned more pages, looked at the cover. "ACC, probably the Alaska Commercial Company." He looked at a few more pages. "They run the village stores." He handed the notebook back. "It's old." Larson thought. "If you don't mind," he took the notebook back, "I know a university professor who can speak a bundle of languages. If there is someone who would know what this is, it would probably be him." He smiled as he continued to look at the pages.

"Sure." Mark wasn't too keen. On the other hand, he wanted a good deal with Larson. What was one notebook?

The university professor, Dr. Cohen, recognized the script, though it took him a bit to believe. He got Mark's number.

"Is this Mr. Aaron? This is Dr. Cohen, Richard from UAF. I have a notebook of yours. Can we meet?"

In this northern land, folks often met indoors at Alaska Coffee Roasters. It was across from the University.

"This is a rare piece of Alaska history." Richard was short of stature while his intellect loomed large.

"I've got twenty. Do they mean anything? I mean, like, are they real?"

"This," Richard held up the notebook, "is real. Quite unique and not what I expected."

"Hmm. Good, right?" Mark wanted to hear something different. "How much is it worth?" He wanted a number.

"That depends." Richard opened to a marked page. "I did not expect this. 'The thirteenth of November, 1877. Strength - the ice is now two inches thick, strong enough yet I don't have the strength to cross. In a sense, I'm strong enough to wait. Strength is a muscle, no matter what one may think. It takes engagement, practice; resistance is what it does. Heat and options are its enemies.' I could go on."

"Gibberish." Mark didn't know what to think. This was a bunch of worthless gibberish.

"Not your typical writing, but not gibberish. The book is filled with topics and reflections. The writer lived a hundred and fifty years ago on the Yukon. Nulato, is what I figure."

"Would you buy it?"

"Ahhmm. Maybe? It again is not typical, but I would not want to take this from you. This is personal. It appears to be your ancestors. Did you know your great-great-grandparents?"

"I've heard stories all my life about Nulato and the Aarons. I'm Mark Aaron. It didn't feel right until I heard of Marky Mark. You know. Like I have a first name for my last."

"Yes. You're not the only one." Richard paused and thought about the Athabascan elder, Bobby Charles. "Could you read any of this?"

"What? Good grief. I thought it was gibberish. Well, it is."

"This," he held up the notebook, "is a mussar journal. It is written in Hebrew script, not something you'd expect from Nulato in the 1870s." Richard paused to see if Mark was following. "Mussar was a Lithuanian moral Jewish practice, some still practice today. To be written in Hebrew script means the person was educated at a yeshiva. Not something that was happening back then in Alaska."

Richard watched Mark's reaction. Did he understand what he was saying?

Did either of them understand? Dr. Cohen was holding one of many moral reflective Hebrew script journals written in Interior Alaska from the 1800s. There was a moment when he realized this Alaskan had more Jewish schooling than himself. The moment didn't last, but the energy did.

Months later, Richard called Mark again.

"For what it is worth, you should hear a few things I found in your notebooks."

"Does that mean you want to buy them?"

"I told you. I'm working with the museum. Honestly, there is a lot within these writings. People need to be able to read them."

"Really?"

"Ok. You've got relatives, well at least you had relatives living in Israel." No response. "Not that they will know of you, but Katz was their surname. From Lutsk - Poland, Russia, now Ukraine."

"Like where that war is?"

"Yes." Richard waited.

"This makes the author of these notebooks Aaron Katz. If you look for documents, check that name." Nothing. "The name appears as an officer in the Russian Navy. Russian merchants needed to be navy officers."

"Ok. That is just weird."

"You may want to write some of this down." Richard paused. "I found a bit about an Aaron in the Russian-American Company reports. He was a big deal in Sitka during the 1830s, quite prosperous." Richard didn't hear any writing. "He may be connected to the coins which were dug up a few years back in Sitka. Remember a bunch of Russian gold coins?" Mark stirred.

"Russian. I didn't tell ya. I found a dozen in the crate. I sold them to Larson. Not a bad find." Mark's tone was upbeat.

"Interesting. Well, I found a few references to burying the dead in Nulato." Richard paused. "The way it was written, I understand it to be Russian coins Aaron was burying. Have you ever heard folks digging up piles of Russian coins in Nulato?"

"Never. I don't think I've ever heard about Russians in Nulato."

"There may have been an old townsite. This is not my area of expertise, but think about Nulato a hundred and fifty years ago. There may be a good bit of treasure out there."

Richard thought more about the notebooks, that's where the real treasure was.

He would take a bit longer to thoroughly finish this one.

Maybe the museum would come through.

Maybe he would find a coin or two to trade Mark for the rest.

Closing Notes

It was a simple sentence from a Revolutionary War article that sparked this story. The line came from a section about Benedict Arnold's invasion of Canada. Upon entering a key fort, on their march towards Quebec, the Americans found a wounded English soldier, an English officer, and a Jew. Who was this Jew?

The story reminded me of Lt. Allen's adventure through the Interior of Alaska. He had survived desperate times for hundreds of miles to then only miss, by a few hours, the last riverboat. His survival fell to an Alaska Native who knew the area and the portage to the Pacific. This human connection saved Lt. Allen's expedition and I often wonder what stories did they tell?

The story of Lt. Allen is recorded Alaskan history, but Aaron Katz is not. This story used reports from Nulato, Unalakleet, Ft. St. Michael, and the Russian/ English/ American exploration of the Yukon River. Histories of English and American ships in Southeast Alaska were incorporated. The 1835 Smallpox Epidemic did devastate much of the territory and the people within.

The Russian-American Company made extensive maps of Alaska, marking the trading posts and forts they built throughout the vast area. They did not see the Americas as separate from Russia as we do today. In 1830, Russia was the world's largest country, still is, and easily had the largest European population. The vast Asia region held diverse Indigenous peoples which challenged Russian domination.

Imagine being an Indigenous Siberian watching white exiled Russians, in chains, marching to Katorga camps. The relationships in Asia, between Indigenous and European Russians, altered the way they engaged the Indigenous people of the Americas. While there may have been eventual peace, the early decades were brutal, used enslavement, and had multiple violent and successful revolts by Alaska Native groups.

Part of the reason Siberia holds a mystique is the intellectual history that emanates from the region. Many of these academic accomplishments can trace their history to the Decembrist exiles from the failed revolt of 1825. The elites of Russia during the Napoleonic Age were Francophiles, which doesn't make sense to most of us as Napoleon invaded these people.

The soldiers and officers who then occupied France, to quell the nation-alistic fervor of 1815, were indoctrinated while they slept. Too rich and too numerous to kill, these elites of Russia were exiled to Siberia. Their influence continued despite the harsh conditions.

Russian Jewish history is deeply tied to today's Ashkenazi. Catherine the Great's partition of the Poland-Lithuania Commonwealth had a dramatic effect on its large Jewish population. What few predicted was that the persecution of Jews increased their numbers. Russian doctrine struggled to accept their growing population in this region. It was a profound 1000-year culture that disappeared during the Holocaust and one worthy of including in today's stories.

Thank you to Caitlin Pollastro who guided my voice and honed the story. Much appreciation goes to Randy Pitney, my neighbor, who graciously did the first reading. A boatload of gratitude goes to Gisela Swift for her guidance and expertise at the formatting and the book design. I had support from many: Elyse Guttenberg, Zack Smith, Barbara Nelson, Marie McMillan, David Crowson, Alex Dunlap, Tammy Boyd, David Mahfouda, and my family: Amy Gallaway and Benjamin Keener. My son, Benjamin, reminded me that I was not the first to be published. Much love to my Jewish Congregation of Fairbanks which held me to Jewish traditions and wisdom. Thank you to my many Alaskan friends and, of course, Alaska.

On a cold 40 below sunny day, the Tanana Flats at 50 and 55 below are hidden by a bank of ice fog. The sparkling mist and soft snow beguile one to the power fundamental in Alaska. Woodstove roaring, a stack of readings, and much to contemplate are indispensable during these prolonged cold snaps. In a sense they are my connection to Aaron.

When Aaron set-off in life he did not expect his inward journey to be as adventurous as his outward. His years wrestling with human traits and sharing of spiritual stories allowed him to flourish in this land. He and all the others would not have been the same if they had stayed home.

May we all enjoy the inward journey.